C000200839

Also available from Unsung Stories
The Beauty

DEJA VU

IAN HOCKING

Published by Unsung Stories, an imprint of Red Squirrel Publishing

Red Squirrel Publishing
Suite 235, 77 Beak Street, London W1F 9DB, United Kingdom

www.unsungstories.co.uk

First edition published in 2014

Paperback ISBN: 978-1-907389-24-5
ePub ISBN: 978-1-907389-22-1

Edited by Olivia Wood (www.textmender.com) & George Sandison

Cover Artwork © Sandro Rybak 2014 (www.sandrorybak.tumblr.com)

Designed and typeset in Minion Pro
by Cox Design Limited (www.coxdesign.co.uk)

Printed and bound in the United Kingdom by Berforts

CHAPTER ONE

Berlin: September, 2023

Saskia Brandt emerged from the shadow of the Brandenburg Gate. She frowned at the Sunday evening sky and turned onto Behrenstraße. Inside the *Föderatives Investigationsbüro*, the EU's Federal Office of Investigation, the lobby was empty apart from a guard at the security barrier. She crossed the inlaid granite seal – '*Ex tabula rasa*' – and dumped her ceramic revolver on a conveyor. She huffed. Stepped through the detector and retrieved the gun while the guard folded his arms and made her feel exposed with her hair down, absurd in her casual skirt, short in her flip flops.

'You should be on holiday,' he said, smiling.

'I should.' She thought about a throwaway remark, but she was too dispirited. 'I should.'

Touched by the air conditioning, her sweat dried cold. She entered the glass lift and waited, biting her lip, until it opened on the fourth floor. Her office was one among dozens. Its plaque read: *Frau Kommissarin Brandt*. She licked her thumb and squeaked away a plastic shaving from the B. There was a picture alongside the name. It showed a serious, beautiful woman in her late twenties. No make-up. No earring in the exposed, left ear. Many photographs had been taken and Saskia liked this one the least. She scowled at herself before opening the door.

Her tidy desk backed onto a window overlooking an expanse of grey blocks; some kind of outdoor art installation. Her secretary had a desk in the corner of the room. Beyond it was a Kandinsky print, and the doors to her kitchen and bathroom.

The office was uncomfortably warm, but Saskia ignored this. She approached her desk and adjusted the position of its antique blotter while she thought about her life. She touched a framed photograph: Simon, her English ex-boyfriend as of five hours and twenty-two minutes ago, allowing for the time difference. She set her watch to Berlin time.

'The air conditioning is broken,' announced the nameless computer that haunted her office. Two cameras hung in the dark corners of the ceiling. Each tracked her mouth.

'Why?'

'I do not know. An engineer has been called. If you are hot, take a cold shower.'

Saskia turned to one of the cameras. 'Thanks for the advice.'

'You're welcome.'

'Beckmann summoned me. Do you know why?'

'No, Kommissarin.'

Saskia had met Simon three years before at a conference on data forensics in Saarbrücken. His talk had been well attended and delivered with self-deprecating humour. She remembered waking up the following morning with a sense that she had found a key to herself in his humour and kindness. Their relationship had been a long-distance one of stolen weekends.

Simon had been planning a move to Siemens in Berlin and was learning German. Saskia had been shopping for flats. Then, five hours ago, he had told Saskia about a colleague called Louise and how life was, you know, shaped by forces beyond your control and, you know, he was being pushed into a decision that would either hurt Saskia or Louise. Life was being tough on him.

Quietly, Saskia had asked him how he was, you know, getting on with his German language studies. Simon had shrugged in confusion.

Saskia said, '*Weißt du was? Du kannst mich mal am Arsch lecken.*'

He seemed to understand.

She had not stayed to collect her clothes – just grabbed her messenger bag and left. On the Eurostar, she had bought a cup of tea and scalded her thumb. That had upset her balance, and she had cried for most of the journey. Her intention was to spend the rest of her holiday in Wannsee. She would lounge and drink; read.

The summons from Beckmann had come half an hour before the train reached Berlin.

'Life is, you know, shaped by forces beyond your control.'

Saskia looked around her office with dry eyes. She entered the bathroom, drew some water and splashed it over her face. Then she went to the kitchen for a bottle of mineral water. As she stepped into the room, her flip-flops splashed in something. There was a large, pink puddle on the floor. She stopped.

The sadness that had followed her from England was overwhelmed by a sense that her world was about to turn upside-down for the second time that day.

Her eyes followed the puddle to the refrigerator. It was an American model, large and black, with a steel handle. The handle had been smudged with something. It might have been blood.

Saskia noticed plastic trays on the draining board. They were deep and clear; the sort of trays one might find in a refrigerator. Feeling nauseated, and breathing through her mouth, she pulled the handle.

Her secretary was sitting inside with her knees against her chest and her face turned away from the opening. Her hands were blue and splayed. There was a cut beneath her ear. Blood had ribboned from it and soaked the back of her dress to a deep crimson.

The woman had been wearing a summer dress when she died, and Saskia, in her shock, found herself fixating on the detail of the pattern – white flowers on a lilac background – as though she were falling into this moment from a great height.

Saskia swallowed. She was on the brink of fainting, so she took a deep breath and held it. But there was a butcher-shop smell, like raw hamburger, and her gorge rose so quickly that she almost had no time to turn to the sink, where she brought up her English tea. The sound disgusted her, threatening to trigger another wave, but she centred, calmed, remembered the autopsies and crime scenes of her short, steep career. She could handle this.

Wiping her hand across her mouth, she looked again at the body.

Why her? Why—

Saskia paused in the wake of this uncompleted thought.

Her name. Why can't I think of her name?

She had no reason to forget the woman who had worked alongside her since the spring. Saskia had last seen her late on Friday afternoon, two days before. This memory lapse had to be shock. The name would come to her.

To kickstart her wits, she sorted her questions. Someone had killed her secretary, which was unusual enough, given what Saskia could remember of the woman's gentle nature and steady life. And she had been killed within the offices of the FIB. That made the unusual extraordinary. It guaranteed that the body would be found quickly, along with all its forensic evidence. Why would the murderer want that?

Saskia pressed hard on the fridge door, making sure that the latch caught. She rinsed the sink and looked down at her flip flops in the pink water. This was a crime scene and she was contaminating it. She slipped her feet from the flip flops and stretched for the doorway.

Out of the kitchen, she closed the door and wiped her feet on the carpet. Then she returned to her desk and turned to the window. She let her thoughts wander through the grey blocks.

The computer broke the silence. 'You have no new messages. However, your refrigerator reports that it is broken.'

'It would,' Saskia said absently. Shock had given way to numbness. 'My secretary was inside. Too much heat for it, I suppose.'

'I do not understand. Why would your secretary be inside the refrigerator?'

Saskia turned to one of the cameras. 'Do you know why?'

'I do not understand. Why would your secretary be inside the refrigerator?'

She looked at the kitchen door. The solution to this crime was a statue inside a marble block; one only had to chip away.

'Computer, we are no longer having a conversation. I need to think.'

The shape of her answer, it seemed, would come with Beckmann. After all, there were two improbable events: a murder, and his summons. They had to be linked.

When Herr Hauptkommissar Beckmann arrived, he was wearing a grey Nehru jacket with a lemon-yellow flower in the buttonhole. Thirty years of criminal investigation had left him a reticent, deliberate man, cold in his outlook. Beckmann was Old School and Saskia liked that. He was holding on for an FIB pension and the long shadows of Croatian twilight.

They shook hands.

'Herr Hauptkommissar,' she said, keeping the urgency from her voice.

'Kommissarin.'

There was an avuncular edge to him. His eyes had the unsettling penetration of a seasoned prosecutor.

'No milk, sorry.' She passed him a coffee in a glass cup. 'Perhaps you could give me the details.'

Beckmann had a habit of putting his tongue tip into a cup before he drank. He swallowed audibly.

'In the early hours of this morning,' he began, 'your computer sent an enquiry to a refrigeration subcontractor about your fridge. I intercepted the email and sent a man to investigate.'

'Diligent of you,' said Saskia, testing.

'A simple statistical test indicated that the probability of it failing within five years was less than one in twenty. I sent the man around as a precaution. He's from the Moscow office, originally. He's called Klutikov.'

Saskia looked from the picture of Simon to the blotter, to the plant in the corner, to the secretary's little desk. She imagined a man with gloved fingers taking the measure of the room.

'Here are the facts according to Klutikov,' said Beckmann. He paid out a silence the length of two coffee sips. 'Your secretary was killed on Friday evening. She died of a single stab wound below the ear. The wound led to a fatal brain haemorrhage. The deceased—'

'Karin,' Saskia blurted, returning from a sidetrack in which she had found the name. '*Karin Haltmayr.*'

'Karin Haltmayr.' He adjusted the flower in his buttonhole. 'Her body was put in the fridge to strain its gas compressor.'

'Whoever did that also broke the air conditioning. That made the air warmer and forced the fridge's compressor to work harder.'

'Inevitably, then, the fridge would fail. The next steps are quite predictable. Your computer would send a request to have the fridge examined and repaired. The repair subcontractor would then send an engineer for Monday morning. He would discover the body and, as simply as that, you would be framed.'

Saskia sat against the desk. She was unused to the skirt and her thighs rubbed together. She was tired but thinking steadily. She had left her office around six o'clock on the Friday evening. If it could be proved that the act happened later than that – which it must have, because Karin was still in the office when she left – then Saskia's alibi would have been provided by witness statements from the Eurostar staff. Storing the body in the fridge had made the time of death less predictable. It had left open the possibility that she murdered Karin before leaving for London. Saskia had not been due back until Tuesday, after the *Feiertag*. By then, it would have been too late.

And yet the idea that Karin had been killed to frame her did not make sense.

'How could this be pinned on me?'

'There were photographs left on your desk. They show you and Karin in a compromising sexual act.' He looked apologetic.

'Forgeries, as it happens. I still don't see a motive. Bisexuality is hardly a firing offence.'

'No, but blackmail isn't the only explanation. It could be a lover's tiff. A quick murder; you panic, put the body in the fridge.'

'And flee to London? Hardly far enough to escape.'

'But far enough to look like you were escaping.'

Saskia sighed. She thought back to her last case. She had tracked down a Polish gang leader called Siudeck, who had been laundering ASEAN currencies from a base in Berlin, and killing competitors with something approaching abandon. Siudeck had been convicted under the Richter ruling, an alternative to capital punishment in which the mind was erased. It was not beyond Siudeck's lieutenants to take revenge by framing her for murder. But killing Karin was too subtle for such a gang, and there was no guarantee Saskia would be convicted anyway.

'But you don't believe it, Hauptkommissar. That's why you sent for me.'

Beckmann placed the empty cup on her blotter. Saskia looked at it, then moved it off.

'The help I can give you is limited,' he said. 'If anyone finds out that I've forewarned you, it will be difficult for both of us.'

Only if I'm guilty, she thought.

Beckmann continued, 'You have until 8:00 tomorrow. That's when the repair contractor will arrive. Nothing we can do about that.'

'Of course there is. We can cancel him.'

Beckmann shook his head as though this would be an elementary mistake. 'That would alert the murderer immediately. If we are to find him, we want his guard to be down.'

'So I have twelve hours?' She felt more tired than ever. 'You must have great faith in my detective powers.'

Beckmann frowned. 'It is not a matter of faith, Kommissarin. You can either have a small chance or none at all.'

'I'm sorry. I appreciate the head start.' She cleared her throat and straightened up, her mind already tracing paths of investigation. 'What if I come up with compelling evidence?'

'If I'm satisfied you've identified the perpetrator, Klutikov can run him down.'

'I'll need to talk to Klutikov now.'

'Not possible.'

'Then I need to see his report.'

'It was verbal. All the evidence he found, including the photographs, is bagged and in your desk drawer.'

Saskia stared, unfocused, at the wall. She rated her chances as one in ten. 'It's not good, is it? If I'm convicted, the courts will have me killed.'

But she was more scared of the Richter ruling. The money launderer Siudeck had been sent back out into the world as a street cleaner. He was now a happy, unaware man with a broom and new, empty mind. His uniform had epaulettes.

Beckmann put the flower to his nose. 'Thanks for the coffee.'

CHAPTER TWO

Hauptkommissar Beckmann had been gone for an hour. In that interval, Saskia had remotely accessed the recordings of the security cameras throughout the building. The videos had been deliberately scrambled. While she worked out implication after implication, circling the fact that the murderer had cracked the FIB's physical and virtual security, two cleaning spiders entered her office. She watched them groom the carpet around her feet – touches to map her calf – climb the desk, lift the blotter's corner, and shoo away the dust. The spell broke when a spider approached the kitchen.

'Computer, get rid of the cleaners.'

The spiders slipped under the door and were gone.

Saskia lingered in her office chair. As she drummed the armrests, the leather stuck to her palms, which were sweaty. Her office was getting hotter.

'Play me some Vivaldi.'

'I don't understand. Would you like to improve your accuracy by reading some training texts?'

'No. Play me some music by the composer Vivaldi.'

'Which piece would you like to hear?'

'*The Four Seasons*.'

'Which concerto?'

'*Winter*.'

It played.

'Louder.'

Louder.

She looked at the photograph of Simon. He had a ginger cat called Charlie. She would miss Charlie. The eyes on the photograph seemed to flash green. Saskia turned to the blinking diode of a camera high on the wall. 'Computer, you use your cameras to disambiguate voice commands, correct?'

'Yes, a multiple constraint satisfaction framework is—'

'Do you capture the video? Show me.'

'Yes, I use it to help process difficult utterances.'

Saskia sat upright.

'I said show me.'

'Raw video or my compressed representations?'

'Raw.'

Four images were projected onto the wall opposite the window. Each showed a live view of Saskia's face. 'Show me the video for last Friday afternoon.'

'It has been deleted.'

Saskia saw herself scowl. 'Is there a backup?'

'Please wait. Yes. Here is the video.'

The squares changed to show four profiles of her secretary, Karin. She was sitting at her desk. The sight of her made Saskia shudder. She felt afraid, squeamish and just plain sorry.

Quietly, she said, 'Overlay a time stamp in the corner of the lower right frame.'

The time stamp appeared. It read Friday, 12:07 p.m.

Saskia nodded. 'Now jump to 7:00 p.m.'

'I'm sorry?'

'Go forward to 7:00 p.m.'

The computer did so. The images showed an empty room.

'Back to 6:30.'

Karin re-appeared.

'OK,' said Saskia. 'Play it in real time.'

The cameras cherished Karin's portrait and made it difficult to see the room around her. Saskia watched as Karin typed at her terminal, as she lived through her last moments, yawning, scratching her nose. She looked distracted.

There was a knock at the door. For a moment, Saskia thought the sound came from her door, now, but this knock was two days old.

On the screens, Karin went to the door and opened it. Her face was expectant, then puzzled, then afraid. The visitor said nothing.

Pull back, Saskia willed.

Two cameras were re-tasked when the visitor entered. They moved from Karin to the murderer. Saskia leaned forward, then swore under her breath. His face was obscured by a broad-brimmed hat. The viewing angle made it difficult to see below his collar. Wordlessly, he moved to Karin. His head tilted as if to kiss her. Then his gloved hand punched at her neck, fast as a chameleon's tongue at an insect. Karin died in a slow curtsy. The murderer caught her weight and laid her down.

Hardly a crime of passion, Saskia thought.

He wiped the blade on her dress. Then he sat her up, put his arms around her chest, and hauled her towards the kitchen – beyond the cameras.

'Go back to the frame where the person walked in.'

'I don't understand.'

'Back five seconds. Forward two seconds. Back three frames. Good. Print that.'

Saskia opened the blotter. It contained a sheaf of electronic paper. On the top sheet was a picture of the murderer mid-stride. His height was difficult to judge, though the computer could calculate it. He wore a long raincoat and dark gloves. His shoulders were narrow. Not enough *detail.* Nothing diagnostic.

Shortly before midnight, Saskia took a cold shower. She dried slowly and twisted her hair into a towel. She examined her eyes in the mirror, then closed the wings of a white bathrobe around herself and returned to the office. The carpet tickled the gaps between her toes. She was hungry and tired.

'Play the video once more. This time from 6:34 p.m.'

Again, Karin was disturbed by a knock at the door. Again, Karin was attacked. Saskia recalled what Simon had said. That life was shaped by forces beyond one's control.

'And stop right there.'

The pictures had frozen at the point the murderer wiped his knife on Karin's collar.

'Zoom in on the blade.'

Camera One, which had the best view of the knife,

expanded to fill the window. The reflection in the metal was distorted, but Saskia hoped it had caught something essential of the murderer.

'Computer, can you analyze the image on the knife?'

'Please be more specific.'

One chance, she thought. *Give me this one chance.*

'I want a true representation of the object that caused the reflection on the knife. The object is a human face approximately thirty centimetres from the blade. However, do not share the analysis with any other computer. Is this clear?'

'If I distribute the analysis, processing will take minutes. If I do it myself, hours will be required.'

'How long?'

'Twelve hours, plus or minus one.'

Saskia looked at her bare wrist. Her watch was in the bathroom. 'What time is it? Around midnight?'

'It is 11:55 p.m.'

'You need to analyse it faster.'

'I can estimate some parameters, but this increases the risk that my solution path leads to a dead-end.'

'Do whatever you need to do. I want the analysis complete by 8:00 a.m.'

'Yes, Kommissarin.'

As the computer set to work, Saskia paced between her desk and the Kandinsky. With a face from the blade, she could exonerate herself. She felt hopeful for the first time since meeting the serious look in Simon's eyes earlier that day. This analysis might save her from the life of a street sweeper, rehabilitated, the crinkles on her brain smoothed clean.

The night was long. Saskia dozed in her chair until 3:00 a.m., then put her clothes back on. She could not bring herself to eat and she was too tired to read the news. She had nobody to call. Finally, she fell asleep on her desk, lulled by the occasional sound of the cameras moving and the swish-swish of the desk's data carousels as, pixel by pixel, the computer formed its answer to her question. She dreamed that she was brushing the streets, swish-swish, until they were as empty as her.

›•‹

Night terrors for the Kommissarin, whose dreams carried her to a fire on a dark plain. Around it sat three old women. Clotho, she spun the thread of life. Lachesis, she measured a length. Atropos, she cut it.

Spin, measure, snip.

›•‹

Awake, she marked each degree of the dawn. The city restarted. The empty streets gathered their people. Saskia watched them. In the bathroom, she studied her reflection. She brought cold water to her face and rubbed her eyes. She pressed until her vision clouded. It was 7:45 a.m. If the engineer was punctual, he would arrive in fifteen minutes. She felt hopeful. Hungry.

'Kommissarin,' said the computer, 'I have completed the image processing job.'

She returned to her desk. 'Print it.'

As the reconstruction of the murderer's face appeared on

her blotting paper, Saskia seemed to split into two people. One person looked at the print out and was defeated by what she saw. The other thought of Simon's words and, for the first time, took solace in them.

'Life is, you know, shaped by forces beyond your control.'

The two Saskias came together.

She thought, *I know*, and all the fear, all the uncertainty, was replaced by a question.

Why?

There was a knock at the door. Saskia cleared her throat. Her breathing felt thick and her mouth dry.

As she folded the printout in half, drawing a slow pinch along the crease, she looked at her right thumb. Flexed it.

Why?

'Computer.' Her voice sounded normal, to her at least. 'Is that the repair contractor? If so, tell him to wait.'

'It is Hauptkommissar Beckmann.'

Saskia felt a weightlessness in her chest.

'Is he alone?'

'Yes.'

'Let him in.'

The door opened. The Beckmann of today was identical to that of yesterday, but a carnation had replaced the anonymous lemon-yellow flower in his buttonhole.

'Kommissarin, have you found our murderer?' He seemed merely interested, nothing more.

'I didn't need to look far.'

She unfolded the paper. It showed Saskia frowning in horror over the woman she had killed.

CHAPTER THREE

'There are fifteen minutes until the engineer arrives. What am I seeing?'

Saskia said, 'This is a computer enhancement of the blade, captured at the moment Karin was killed.'

Beckmann looked from the picture to Saskia. 'So you used the computer-interaction cameras,' he said, quietly. 'Bravo. And now you will tell me it's a fake. That data can be falsified.'

Saskia looked for a path through her terrors. There was a way out of here. There had to be. She would move slowly, keep to the small facts until the larger ones became clear.

'Let's put aside the question of falsified data for now,' she said. 'First, the mechanics of the crime. They are consistent with the notion that the murderer is a woman. Karin was killed by a single stab wound below the ear. Though that requires skill, it does not require overpowering strength. In the video of the murder itself, the perpetrator struggles to move the body.'

Saskia held out her hand.

'Do you see my thumb?' she asked.

'Your thumb?' Beckmann's voice carried a warning tone.

Saskia waited for a response. In Beckmann's impatience she saw further clues to her situation. More routes through her terror. Why had he *really* summoned her from London?

'Very well,' he said. 'It is a perfectly ordinary thumb.'

'And yet this thumb was scalded badly enough yesterday to need a plaster. It happened on the Eurostar. I remember holding a plastic cup of tea. As I sat down, it spilled over my thumb. Scalds can heal quickly, but not that quickly.'

Beckmann seemed to look at her with a mixture of curiosity and admiration.

'What does this tell you?'

'On the assumption that I am not hallucinating at this moment, then it must be true that I was never burned.'

As Saskia spoke, she divided once more: her rational self acquiesced in the conclusion, while another part writhed.

'Meaning?'

'Perhaps I was never on that train. Perhaps—' she lost her voice for a moment. 'Given that at least some of my memories are unreliable, and that I have no reason to believe the computer's analysis of the blade is incorrect, I should accept that I—' Again, her voice emptied.

'That you killed Karin?'

Beckmann was smiling, but he had lost his avuncular edge.

'I *killed* her,' said Saskia. She felt utter defeat now. 'Perhaps we were lovers after all. Perhaps, before killing her, I lost my mind.'

'But you've seen the video of the murder itself. Did it

strike you as a crime of passion?'

She shook her head. 'Perhaps,' she said, struggling, 'it had been long planned—'

'And if your memories of the weekend are false, where do you draw the line between falsehood and truth? What can you be sure of?'

'But I remember working with Karin for months. She came here in the spring. And then there are my cases, my training.'

'Details? Specifics?'

Saskia opened her mouth, but her thoughts were interrupted by the realization that there were huge gaps in her life story. Who were her parents? Where had she gone to school? Who was her first love? What music did she like?

She found nothing.

Unstoppably, other certainties followed. She had remained in the office overnight because she had no home. She had called no friends because she had none. Even Simon was an indistinct shape in her recall. There was no substance to his kindness and his humour. She took his photograph from the desk and opened the frame. She found a yellowed advert for stationery on the reverse.

Oh, Christ.

Saskia planted her feet apart and leaned on the desk for support. Through her vertigo, and the warping of her tears, she saw Beckmann staring. He might have been a scientist observing a chemical reaction.

Without moving her eyes from his, she felt for the second drawer of her desk and removed her revolver. She aimed it at his chest.

'There's something more to you.' The barrel of her revolver

trembled. 'You've been… *strange* since the start.'

Beckmann laughed. It was deliberate, signalling satisfaction more than humour. Saskia gritted her teeth.

'Oh, Frau Kommissarin. You are so worried about being caught for your secretary's murder. You think they'll wipe your brain. It's too late. They already did.'

Saskia let the gun drop to the desk. 'What? *What?*'

'Put the gun away.'

'No. Keep talking.'

'Several months ago, you perpetrated a thorough and meticulous example of multiple murder.'

Saskia struggled to assimilate his words. 'But Karin died on Friday.'

'I'm not talking about Karin. I'm talking about before. You killed a group of people. I must be vague on the details, you understand. Your conviction was fast-tracked and, as part of your sentence, you were released into my programme. Do you know the expression –' here he switched briefly to English – '"Set a thief to catch a thief"? People like you, Saskia, have a talent to know their own kind. I want that edge. The FIB wants that edge.'

'People like me?' Even as Saskia felt the rise of madness, her intellect pushed on. 'So this is an interview? A test to see if I could catch myself?'

'Identifying the murderer wasn't so difficult. Your acceptance of her identity, however, suggests that I was right about you.'

'Who was Karin?'

Beckmann said, 'Computer, show the video.'

He nodded towards the wall as a video appeared. It showed the corridor outside Saskia's office. Although it was empty, what struck Saskia was the dishevelled floor and exposed fittings. It was abandoned – or unfinished. The date stamp was Friday.

FIB headquarters would never look so untidy. This building is just anonymous office space. They decorated the parts I would see.

She asked, 'Where is the real FIB?'

Beckmann smiled and put a finger to his lips. Then he pointed at the video screen.

As Saskia watched, a woman came into view. She was being frogmarched along the corridor by a tall man. Even before Saskia recognised her blue dress, she knew it was Karin. And the tall man was the guard who had greeted Saskia when she entered the building the day before.

'You should be on holiday,' he had said, smiling.

'I should.'

The guard was fake, too. Part of the decoration.

As Karin approached the door to Saskia's office, she began to fight against the guard, but he was too strong.

'No!' the woman begged. 'I'll try again. I'll do better next time. The test wasn't fair.'

The guard said nothing.

'Are you listening to me? Are you—'

She broke off and stared at something behind the viewpoint of the security camera. With slow, echoing steps, Beckmann walked into frame.

'Your story is over, Karin,' he said. 'Now you're just a doll within a doll.'

'What do you want from me?'

'I would say your cooperation,' said Beckmann, 'but it won't come to that.'

He raised his hand. In the high resolution image, Saskia could see a silver ring. He reached across with his other hand and touched it.

Immediately, Karin relaxed. She assumed an upright posture. Her eyes looked sleepy.

'Karin, you are the secretary of Frau Kommissarin Saskia Brandt. She's coming back to the office very soon. Do you understand?'

'Yes.'

'Then be a good secretary and go about your duties.'

With that, Karin opened the door to Saskia's office and walked in, closing it behind her.

The video stopped there.

There are others like me. If I had failed the test, I'd have become the test for someone else.

'Don't be sorry for Karin,' said Beckmann. 'She was one of your kind. She won't be missed, particularly by her victims' families.'

'How did you make me kill this woman?'

'Anything is possible given the right technology.' Beckmann held up his hand to Saskia just as he had held up his hand before Karin. 'There is something inside you now, Saskia, that works for me. I pull the strings and you move.'

Saskia looked at him. 'You are grotesque. This whole thing is grotesque.'

'As you are a convicted criminal, I question your judgement on the matter.'

'What happened next, after I killed her?'

'We kept you in a dark room until Sunday afternoon. Then we dressed you in casual clothes, drove you around the block and let you out of the van with instructions to return here.' Beckmann leaned over the desk. 'Now, will you work for me?'

'Since you've taken me into your confidence, you think I have already decided. What's the alternative?'

'You'll be destroyed and your ashes scattered across the Spree.'

'So why don't I just put a bullet in you and leave for Siberia?'

Beckmann looked at the gun. 'What bullet?'

She checked it. There were no shell rims visible. She flicked out the cylinder and found one round in the topmost chamber. She clapped it shut and pointed it at Beckmann. 'This bullet.'

'Saskia, do you know the true significance of Russian roulette? During the First World War, senior Russian officers would test the cleanliness of a junior's revolver in a peculiar manner. The gun was loaded with one bullet, the cylinder was spun and the weapon fired at the junior. If the gun was well maintained, the cylinder would come to rest with the bullet at the base. The pin would strike nothing. However, if the gun was poorly maintained, the bullet could stop anywhere. Beneath the firing pin, for example.'

Beckmann touched his ring. Immediately, Saskia felt another separation inside herself. He raised his arm so that it was the perfect mirror of her own. At the same time, pain ripped along her gun arm. She felt the joints flare and her muscles tremble with effort. Despite her will, her arm began to bend. She could not move any other muscle.

'Your arm becomes my arm,' Beckmann said, 'if I wish it. Think of it as a safeguard.'

She strained until her jaw creaked and her chest bulged with trapped air.

'Don't fight me,' said Beckmann. 'Listen. The purpose of Russian roulette is edification. A lesson that poses the question: is there a bullet or is there not? Some officers were hanged because they did not have the courage to ask.'

Her eyes, which she could move, beseeched Beckmann, but he did nothing. She – or he – dashed the cylinder across her thigh. It spun. Then the revolver was raised to her temple.

Beckmann's eyes drank in her body from toes to crown. 'Now,' he continued, 'do you commit? If so, you will become my property. You will investigate federal crime as a probationary officer within the FIB. You will not be permitted to leave the EU and you will not attempt to rediscover your past. You will tell no one your true circumstances. You will accept anything I care to put in your brain. If you break any of these rules, you will become the recruitment participant for your successor. Do you understand? Answer me now, or the gun will fire.'

She felt her jaw unlock and understood that she had been given the power to speak. 'Yes,' she said.

Beckmann waited. He looked at her grubby T-shirt and cheap flip-flops, both souvenirs of a holiday she had never taken. 'Good.'

The spell broke. Saskia staggered to her chair and collapsed into it, spinning with a clicking sound that recalled the revolver's cylinder.

'In my briefcase you will find, among other things, some money and the keys to an apartment. I suggest you go there and calm down. This is your new life. A second chance.

Here is your badge.' He put a leather wallet on the table. 'Oh and...'

Beckmann stopped. Saskia was pointing the revolver at him. She pulled the trigger. Nothing happened. She pulled again and again. On the sixth click, Beckman shook his head.

'...you'll find live ammunition in the briefcase too.'

She regarded him blankly.

'Saskia?'

'What?'

'Remember you're on probation. If you fail, you die, and at length. There will be another like you. There always is. Dolls within dolls, *und so weiter.* Good morning.'

'Beckmann.'

'Yes?'

Despite everything, she felt that something of herself had survived this day.

'How did they recruit you?'

He smiled. 'That would be telling.'

CHAPTER FOUR

Professor David Proctor awoke with a stiff neck. He looked at his bedside table for a flat device the size and shape of a business card. It was vibrating.

The card said aloud, 'Good morning, Professor. It is 7:03 a.m. The weather looks good for today. You have sixteen appointments, the first of which is with your PhD student Sandra Xiang at 8:30 a.m.'

'Right.'

David pressed his eyes and rubbed hard. Then he swung his feet onto the wooden floor. His legs had been carrying him around for more than fifty years and the older he became the greater the need to crack them each morning like a big pair of knuckles. Not a good sign. Still, his weekly squash game was scheduled for lunch time. He had played Gregory Kleczkowski every week since joining the university ten years ago, and, he sometimes admitted with a smile, lost each time.

He went to the window and inspected his garden for the

neighbour's cats, which he had named Bastard Tabby and Bastard Ginger. Collective noun: the Cats Bastard. This morning, they were absent. He turned his attention to the hedge at the end of the garden. 'Ego, remind me to trim that hedge.'

'I'll do that.'

David practised his yoga and tried to remember whether Sandra was the student who had failed her upgrade or the one who had published in *Cognitive Science*. He thought of asking Ego, which, though only a prototype AI unit on loan from Marquis Computing, was capable of answering complex queries. He decided to tax his brain instead.

It didn't work.

'Ego, which of my students published a paper last month?'

'Sonia Wakeman. Would you like me to summarise the paper?'

'Thanks, no.'

When he was finished with the yoga, he dressed in his usual loafers, chinos, shirt and blazer; clothes that Joyce, his girlfriend, called CGC, or Consultant Gynaecologist Chic. David pulled a face when he remembered this. His wardrobe was full of this stuff and he wasn't about to chase his youth by dressing up like his hipster colleague Zoltan Rogers, who had acquired a Porsche and toupée when he clocked fifty.

David went to the bathroom and brushed his hair. It was thinning yet voluminous. He opened his mouth, inspected his tongue, and checked his nostrils for protruding hair. Not a trace. David had reached the age where his features, once unremarkable, had sharpened against his bone structure, and he seemed to inspire confidence in strangers. People in the street asked him for directions and, whenever something vaguely non-conforming happened – an ambiguous remark in a faculty meeting, or a person smoking on campus – it was to David that people turned.

In his farmhouse kitchen, David made coffee using a large, expensive machine. Grumpily, he took out the marmalade and asked Ego to tell him what was happening in the world. At the same time, he put the toast on and turned to a stack of printouts dealing with Lorenz mathematics and embodied cognition, wondering what bright spark had decided to combine the two. Holding the coffee with his left hand, he walked the fingers of his right through the sheets. One of his postgrads had highlighted sections that might be important to their lab.

Ego told him about a friendly fire incident between the US and Chinese fleets in the Pacific, the death of a musician David had never heard of, and the birthday of a minor royal.

Some of his attention went to Ego's voice, some to the papers, and the rest to a pink sheet of paper that he had stuck to the fridge door with a magnet years before. It showed a boxy house with square windows. It had been haphazardly coloured in orange. The house had two trees – one either side – and below the left-hand tree were a man, woman and child. All three were stick figures, but the woman had a scribble of yellow hair.

'Professor, there is an incoming encrypted call from Marquis Computing. Would you like to take it?'

David forced himself back to the moment. 'Encrypted? Go ahead.'

The call came through as audio only. The quality was poor. A man said, 'David? It's Sam from Marquis.'

'Sam.' David picked up one of the papers. The title referred to eigenvectors. He held it at arm's length and squinted to read the abstract. 'Must be the middle of the night for you.'

'Actually, it's four in the morning.' Sam cleared his throat. David had met him in Boston the previous year. He remembered him as a quiet, persuasive man who worked in the Marquis sales division.

'Everything OK, Sam? Don't tell me you want your Ego unit back. He's in the middle of reading me the news.'

'I'll make this quick.'

The absence of a reply to David's rejoinder struck him as a little rude. His attention drifted back to the paper. There seemed to be an error in a graph showing a transformation matrix.

'Okey-dokey.'

'We had a break-in last week.'

'Commiserations. Was anything taken?'

'Yes, the second and third Ego prototypes.'

David looked at his own Ego unit on the table. It was a combination of advanced software and rare materials, and years ahead of the market. 'You want this one back? I understand. I'll—'

'Listen.' Sam paused. He sounded anxious. 'I wanted to tell you that our servers just picked up the location of the second Ego unit. It's in Oxford.'

David dropped the paper. What were the chances of that unit turning up here? Low. He was still thinking this through when a silent shape crossed the hallway, just a momentary dim in luminance, only registered peripherally.

Without moving his head, he said, 'Can you be more specific?'

'Not right now. We'd all be happier if your prototype could be returned ASAP.'

David nodded. 'I understand. Bye.' He whispered, 'Ego, cut the call. Replay the conversation at a volume consistent with me standing in this room. Don't acknowledge me verbally. Just do it now.'

David waited until he heard Sam's voice, almost perfectly real, say, 'David? It's Sam from Marquis.'

Under cover of their recorded conversation, David moved into the hallway, which ran unbroken from the front door to the back conservatory. He kept an old cricket bat named the Red Special in the hatstand the better to dispatch the occasional rat, and he reached for it now, lifting it with a practised motion. David had boxed as a teenager and moved on to full-contact karate at university. He had only stopped when he broke a finger and it affected his guitar playing. He hadn't trained for years, but the eagerness was there, as well as the lightness in his steps.

He heard a noise from the parlour. Its door was open a crack. He pushed it aside and stepped through. He did not know what he was expecting: perhaps a deranged geek, or an international thief of cutting-edge computing equipment.

What he saw was Bastard Tabby from three doors down.

The cat was sitting on a chair in the corner, below a photograph of David's late wife, Helen. It was licking its front paw and rubbing it over its forehead.

'You.' All the excitement dropped away. He felt absurd and a little disappointed.

Then he thought, *Who let him in?* and the excitement came back, humming.

But before he could turn, he felt something press into his

lower back. It had two prongs. Whatever it was, David froze. He raised his arms. He was still holding the Red Special but he knew he could not turn quickly enough to use it. The prongs, he realised suddenly, represented the business end of a taser.

Whoever was holding it said nothing.

David felt a gloved hand touch his shoulder. It was more personal than the taser, and, paradoxically, seemed to scare him more.

'What are you playing at? This is my house.'

If he hasn't fired the taser yet, he probably wants something.

His body ached with the need to play out old patterns. He wanted to twist left and right, treat his intruder to elbow strikes, but those were the thoughts from a mind that had not aged as fast as his body. Shenanigans like that were apt to burst a disc.

The gloved hand shifted. David felt himself being guided, so he let the intruder take him to the kitchen. They both stopped facing the picture on the fridge door.

'Professor Proctor,' said Ego, 'I have been hacked. The following message comes from the person standing behind you.'

'Who are you?'

'My name is not important,' continued Ego. 'Be aware that the taser in my hand will incapacitate you if you try to turn around.'

'Consider me aware.'

'I belong to the Neohuman Cooperative. We have been watching you for a long time. We believe that machine life has certain rights and we repudiate modern society's use of machine life in slavery. In a few minutes, you will receive a communication from your acquaintance, Colonel Harrison McWhirter. He will ask you to travel to Scotland on a matter of national security. You will do so. McWhirter will pretend that your mission is humanitarian, but it is not. He wishes to recapture the virtual world of Onogoro, which we know all about. With my help, you will stop him. Onogoro must fall.'

Onogoro. That was a word David had not heard for a long time. Tears came to his eyes. He remembered his old friend Bruce Shimoda. *What happened to you?*

'Why would I help you?'

'Because, by doing so, you will help yourself. This is the first step on a path that will lead you home.'

He frowned. 'I am home.'

'You haven't been home for years. Look at the image on the fridge door, the one drawn by your daughter Jennifer.'

'I don't understand.'

'Listen to me. I will give you the tools you need to reach your home. You must decide whether or not to use them.'

David sighed. The contrast between the house in the picture and the house around him reminded him again of Zoltan's Porsche. This house, the fancy toaster he could barely figure out, his Consultant Gynaecologist Chic – all of it was an escape from the gloom that had stalked him since Jennifer, his daughter, left his life.

'What tools?'

CHAPTER FIVE

Helix Base, Nevada, USA: the day before

Half an hour before dawn, John Crane turned his *dorado* watercraft east on Lake Mead, leaving the lights of the small harbour behind. The lake was a grey plane and the mountains a black serration. The transparent carapace of the *dorado* was open to the stars and the spray. A proximity system would warn him of other craft on the lake, but he had never encountered one this early, which was his preferred time to enter Helix Base.

His course followed the Nevada-Arizona border. He looked left towards Swallow Bay, and remembered taking a prostitute there. Suzanne. Her face was lost in the static of the years. This, now, today, was the signal in the noise.

There had been a breakthrough.

What is the phrase? Crane thought. *Something about luck. Being in the right place at the right time.*

He increased the thrust and felt the seat gel redistribute. The angle of the windscreen became shallower and spray moved radially from its centre: a personal star-field lit by the dashscreen. He would not ruin the effect by turning on his navigation lights. To anyone in the desert, the *dorado* would only be heard, another noise in the night.

There was a tight S-shaped channel coming up. The watercraft reached a speed where it rose on its hydrofoil, and the buffeting stopped. Crane looked at the speedometer. It was still climbing. Crane swept through the channel. At last, as it widened, he turned to port, where an outcrop of rock formed Crescent Cove.

The outcrop grew large. It triggered the proximity system. Crane's yoke vibrated.

'Warning: terrain. Warning: terrain.'

In a voice that was equally robotic, Crane said, 'Override.'

The phrase about luck was 'Fortune favours the prepared mind.'

He reached for a lever. He squeezed its end to disengage the safety, then pushed it forwards. Immediately, the nose of the *dorado* bit the water. He was too fast for a smooth dive but the impeller outlets compensated by shifting upwards, adding downforce astern.

Crane was pushed forward in his seat. He heard the whine of the dive fins extending. The lobstered carapace closed rapidly, sealing him a moment before the lake washed up and over.

And then he was diving at a steady ten degrees.

The *dorado* projected a contour map of the rocky floor. Crane adjusted his course and approached the middle of three water intake pipes. Each opening was wide enough for him. He spiralled down.

A light blinked on the dashscreen. Crane touched it.

'Welcome back, sir,' said a male voice.
'A black coffee. Some eggs.'
'Of course.'
The grills blocking the pipes lifted.

›•‹

After breaching in the first of six underground pens, Crane retracted the carapace. He breathed the dank air. The chamber was low-ceilinged, stuffy and cold. Its walls dripped. Light flickered from the concrete steps near the *dorado* to the junction thirty yards upslope, which opened onto a road tunnel. The tunnel led to the old fresh-water pumping station that used to serve Vegas.

A short man wearing a battered hard-hat approached him. Crane stood carefully and tossed him a mooring rope. Then, when the watercraft was secure, he stepped onto the jetty, turning to drop his gloves into the cockpit. He followed these with his overalls. Beneath them, he wore a grey suit. He reached for his Stetson, which hung near the starter button. It had been a fiftieth birthday present from his brother, Jacob, and was stiff around the brim.

Crane's mind was blank, all static, no signal.

He said, 'I'll be one hour.'

›•‹

In the Valley of Fire State Park, north-west of the lake, there was a lone column of rock with two cabins and an array of weather instrumentation. This was Met Four. Inside, protected by smiling soldiers in plain clothes with permission to use deadly force, was a secret lift leading to a massive bunker called Helix Base, constructed between 2008 and 2014 using a small portion of the US Black Budget and a major part of John Crane's own assets. For this reason, Crane was allowed to enter the base through Lake Mead, whereas most entered through Met Four.

The enormous, helical cavity of the base had been melted by a nuclear-powered tunnelling machine called a subterrene. Most of the operational departments – power, communication, food, water and air services, as well as administration – were located in a central column that ran vertically through the helix. At its top was the Met Four weather station. The service tunnel used by Crane touched the central column at its midpoint. At the terminus of the main helix, the subterrene tunneller remained. Its energy would power the base for another twenty-five years, or, should the need arise, annihilate it with an inferno that would roll up the excavation like a fuse, thanks to compressor modifications insisted upon by the US government.

John Crane was an anonymous figure in the anonymous corridors. A few civilians and scientists recognised him as he passed. They stared. The military personnel did not. Eventually, he reached the central column, itself the size of a tower block, then headed down to the lowest level, where he stopped before a large blue door. Above it was the symbol of the base: the serpent entwining the Rod of Asclepius. Below, sprayed in white paint, was: 'Project N83261'. Underneath this, in magic marker, someone had written:

We like to call it "Déjà Vu".

And underneath that:

But you knew that already. ☺
Crane stepped through.

›•‹

Project N83261 had a long section of the helix. Its vitrified roof glistened. The floor was terraced in three sections, each eighty yards long. The highest terrace held a control room with a semi-transparent screen overlooking the lower sections. The middle terrace was a bank of sand, large enough to protect the personnel in the control room from catastrophic failure of the two centrifuges in the third, lowest terrace. Scattered throughout the chamber were equipment crates, vehicles, work cabins, and construction materials. The air was dry, dusty and cold.

It was still two hours before the working day began. Most of the scientists and administrators would have gone home the night before, or taken temporary beds in the central column. But Crane found the person he was looking for, Jennifer Proctor, stretched out on a chair at the back of the empty control room. The giant screen was still showing line graphs and tables. The desk in front of her was covered with computer displays, pads of paper, and plastic cups that smelled, faintly, of alcohol.

Crane did not wake her immediately. He stood there and looked. She was a short, young woman with a plain face. Her arms were folded across her lab coat. Someone had taken another lab coat and thrown it across her legs.

Crane found himself wondering how old Einstein was when he published his Special Theory of Relativity. Mid-twenties, he guessed. And Newton when he made his own advances in mathematics and optics: early twenties. And here among the cups of flat champagne lay Jennifer Proctor, the first person to send an object through time. She was twenty-one.

From Einstein to Proctor: younger and younger. Newton, of course, stood on the shoulders of those who came before him. Einstein had Newton. And Jennifer...

He thought of Jennifer's father.

David Proctor. What role had he played? What role *would* he play?

He cleared his throat and touched one of her clogs.

'Jennifer Proctor?'

Her eyes twitched open. She stared at him for a moment, her fright subsiding to irritation.

'Who the bloody hell are you, cowboy?'

More than twenty years before, Crane had been riding a thoroughbred at his Kentucky home when he lost consciousness and fell from the saddle. Doctors diagnosed a malignant brain tumour. In the months that followed, he underwent a series of treatments, all of which failed. That was when he decided to go public. He offered one billion dollars – a twentieth of his wealth – to anyone who could cure him.

He was approached by the usual con-artists and idiots. But one email intrigued him. It was from an Argentine medical student with an idea for a non-surgical treatment involving nano-scale robots. In its initial animal testing, non-cancerous cells were also attacked, particularly neurons associated with higher brain function. In that respect, it was as blunt an instrument as chemotherapy. But, with only hours to live, Crane had taken the treatment.

Waking the next day, looking into the anxious eyes of Dr Orza, Crane could have had no idea of the bargain he had struck with death. His life was forever changed. Where once he had been a masterful reader of people, faces were now only muscle activity and moving folds of skin.

The prototype treatment, which had later been perfected, had not made him a bad person. He had been that long before.

Crane had first killed a man when he was on summer vacation from his finishing school. In the logging country north of his home, there had lived a derelict called Gregory–whether his first name or last name, Crane would never know. Gregory was a figure of fun among the town's teenagers. He habitually came through during the summer, heading south. Crane would track him like game.

Crane had already despatched the family dog, drowning it in their fountain because it used to disgust him during mealtimes, but that killing had been improvised and difficult. There had been questions and he had been lucky to get away with it.

For Gregory, Crane assembled nylon cord, a hunting knife, and a change of clothes.

Fortune, he thought, *favours the prepared mind.*

›•‹

'It happened quickly,' she said. They were walking down the aisle of the control room. In her high, Transatlantic voice, she continued, 'One hour before we received presidential authority, the re-injection alarms sounded. These alarms are designed to respond to certain gravitational anomalies that correlate with the re-injection of matter. They're automatic.'

'May I see it?' Crane had read about the watch in his report. It was suddenly very important to touch the thing; to reassure himself that this was real.

Jennifer took the watch from her back pocket. It was a silver pocket watch with a chain. 'Here.'

'You should be more careful with this. One day, it will be in a museum.'

She smiled. 'I try to focus on the science. Not just the day-to-day running of this place, but dealing with problems, large and small.'

'I interrupted. Please continue.'

'The reception centrifuge began to spin up at 11:52 a.m. At precisely noon, with the rotation arm at full speed, our cameras captured the materialisation of a plastic box at our chosen location: the reception container. Splashdown. Turn the watch. You see the time and date?'

'Yes.'

'I wrote that at 2:00 p.m., two hours *after* the watch materialised.' She laughed.

Crane tried to reconstruct the moment from her point of view, and failed, as he always did. But: was her attitude to failure the key to understanding her? He looked at her neck, the blushing blood. The time machine was her triumph. Not long ago, the only reports coming from Project Déjà Vu were ones of malfunction, injury, and ignition failure.

'I truly couldn't believe it,' she said. 'I ran to the office, opened a drawer, and took it out. The same watch, that is. There was a moment when I held both watches. In my left hand, the original showed the time at that moment. In my right, the duplicate was two hours ahead. The *same* watch. We had done it. But we had only two hours to prep the machine.'

Now, thought Crane. *We come to it.* He said, 'What would have happened if you hadn't sent it back?'

'I don't understand.'

What was her expression now? Had he amused her? Did she think he was stupid? If only this kind of perception were still in his power.

'Were you tempted to let 2:00 p.m. pass by without firing up the machine and sending the watch back to 12:00 p.m.?'

The muscles in her forehead pinched together. Either she was upset or she was concentrating.

'That would create an inconsistent causal loop, Mr Crane. The effect of the cause had already been observed. You can't have an effect without a cause.'

'What would happen if you tried?'

'The Novikov self-consistency conjecture would apply, I hope. A series of unlikely events would occur leading to the effect we have observed. A technician might accidentally lean on a keyboard, initiate part of the process, triggering a bug in the code, or whatever, leading to an activation of the machine.' She looked at him. 'That might be difficult for you to grasp. It's easier to think of it the other way around. What if the watch had not appeared earlier, suggesting that our machine wasn't going to work, and yet we tried to send the watch back anyway? In that event, a technician might trip over a power cable. Or we might see a simple failure in the nuclear bomb beneath our feet.'

'You say the paradox is impossible.'

'There is another possibility,' she said, not appearing to listen, 'which is that an object travelling backwards in time winds up in a universe different from ours.'

'But that doesn't explain the fact that there were two watches. You must have sent it back into our past.'

'It's not as simple as that.' She smiled. 'The watch we received could have been sent by a second team.'

Crane simulated a cold stare. 'What are you talking about?'

'Given our understanding of reality at this point, we should expect there to be other Déjà Vu projects in nearby universes, doing something very similar to us. Whatever the case may be, we need to do further testing, starting with a minute examination of that watch to see whether it did indeed come from our own universe or a parallel one. There is great danger involved.'

Crane put the watch to his ear. He closed his eyes. 'It's running fine.'

'Actually, each tick is marginally slower than the last. The error was three nanoseconds per second on Tuesday. Now it's three microseconds, an order of magnitude greater.'

'Is that why you can't send a living person?'

'You're asking Wilbur Wright how to put a man on the moon.' She took the watch and let the chain spiral into her left palm. 'The two things are entirely different. But the danger I'm talking about isn't to the watch. A time paradox is something that might threaten the fabric of the universe, perhaps all universes, and we can't yet be sure how resilient that fabric would be to such a violation of causality. The effect might be catastrophic.'

They walked a zigzagging channel in the sand barrier. The walls were translucent plastic. Ahead, Crane could see a gantry spanning the gap between the two centrifuges.

'How soon before the machine can be used again?' he asked.

'A couple of days. There are rare elements to do with carbon focusing that we can't source easily. And we need to be careful. Now that we have the proof the theory holds, we need to work through the implications.'

'When will Patrick Harkes assume control of the project?'

'Two days.' She smiled. 'I'm looking forward to stepping down, frankly. There are lots of kinks in the theory that need working out. I'm a theory girl.'

Crane looked at her.

Only two days.

He had conducted this conversation according to a plan. It was his habit. He found that conversations did not work otherwise. This one had deviated from the plan somewhat, but stayed within its bounds. Now he came to his last topic and found that he could not decide on an appropriate way to introduce it. It would surprise Jennifer. He wondered if she would become uncooperative before he could tell her what she needed to know.

'Jennifer, your father once worked for me.'

She did not seem angry or unsettled. But she stopped. 'Dad? You were involved with the West Lothian Centre?'

'More than that, I owned it, and others. These were investments I was happy to make. I owe my life to science.'

'But you owed nothing to my father.' Jennifer's anger was easy to see now. Her expression was easy to interpret. 'I remember the problems he had when I was growing up.

Doors closing, friends not returning his calls. Was that your doing? Because you thought him responsible for the bombing?'

Bombing, thought Crane. The word touched memory after memory. Back then, he had been a different person. He had taken pride in destroying his enemies personally. Was David still an enemy? Crane had never fully decided on his guilt

'Your father was found innocent in a court. He returned to academia and recovered his career.'

'And my mother?'

Crane leaned against the plastic wall. Behind it, he felt the tonnes of sand, pressing.

'Jennifer, I do hope I haven't offended you. I came here to offer congratulations. And, because your father and I were once friends, I need you to do something for me. You need to warn him. He is in danger.'

'What kind of danger?'

'We've had a tip-off that he might be mixed up with some bad people. Did your father ever tell you about his work in the West Lothian Centre? It could be a target.'

'But that was destroyed years ago.'

'Not completely. The thing about these people, Jennifer, is that they manipulate others into doing their work for them. He may not even know what these Neohumans are truly planning.'

Emotions passed across her face too fast for Crane to register.

'Dad wouldn't be fooled like that.'

'Please call him. Talk him out of it.'

'*You* call to him,' she said.

'He wouldn't listen.'

Crane waited. He knew he only had words to persuade her. He knew he had a blank, closed face; unnatural body language. He waited.

'What should I say?' she asked.

'Tell him to stay in Oxford.'

'Oxford.'

Crane remembered what she had said.

'You can't have an effect without a cause.'

Jennifer folded her arms. 'Or, what goes around comes around. Is that it?'

Crane looked at her. Was she joking? Threatening him?

'That too. Thank you, Jennifer. I'm glad we met. Congratulations once more.' He raised his hat. 'Goodbye.'

›•‹

Minutes later, as he was at the blue door to the central core of Helix Base, he heard Jennifer run up behind him. She was out of breath and her face was a moving puzzle.

'Mr Crane, before you leave — sorry I didn't recognise you at first.'

'I don't understand.'

'When I woke up just now, I didn't recognise you. I called you "cowboy". What I should have said, on behalf of the team, is that we all appreciate your funding. This couldn't have happened without you. We raised a glass to you last night.'

'We raised a glass to you last night', thought Crane, turning over the sentence for its outward and inward meanings. Was she joking?

'I'm sorry I startled you. Goodbye.'

'Mr Crane?'

'Yes?'

'Forgive me, but what do you care if Dad goes up to Scotland?'

'You might say that I care because you care.'

Her features moved through different arrangements. One might have been disgust; another surprise. At length, her face became still. She smiled. He could tell it was a simulation, like his. 'Well, thank you and goodbye for now.'

'Goodbye.'

He walked out of the chamber and the door closed behind him. Before continuing, he turned and looked at the graffiti.

We like to call it "Déjà Vu".

But you knew that already. ☺

He lingered on the smiley. Then he returned to his *dorado* in berth six.

As he settled in the cockpit, putting his Stetson to one side, he watched the transparent carapace close over his head. He was so close to his goal. He had two days until Harkes took over Project Déjà Vu and had its equipment shipped out piece by piece to a bunker somewhere near Colorado. Once there, Crane would never see it again.

The movements of David Proctor worried him more than he would admit to Jennifer. Proctor the elder was too unpredictable. What if these Neohumans had told Proctor about the connection between his work at the West Lothian Centre and Project Looking Glass, here in Helix Base? The man was like a chess piece from a different game relocated to the centre of Crane's board. Proctor could be snuffed out, yes, or taken away. But it would be difficult to isolate

Jennifer from news of his disappearance. The solution Crane had suggested to her was elegant. Even an egotistical man like Proctor would listen to a plea from his long-lost daughter. She was scared enough.

Crane considered his memories of the conversation. *Yes,* he thought. *Jennifer will warn him off.*

The dorado sank and darkness closed in. There was the comforting pressure of water.

Fortune favours the prepared mind.

CHAPTER SIX

West Lothian, Scotland

David Proctor forced himself to breathe with tidal ease, to wax air, to wane. He counted the blown specks on the taxi's windscreen as it idled. The hotel seemed to watch him. Twenty years ago, he had worked beneath its vast grounds in a research centre whose entrances were now capped. He thought about the cut plumbing, the emptied kitchens, the barge-long conference tables splintered, the coffee pots emptied and the conversation silenced. He thought about it all. The young David Proctor was gone. Oxford was gone, too. He opened his briefcase, took a brush, and tidied his hair.

Now or never, Proctor.

He opened the door and, without emerging, breathed the Scottish air. Nodding firs. A cloud-shot sky. For a moment, he was inside his memories of twenty years before.

Through his earpiece, Ego said, 'Professor, you have a call.'

'I'm supposed to be stealthed.'

'The call is encrypted but lacks any metadata referring to the encryption method.'

David frowned. Most of his friends used PGP encryption. He had only once used a different encryption method, and that was between him and his daughter before she disappeared.

'Could be my daughter.' He looked at his flat shoe on the gravel. He decided to take a chance. He closed the door. 'Access my medical records, please.'

'Just a moment. What am I looking for?'

As David opened his wallet, looking for the Ego unit itself, he told the computer what to look for. Then he placed Ego on the slope of the dashboard and sat back. An image of his daughter appeared on the computer's exterior. Her skin was puffy and her eyes were ringed with the sediment of hard work. For a moment, David was shocked by her resemblance to her late mother, whose head David had cradled in the last moments of her life all those years ago, not far beneath where his taxi was now. He touched his trouser pocket. In it, he had the picture of a house that Jennifer had drawn as a child, the picture that had been on his fridge door.

'Hey,' he said, unsettled by his nostalgia.

'Dad.' Her tone was neutral, lawyerly. 'You're not easy to find.'

'Jennifer, I'm really glad you called.' He told himself he was, and, on some level, this was true, but right now his heart thudded and his hands were making fists. 'Really.'

'You seem shocked.'

He forced a smile. 'It's your accent.'

Jennifer did not smile back. Drily, she said, 'You sound as British as ever.'

David had thought about Jennifer every day since they had become estranged, but he had never rehearsed how a conversation might go. He had always assumed it would be as natural as their long-ago discussions of maths or psychology. Despite his discomfort, he recognised the opportunity here. She might not contact him again.

'Jesus, sweetheart. We need to talk.'

Her expression softened. 'Go on.'

'The truth is,' David said, wondering how his mistake would sound when spoken, 'I sent you to New York too soon.'

'You sent me away, Dad.' Her voice was still toneless, as though she were maintaining a deliberate distance. 'You sent the freak to the freaks, then skipped the country.'

That hurt.

'You couldn't stay in Oxford any more. You wouldn't have realised your potential.' David rubbed his sore neck. 'We've been through this.'

'I was the one who had to go through it, not you. Do you know what it was like in that school?'

'I got your emails.'

Quick as a wasp, she replied, 'I didn't get yours.'

Now his anger threatened to match hers. 'Jennifer, this is the first time we've spoken in years. Did you call just to start a fight?'

She took a breath and closed her eyes. David recognised it as a trick her mother had used when settling herself.

Jennifer said, 'Just tell me where you are.'

'I'm at the old research centre in West Lothian.'

'Already?' She was scared. How much did she know? 'What are you doing there?'

'I can't tell you that on the phone. I'm sorry, but I can't.'

'This isn't a phone, Dad.' She sounded amused.

'I know. Even an old duffer like me can tell the difference.' He waited for the hint of on a smile on her face. 'I even figured out your encryption.'

'You mean your Ego unit did. Sounds like a nice toy.'

'He's clever, but a bit buggy. A prototype.'

'Dad?' Jennifer was serious now, her iciness gone. 'I want you to listen to me. Just turn around and go back to Oxford. Go home.'

The high ribwork of the orangery joined a sternum thirty feet above the floor. Evening had turned the panes dark blue. Rain sputtered. McWhirter, the West Lothian Centre's former Chief of Security, sat in a winged chair and David stood with his elbow on the mantel of the unlit fireplace, spinning the ice in his whisky with metronomic tips of his wrist. Otherwise, the orangery was deserted.

'Somehow,' said McWhirter, scratching the translucent skin of his knuckles, 'Bruce broke into your old laboratory.'

'First, tell me what it's like down there.'

'A steady five degrees.' McWhirter paused. 'Structurally, it isn't safe. We've had two cave-ins.'

'His physical condition?'

'Uncertain. I thought you could take a look at him.'

'Medical school was a long time ago. Don't you have your own people for that?'

'You'll do.'

David abandoned the hearth for a chair opposite

McWhirter. There was a pile of broadsheet newspapers on the table. Dead-tree editions for the old fossils of the Park Hotel. How long had the hotel been closed? He disliked the malt, but sipped. 'So you want me to go down there. Triffic.'

'You know the layout as well as anyone.'

'I worked there. So did you. What say I guard the whisky and you go down?'

'The bomber knew this place too.'

David studied his glass. 'No argument. It was an inside job.'

'He knew where to set the explosives.' McWhirter stared at him. 'He knew when the scientists would be in the hall and away from danger. He knew which project to bomb.'

David could hear the pings of his heartbeat. 'Aren't you a bit old to be playing games?'

McWhirter leaned forward. 'Just between us now. We're alone. Did you do it?'

'You know, there are rumours that someone infiltrated the research centre that day. If so, a person in authority must have covered up the evidence.'

'There's a another rumour,' said McWhirter, 'that you and Bruce were planning to destroy Onogoro.'

'So what if we were? Under pressure from Crane, Onogoro became a torture chamber for the artificial organisms trapped inside. I made that clear to the committee. That doesn't mean we went through with it.' David let the moment stretch out until it snapped. 'My wife died in the explosion. My Helen. There was nothing left for me after that.'

'You had your daughter – only she ran away, didn't she? Disappeared into thin air.'

David looked at McWhirter. 'Whoever put you in charge of security made a mistake. You've both had twenty years to get over it.'

McWhirter crossed his legs. The faded jeans were at odds with the smartness of the man David remembered. His crew-cut hair and combed moustache had whitened. McWhirter tapped a nail at the side of his glass. 'Bruce has put Onogoro back online.'

'Bollocks he has.' David tried to sound surprised. 'It was destroyed.'

'Evidently not.'

'It needs a dedicated power plant just to boot.'

'Twenty years ago, maybe, when you and I were lads. Welcome to the future. The power spike is how we got wind of the whole business.'

'I thought the entrances were capped.'

'We cut through them.'

'"We"?' David surveyed the neat, empty tables and chairs. 'So you and I are not alone.'

'This is the future. Nobody's alone anymore.'

'You got grumpy with age, McWhirter.'

'I was always grumpy. Now I've grown into it, like my ears. Professor Proctor?'

'Colonel?'

'I can't send any more of my people down there. It's too dangerous.'

'But my death is a risk you're willing to take?'

'Aye. Nobody else can operate that device. And remember that Bruce needs you. He was your best friend.'

Idly, David put his nose into the whisky glass. 'He was.'

›•‹

The preparations for David's descent into the abandoned research centre were carried out by McWhirter alone. He claimed that this would protect the identities of his team. David appreciated that this made his presence ever more ghostly and asked McWhirter, with a crooked smile, whether he had anything to worry about besides the airborne contaminants down there.

McWhirter gave him a serious look. 'The cold. Put this on.'

It was an all-in-one encounter suit with a clam-shell helmet and respirator. There was a medical kit strapped on the back. As David climbed into the suit, he looked around the cloakroom. All those years ago, he would have stood exactly as he did now, placed his thumb on the wall and waited for the computer to scan his blood. Then the room would drop. But there was no longer a computer. Instead, there was a rough hole in the floor with a ladder leaning against its edge.

David fastened the collar.

'What happened to the lift?' he asked.

'It was dismantled. All part of the clean-up.'

David paused. He did not want to talk about that. The regrets were shards of glass.

'Anything else?'

McWhirter nodded. He took a body-harness – the kind a mountaineer might wear. David put it on.

'Am I going potholing too?'

'It's a possibility. One of my men fell into a void and was badly injured. Now everyone gets one of these.'

'Bloody hell.'

'Pay attention down there. When you get to the bottom, attach both the carabiners on that harness to the safety line. It runs all the way to your old lab.'

'Anyone else down there, or is it just me?'

'Just you.'

And Bruce.

David closed the clam-shell helmet and tested the respirator. When the valve opened, his forelock moved in the dry air.

'Are they going to give me a medal for this?'

'Down you go. The clock's ticking.'

›•‹

David sat on the edge of the hole, slid his weight forward, and began to descend. When his head passed below the level of the floor, he looked down and saw a circle of lighting twenty metres below.

›•‹

As he stepped off the base of the ladder, David shielded his eyes from the spotlights, which put irregular shadows over ruptured cabinets, broken chairs and blackened computer screens. Shredded paper lay like snow. He could hear the faraway growl of a diesel generator. There was a rack of recharging torches next to the ladder. He took one and clipped himself to the safety line that disappeared into the darkness.

His torch beam reflected from the ashy airborne particles.

As he breathed, his mouth dried.

David remembered the corridor as a bright, air-conditioned expanse dotted with abstract art. Now there was just ongoing black. His feet settled feather-light, careful as an astronaut in moon dust, but the corridor sediment stirred nonetheless. His heavy-duty trousers snagged on cabinets, splintered wood, and stalagmites of glass. He stepped around one of the many cables that looped down. Occasionally, the ceiling made a purring sound.

He fought against the silence but the silence won. Its negative pressure drew out the memories. He pictured Helen, his wife, leading Bruce into the dining room of their new house; Bruce noting the layout of chairs, counting the paces between the kitchen door and the patio. Helen had watched Bruce from the doorjamb. Her hands had rested on her swelling belly. He remembered how at ease Bruce had been, the way he had laughed.

There was another purr from the ceiling.

David's tears grew, unwipable, behind his visor.

Ten metres ahead, a light bobbed. Was it a reflection? David thumbed off his torch.

'Bruce?' he called, muffled.

He pressed forward. Cables snagged at his chin. Then he heard a sound from his teenage years. It was the tight creak of rigging when the sails took wind. He looked up and saw the ceiling distend. Dust fell, absurdly liquid. He scrambled clear but tripped. His head struck a rocky swelling of concrete. The world swayed and he could not stand. He heard the ceiling collapse behind him; the vibrations coursed through his belly. In the stillness afterward, he realised that he had lost the torch. The corridor was black as burial. The collapse had missed him by centimetres.

The pip in his ear said, 'Professor Proctor, you have lost your telemetric connection to the surface.'

'There's been a cave-in. Looks blocked. Is there another way out?'

'Not directly. But McWhirter's team left an extremely low-frequency transmitter in your former laboratory. You could send a message.'

'I think I broke the torch, Ego.'

'Your visor is equipped with a zero-light mode. Would you like me to activate it?'

'Please.'

›•‹

Above ground, McWhirter completed his nightly exercises with ten last press-ups on his knuckles. Sweat dewed his chest hair. He moved into a crouch and pressed a towel against his forehead and each armpit. There were eight mirrors in his Victorian suite. The full-length glass in the living room showed him what he wanted. He walked through the French doors to a balcony set with hardy, dark green plants. McWhirter had such shrubs in his own garden, where they defined a pet labyrinth. He hung the towel around his neck and looked down the hotel's gravel drive – footlights marked its edges – while his sweat dried in the wind.

His telephone rang.

'McWhirter.' He sat on the bed and rolled his head to treat a crick. 'Go on.' He removed the towel and sat on it. 'What? Fuck.'

CHAPTER SEVEN

David stopped in the doorway of his former laboratory and studied the ceiling. His visor gave him a false-colour image. Fire had taken the tiles. Exposed cables trailed.

His first footfall crunched.

'Ego, can you analyse the air?'

'There are fine transition metals, some acids – chiefly sulphuric – and insoluble particles. The atmosphere is acutely carcinogenic.'

'Remind me to give McWhirter a slap.'

'When would you like this reminder?'

'Forget the reminder.'

'Very well.'

The liquid storage device had once prompted a joke about LSD, but David could not remember which of the team had cracked it. The transparent chamber was the size of a car, and the soup of liquid polymer, the tonnes of it, rolled in huge fronts of colour. Once it had reminded David of the surface of Jupiter. In contrast with the darkness, it was nova-bright.

'Ego, I will place you beneath the forward stanchion of the device. Do you understand?'

'Perfectly.'

David slid Ego into the drifts of dust.

›•‹

Though the laboratory had never stored hazardous materials, it contained a decontamination room as standard. There was a shower, a bath, and a huge sink. The concrete floor sloped towards a drain on the far wall. The emergency lights were dead behind their grills. David walked across the broken tiles and burst pipework, and knelt in the corner, where a body lay in a sleeping bag. He peeled away the fabric.

Bruce might have been dead. His face was sunken and his mouth lopsided. His hands were drawn against the chest. There was a blanket over his legs. When David moved it aside, a writhing ball of blackness fragmented into rats – their tiny feet pink, their eyes winking – and he checked the urge to scoop them away. Gently, he examined Bruce's trousers. They were intact. The rats were in it for the warmth. If Bruce got some warmth in return, David was easy. He resettled the material.

Bruce lay on a mortuary headrest. David felt underneath. Sure enough, there was a neural bridging unit.

'How long have you been inside, Bruce? Two days now? Soon after you broke in, I bet.'

His unconscious patient said nothing. David considered ripping the cable from the man's brain, but the lab mice had all died when unplugged. He thought of Bruce moving around in the inkiness of this place – making his nest, his grave. The darkness of it. The same darkness that had fallen on Bruce at the age of ten. The blind man navigating by touch; coughing in the dust.

David pushed these thoughts aside. He went about his work efficiently and calmly. He put a saline drip in the left arm and an antibiotic drip in the right. It was impossible not to think of former, better times. He and Bruce had been inseparable. He found a note in Bruce's trouser pocket. In handwriting frozen at ten years old, it read:

Well well well, after all these years! I'm looking forward to seeing an old friend. Come into my parlour said the spider to the etc.

David rocked back, hugged his knees and stared at his oldest friend.

Later, he left the room, crossed the main laboratory, and entered the suite of immersion chambers. There were six of them arranged either side of a walkway. Their transparent doors were blackened but otherwise intact. The first one opened easily. David put his head inside and tried to inspect the vents in the ceiling of the cubicle, but his helmet was too cumbersome. The visor's alarm whooped as David broke the seal. Perfect darkness slid up. When, finally, he took a breath, he gagged on the air. It stank like an old incinerator. He looked again at the cubicle vents. They were clear. He put the helmet on the floor, imagining the spill of dust, and removed his clothes. His bare feet stepped on silky sediment. The chamber was no larger than a shower stall.

'Ego?' He pressed his earpiece. 'Has the computer finished the diagnostic program on the fines in this cubicle?'

'Yes. The diagnostic has been passed. The machine is safe.'

Next to the vents in the cubicle ceiling was a full-face mask. It slid down like a periscope. David turned aside as two decades of dust hissed out. When the apparatus was producing good air, he attached it to his head, which was now held in a fixed position within the cubicle. The door closed automatically. Next he heard a whine from above. A warm, viscous liquid poured on his head. White droplets covered his mask, and then his vision was obscured entirely by the deluge.

The liquid evaporated to a crumbling residue, which soon lifted from his body as though blown by a wind from below. It formed a swirling, buffeting storm. Each microscopic mote in that mist was a 'fine': a smart particle not unlike a bumble bee in appearance. The uncountable billions of fines could move according to instruction and induce temperature through friction. They were a haptic cloud of edges, shapes, and objects. They recreated the solidity, texture and danger of physical reality.

David watched some log-file text slide across the internal screen of the mask.

'My voice is my passport,' he said. 'Verify me.' The computer heard the key phrase and checked his voice against a database. Its essential components had not changed in twenty years.

The log-file text was replaced by an epic vista. As always, its beauty staggered him. He was looking over the ocean of Onogoro. The dawnlit waves at his feet lapped against a sugar-white shore. The grains beneath his feet were virtual surfaces created at whim by the fines; but the feeling was like coming home. It conjured a sudden, painful nostalgia for the glory days.

A virtual square appeared. On it was a user interface. One icon would summon The Word, the programming language that controlled the universe. He moved his virtual hand over this panel and a blue dot appeared beneath his index finger. He hesitated over 'Shut Down'. A gesture would stop the program. It would send him back into the real world forthwith. He could not guess where it would send Bruce.

He touched another icon. It was a picture of his younger self. His old account.

'Professor,' said Ego, 'the low-frequency transmitter has received a response from McWhirter. He seems upset.'

'Go on.'

'I will paraphrase. He wants you to cease all activity while an emergency shaft is sunk to remove you from the laboratory.'

'How long do I have?'

'The estimate is one hour. McWhirter already has the equipment on site. Do you have a reply?'

'Tell him to go fuck himself. No need to paraphrase.'

CHAPTER EIGHT

David rushed into the image of the ocean and shore, which blurred away as though he had been accelerated to the speed of sound. He flew over lakes and trees, through pristine mountain passes, across waterfalls, into grasslands and desert, over ice floes and volcanic islands. Night fell in seconds. He slowed, felt vertiginous, and landed in a tropical glade. The mimetic cloud of fines rendered the springy crunch of the undergrowth perfectly. Experience told him not to think about his real body. He made a mental effort to accept himself here, now, walking in the woods: its dampness; its predators. Onogoro had no moon, but David could adjust the brightness using the command console. Doing so, he walked on through this alien world. Its plants were blue, not green, and typically angular. Through breaks in the canopy, he saw a snow-smudged mountain. The peak was bright with dawnlight. Was he being watched by a predator?

As he walked, he smiled to himself. If a race of intelligent beings had evolved in this universe, and developed science, their physicists would discover that matter was continuous, not discrete. Their astronomers would find that their planet was the only planet, their star the only star. They would correctly place themselves at the centre of the universe. Should they build a computing machine, it would never outrun the computer that ran their universe: and what, indeed, would they hypothesize the limiting factor to be? God?

The ground inclined. Ahead, David saw a cabin that had been modelled on an Alaskan hunting lodge from a hiking magazine and, by dint of Word, conjured into being. It overlooked the forest below. David turned to the vista, which opened up to the east. He could see the mist of a waterfall and a double rainbow in the eye of sunrise.

It began to rain.

'Quite a view,' called a man.

Bruce Shimoda, whose body was lying not far from David in the abandoned laboratory, stepped from the cabin. He wore a haphazard patchwork of fronds. The computer had used the instructions in his DNA to forge this body anew in zeros and ones, so he was twenty years old once more and bearded. Yet there was a greater, unplaceable difference.

David said, 'I didn't know about the fancy dress code.'

Bruce smiled. 'That's rich, coming from a giant, sparkling bogey.'

The difference: his eyes were clear and steady. Bruce Shimoda, blind in the outside world, could now see.

Bruce stirred the fireplace. He was crouching on the edge of a grizzly bear pelt, a photographer's idea of a lodge *accessoire*. The kitschery continued with tasselled lamps, a mahogany bar, shotguns, and mounted animal heads.

David moved towards the fire. He felt the fines mimic its temperature. This reminded him of McWhirter. 'I've got about half an hour, Bruce. Can we talk?'

'I jinxed the room. It's encrypted.'

'For you, maybe. McWhirter could be listening at the door to my immersion chamber.'

'Jesus, is that old dog still alive?'

'And learning new tricks, you bet.'

Bruce sighed. 'How much do you know, David?'

'Not much. Our mutual friend, whoever that is, told me to accept the summons to Scotland, which I did. I know I have a job to do.'

Bruce leaned on his hand. He coughed with a scraping sound that David associated with the pneumonia cases of his junior doctoring days. When the fit passed, Bruce looked up. There were red flecks on his teeth.

'What's up?' asked David.

'I'm infected. On Onogoro, we've got all kinds of animal – analogues of them, anyway – from birds and fish to viruses. I wasn't born in this world. I have no history of exposure. My immune system hasn't been toughened up.'

'The program I wrote should have compensated.'

'Yes, but it was never tested.' Bruce made an explosive sound with his lips and pointed to an imagined horizon. 'Bruce Shimoda. The test pilot. The dog in orbit.'

David's tired eyes dropped to the floor. 'It's a new trick, mate. I'll give you that much.'

They said nothing for a few seconds. The fire crackled and the wind was a low hum in the eaves.

'Dave?' began Bruce. There was a serious look in his eye. 'I'm dying. But…'

'But what?'

'I haven't seen hills and trees for years.'

'Was it worth the wait? Honestly.'

Bruce grinned. 'Honestly? Every bloody second.'

The estranged friends looked at each other. David remembered their first meeting, remembered the impressiveness of this blind man who moved unstoppably around new rooms, smiled with delight at the smallest kindness, and loved nothing more than long hours with his genetic algorithms, his virtual toys. A tiny crack in their friendship had formed back then, after the bombing, and David didn't know who to blame for the gaping hole of today.

'Bruce, talk to me.'

'I'm effectively already dead, if that helps. Unplug me, I die. Shut down the computer, I die. The computer has me by the balls.'

David drifted to the edge of the room. Rain sizzled on the pane.

'What does this have to do with our mutual friend? The person who sent me here?'

'I don't know yet.'

David sighed. 'How did it get it to be twenty years, Bruce?'

'Time takes what it wants. We give what we must.'

There was a distant boom and David felt the floor shake.

'Did you hear something?' he asked.

'Nope.'

'If you didn't, it must be McWhirter's men. They've blasted through.'

'Like I said, we give what we must.'

David heard breaking glass, but the cabin window remained intact. It had to be the immersion chamber smashing. Abruptly, his visual field scene shifted. Somebody was trying to remove the mask from his face.

'Bruce,' he said. 'I'm sorry. I'm really sorry. For the time.'

Bruce pointed at his eyes and then at David.

'See you later, alligator.'

In a while—

›•‹

They swirled, the dark swathes of bubbles, and the half-seen flick of a reptilian tail stirred David from his hallucination, brought him gasping to the surface of his consciousness.

Room. I'm in a room.

He went under again. The memories of childhood holidays around the beaches of Padstow – deep water – pushed hard against him. He tried to wipe his eyes but his wrists were bound to his chair. He slumped asleep. Woke again. Slept. Troughs of anxiety. Peaks of fear. David rolled through the minutes.

'Professor Proctor,' said McWhirter, as though distracted by a certain quality in the alliteration.

A nurse.

A nurse moved away from David's arm, where she had stopped to tend something.

To adjust.

A drip.

Chemicals; drugs; right.

'Mc—' David said. 'Whirter.' His voice was crumbly, flawed.

'That will be all.'

'What will be?' asked David.

'I'm not talking to you.'

David sensed the nurse leave the room. He forced his eyes wide and looked around. He was in an empty luggage store. Still in the hotel, then. An empty table separated him from McWhirter. He noted the clear, hanging bag and tried to guess which chemicals it contained, but the only memories at his recall were sentimental. His father painting the house with a brush like McWhirter's moustache. Two-tone. Black and white. His daughter as a girl, drawing a house on sugar paper.

'Beautiful, Jenny. Do you think you can draw it without taking your crayon from the paper? Good girl. And can you do it again without tracing the same line twice. Jenny? Hey, clever girl.'

He swallowed. 'How long have I been in here?'

'Let's start at the beginning. Why did you come, Proctor?'

'You invited me as a consultant.'

'Isn't there another reason?'

David felt more clear-headed. Perhaps the nurse had administered something to diminish the fog. Despite this, he pretended to remain groggy. There might be an advantage in that.

'To talk to Bruce. To find out why he came. Is he still down there?'

'Yes. Why?'

Jenny asking, 'Why?' and David answering over and over,

each explanation a cheerful retreat, until he backed into atoms, to orbits, quarks, the Higgs field.

'I'll tell you everything,' said David, 'if you'll tell me one thing.'

'Let me guess. You want to know if the research centre has been evacuated. Well, it's your lucky day. It has.'

A sucking, heavy despondency pulled at David. What did McWhirter know? What had David already confessed, and perhaps forgotten?

'Why?' asked Jenny.

'Looking for this?' asked McWhirter, holding up Ego.

'Fuck.'

'My security staff found some kind of MEEC tech inside this thing. Yeah, I know all about it. High efficiency mass conversion could turn this into a handy demolition charge.' McWhirter now swapped feigned amusement for feigned disgust. 'You weren't happy with the destruction you caused the first time, were you? You wanted a second go. But why this?' He shook his head. 'You would have killed your friend, man.'

In a tired voice, David said, 'The Onogoro computer needs to be destroyed.'

'Listen to me. See that drip? One twist of that valve and you'll feel the lights going out, one by one. Now. Why destroy Onogoro?'

'To stop…'

'Concentrate. Who?'

'Crane.'

'Crane who? John Crane?'

'And to kill Bruce.'

Loudly, McWhirter said, 'Bruce is your friend.'

'Dead anyway. Viruses.'

McWhirter slapped him.

'Sleep later. How did you expect to get away with it?'

David licked his lips. 'Relied on a weakness.'

'What weakness?'

'You.' David opened his eyes. 'As head of security in 2003, you failed. Now, in 2023, you've failed again.'

McWhirter now looked genuinely scared. 'Talk to me.'

'You're a one-trick pony. I knew you would order a quick search of the laboratory, find the card, and wave it in front of me. But think. How could I, above ground, expect to send a signal to a computer in the research centre?'

'A timer,' said McWhirter, though he did not sound convinced.

'A timer? Then why would I want to know if the centre had been evacuated? The logical solution, Colonel, is two computers. The Ego unit in your hand has already interfaced with the local ELF transmitter. Now it is ready to trigger the second Ego unit I hid somewhat more expertly. Is this not true, Ego?'

'Yes, Professor,' said the card.

McWhirter held his stare. 'You have control, Proctor. Fine, I concede that. Now take it easy. Think about it.'

'Get fucked, McWhirter.'

Ego bleeped. 'Key phrase recognised and signal transmitted, Professor.'

McWhirter threw down the computer like it was a losing card. 'Is it on a delay?'

'A while, crocodile. Two minutes.'

McWhirter took out his mobile phone and dialled. He said, 'Confirm everyone is out of the Centre.' A pause.

'Then confirm it again.'

The explosion, when it came, was a croak of thunder. The table buzzed against the metal band of McWhirter's watch. He did not move his eyes from those of David, and when a uniformed officer returned with news of smoke from the evacuation shaft, McWhirter simply nodded and told him to take appropriate measures.

The minutes collected. David watched the questions pass. They did not touch him. He smiled and remembered the questions of his daughter.

Jenny asking, 'Why?'

CHAPTER NINE

Berlin

Saskia wore an FIB standard issue outfit for women field agents: black trouser suit with a short, double-breasted rain jacket. They had thrown in ankle boots. In these, Saskia was now walking around Berlin. With the wind in the north-east, she looked at the Brandenburg Gate and wondered if her memory of passing beneath it was implanted. Greened steel horses looked east. Saskia turned too. Pariser Platz stretched out. A drum skin. Her eyes dropped to a human street cleaner. He was too distant for her to see his epaulettes. She thought, again, of the Soviet memorial to the west.

I know what Soviet means, at least.

I know what meaning means.

The Gate's sad blocks, its darkness, its gold lettering: these said nothing to her. What did those with memory read in the stones?

Her coat was swept open by the wind. It exposed the dark handle of her gun in its pancake holster. She gathered the coat about her, embarrassed, and walked towards the shadow of the Gate. She collided with a man. He took her wrist and said, '*Seien Sie vorsichtig, Frau Kommissarin.*' The Russian accent was strong like his grip. He opened and closed an FIB badge and then she remembered him in the lobby of that building on Behrenstraße.

'*You should be on holiday.*'

'*I should be on holiday.*'

'Klutikov?'

Coffee in a dark, long room where flowers in wire spirals sagged across the tables. Amaretti biscuits. Coffee with her past in the form of an over-tall man called Klutikov – FIB, Moscow Station. He had a translucent raincoat. It hung now behind them on an antique coat stand. Saskia kept her jacket on. It covered her holster, her speed-loader and her shape as a woman before the eyes of the man who could thumb through her identity at will. Coffee with memory. Klutikov licked sugar from his palm.

'Cigarette?' he asked.

'Here?'

'It's the only place.'

'I don't smoke.'

'Take one. Draw it beneath your nose. Now. Want a cigarette?'

'God, yes.'

He laughed as he put the lighter to the cigarette. Saskia saw something important in its golden reflection, but he withdrew it before she could pinpoint what had aroused her curiosity. The smoke left her mouth slowly. She spread out in her chair.

'Better?'

'Sure.'

He showed her his empty palm. Then he touched his fingertips in order: 'One, no names, ever. Two, after this coffee, you forget you saw me. Three, smile.'

Saskia blushed. She drank some coffee. It was ashy, like the cigarette.

'Any synaesthesia?' asked Klutikov.

'What's that?'

'You never need to ask that kind of question again. Ask yourself.'

'What?'

'Do it.'

What is synaesthesia?

An answer entered her head. It had a fundamental strangeness that took her a moment to identify: it did not use the same voice as her thoughts.

Synaesthesia, in this context, is the experience of sensation in a modality that did not trigger the initial sensation. For example, a voice might be described as 'crumbly, yellow'.

'What was that?'

'Intel. Don't worry about it. The important thing is that you haven't had any synaesthetic experiences. Synaesthesia is an indicator that the operation went wrong.'

'Operation?'

Klutikov exhaled smoke from his nose and beckoned Saskia. Again, her understanding lagged. Oh, he wanted her to lean forward. When she did, he put his hand on the back of her head. He touched a scab that Saskia had not noticed.

'This is where they fired it in.'

'*You* lean forward.'

Klutikov paused. Then, with a nod, he bowed. He let Saskia search his hair. She found a knot of skin no larger than a vaccination scar. Klutikov sniffed and checked the other customers.

'The chip is a small computer, but quite powerful. One of its talents is telecommunication.'

'It connects to the Net?'

'Just so.'

'What else?'

'The specifications aren't well known. To me, at least.'

'Who made it?'

'That's above my pay grade.'

'Does it suppress my memories? Why can't I remember anything?'

'No, that's not it.' He jammed his cigarette into the ash tray. 'Your brain is made of little cells – following? The reason that I'm me and you're you is that the cells are wired differently. One pattern of wiring is me, one pattern is you, and another is the King of England. It's all about the pattern. If you took a recording of my brain and imposed that pattern on another brain, then that brain, and therefore that person, will start to sound and act like me. They'll think that they are me, and, in important ways, they will be. Your chip contains the memories of another person in a compressed, digital form. Reasonably high fidelity. It would take an expert to tell the difference.'

'An expert?'

'The chip is connected by tiny filaments to more than half the neurons in your neocortex. Your neocortex is where the more "human" functioning goes on. The chip remains in contact with your brain and constantly imposes the donor pattern over your own.'

Saskia looked at her hand. She realised that she did not know whose hand she was looking at. *The chip is like a parasite with its feeding tube in my brain.* She moved a finger. *No, the parasite moved the finger.*

'That's enough, Klutikov.'

I'm the parasite.

'No names. Are you going to be sick?'

'No.'

'Good, because I haven't finished. The imposition of the donor pattern must be constant. If not, the original pattern – that is, the personality and identity extant in your brain – will resurge. If you switch off the chip, you switch off "you", the you *you* know as yourself.'

'My... body's personality – my original brain and body before the chip – was convicted of murder.'

'Don't get distracted. You need to protect that chip. If you ever receive an electric shock, it's over. Likewise don't let yourself be put in a scanner that uses magnets. You could get a bracelet like mine. It says I have metal in my head from a hunting accident.'

'I can use a gun, a computer, and I know the layout of this city. Why can't I remember anything else?'

'Slow down. You're conflating episodic and procedural memory. Speech, for example. You haven't forgotten that. Walking, too. That's all procedural memory. Some of those skills will come from your brain, some from the chip. If you're talking about memories of people, holidays, and your childhood, that's episodic.'

'Then why don't I have any of those memories?'

'I guess our boss didn't think you needed them.'

Klutikov shook his wrist to expose his watch. 'I have to go soon.'

'So what's your story?'

'My story?'

'Why did our boss recruit you?'

'The same reason he recruited you.' He lit another cigarette and gave it to her. 'My body, the criminal, will talk to me through inspiration, intuition, gut feeling – call it what you like. That gives me an operational advantage. My mind – the donor pattern on the chip, what I feel is the real me – gives me the discipline, the analytical firepower, and keeps the instinct in check.'

'What you're telling me is unbelievable.'

'Then you must concentrate. First, you need to understand that you're not responsible for the crimes of your body. You – the person I'm talking to – are completely different. You're brand new. You're not answerable for the crimes of your body any more than you're responsible for the crimes of your parents. Understood?'

'No.'

'Good. That's honest.' He looked past Saskia's shoulder. 'One year ago, I discovered that I was a fraud. In my own mind, I had been working criminal cases for ten years, but, of course, the truth was that I'd been active for less than two months. Before that, I – well, this body – had been a real terror. When our boss told you what you were, he let you keep your memory of the event. You have Beckmann's explanation for why you are who you are. Not me. He wiped my memory soon after telling me. My big wake-up call came this summer when I was on holiday in Poland.

'I was out fishing. A man walked by with his two sons. He took one look at me and literally had a heart attack. Fortunately, I had my field kit, so I could treat him. Shouldn't have bothered. When he woke up, he shouted to his sons that I was the bastard who killed their mother during a bank robbery the year before. I...' he shrugged. 'I buried them where I shot them, the sons and the father. By morning, I was two hundred miles away. I went straight to Beckmann, confronted him, and he told me everything. Since then, I've found it difficult to concentrate. So I do odd jobs.' He paused. Saskia did not know what to say. 'There is one more thing,' he said. 'It's the answer.'

'The answer to what?'

'The question you've been asking yourself since yesterday.'

Klutikov reached for his coat. He withdrew a broadsheet newspaper and handed it to Saskia. The script was Cyrillic. The lead story was accompanied by a picture of her.

No, not me; this body I've infected.

Her hair was much longer and the wind had blown it wide. Two police officers held her arms.

'Sorry, it's in Russian. If you learn something significant about your previous life, that risks tripping the safeguards Beckmann put on your chip.'

'So my chip can't translate it?'

'Given time, you will be able to translate any language.'

'What does this bit say?'

'"Angel of Death in Custody".'

Saskia felt the words in her belly. 'They call me the Angel of Death?'

'Yes. As Beckmann told you – you were a multiple

murderer. You were captured at the German border.'

'No. *No.* ' She wiped away a tear with her knuckle.

'Listen, you *were* a murderer. Past tense. That was just your body. You're a blank slate now. Look at your badge. *Ex tabula rasa.*'

'But surely I'm still responsible?'

'Don't get philosophical about it. Be pragmatic. Do you feel like a murderer? Could you kill someone now in cold blood?'

Saskia's eyes were fixed on the article. The Cyrillic letters seemed to warp. 'You did,' she said. 'That Polish man and his sons.'

Saskia put her lips to the cooling rim of her cup. The end of their conversation. Coffee in a cinder-grey room, murderer to murderer. Klutikov gathered his cigarettes and flung his coat about his shoulders.

'Where will you be?' she asked.

He took the newspaper. 'East of the Urals, if not west. Remember, your past is just a tabloid horror story. Give it up. If our boss finds out I told you, he'll kill us both. But I thought you should know.'

As he left, Saskia sent a thought to her chip.

Who am I?

There was no answer.

CHAPTER TEN

David had been given orange overalls and cuffed to the floor of the hotel's wine cellar by a short shackle, which forced him to crouch. He wore a hangman's hood. A nearby speaker blasted static. He remained still and silent. Let his captors think he was about to break. He daydreamed that he was poised on a starting block. He could maintain the stance. He played squash once a week. Cycled to and from work. The room here was cold, but he had known colder.

He calmed his thoughts through the slow recall of his graduate seminar on psychological interrogation. The unremitting stress of the crouch was designed to weaken him physically. The static filled his hearing; the hood removed his sight. Given time, such sensory deprivation would turn his mind upon itself, trigger an incestuous multiplication of thoughts leading to hallucination and despair.

There was a crack in his composure that McWhirter could probe. Bruce was dead. David had murdered him.

The stain would mark David forever, but his deeper fear was his daughter's reaction.

Any further thoughts were interrupted by the sudden silence. The static had stopped.

David heard flat shoes approaching slowly.

A woman said, 'I can get you out if you come with me and ask no questions. Deal?'

'Deal.'

The hood was pulled away by a woman whose seriousness reminded him of Jennifer, but whose eyes were bottle green. She was dressed in black, had a slim build, and was perhaps in her forties. She was crouching close to him. He looked at her as her power-cutters clipped through his chain. She did not meet his eye. Instead, she took his hand and touched the sound system. Its speakers roared with static once more. *Like rapids*, thought David. *Ride them out of here.*

'Quickly,' she said.

They left the cellar and ran through a corridor into a kitchen – mortuary-clean, prepped for new day – and into a pantry, and through chambers where old washing machines had once laundered the clothing of the great and the good, and down spiralling, wobbling stairs into darkness. Then she turned to him and said, 'They've realised you're gone. Faster.'

The door ahead was haloed with light. She barged it open and they were outside the hotel, in a yard. Recycling bins lined a low wall.

'It's daytime,' said David.

'Quiet.'

She pulled him into the gap between a bin and the wall. There was a police motorbike on its lay stand. Its white panniers gleamed in the nodding shadows.

'Get behind me,' she said, swinging herself across the seat.

'Don't we need helmets?'

'Come *on*.'

David heard a shout pass through the firs upwind of them. He settled behind her. Oddly intimate. Her long hair smelled of coconut.

She touched the ignition. A windscreen rose from the fascia and fairing grew out around their legs. The noise-cancelling system started with a whine. Something in the sound reminded him of the artificial voice used by the person who had broken into his house. He asked, 'Was it you putting a stun gun in my back yesterday?'

They erupted from the hotel. The accompanying wind recalled the interrogation static. David put his cheek to her ear, trapping her whip-like hair. His trouser cuffs buzzed. He looked up. They left the grounds and a tunnel of trees closed over them. The woman downshifted.

She turned her head and nodded. 'That was me.'

The bike shuddered. She cut left, through an open gate, and skidded across a slush of mud and leaves. Then the bike found its grip once more. They rode uphill.

The bike shimmied briefly and David, unbalanced, dropped his grip to her hips.

'Sorry,' he said.

They kept to the incline. Ahead, panicked sheep had clotted in a corner. The woman swerved across them and abandoned the field through another open gate. She downshifted again and shouted, 'Lean with me.' They made a deep turn that scraped the fairing. The corner opened to reveal a dozen more sheep. *Escaping too*, David thought. *Go.*

She slalomed through the animals.

David waited for a straight section of road before he glanced back. Behind them, a marked police car canted on its suspension as it emerged from the bend. Blue lights flickered.

The next few minutes passed in a tiring series of accelerations and decelerations. They took the bends hard and roared along the straights. The road steepened. Soon, David could see the valley floor. It was bluish with distance. Above them, a helicopter moved into view, rotors thudding.

'Hold on,' she shouted, and David tucked himself into her shape. The lane lost its hedges. She swerved onto the stony, grass-splattered shelf that overlooked the valley, hundreds of feet below. She wove around the rock piles. David struggled to look back. The police car had parked and its doors were open. Black-vested officers, their arms open for balance, teetered through the uneven rocks in pursuit.

She stopped.

'Get off the bike and run.'

He hopped sideways. His legs were weak with cramp. 'Where?'

She nodded at the house-sized pile of rocks in the near distance. Then she pulled away towards the cliff edge. David glanced at the policemen. They had slowed to a walk. It was no challenge to understand their complacency. With the helicopter, David could not hide from surveillance, and the foot officers had him trapped against the sheer drop.

He looked for the woman, but the motorbike had disappeared, sight and sound. Gasping, he loped towards the rock pile. His shoes slipped on the stones and the wind cut through the fabric of his orange overalls. Finally, he rounded the granite slabs and settled in their lee. He hugged himself and considered the lip of grass only twenty feet away, and the valley floor so far below that. He was in greater trouble than ever. His career was over. Bruce was dead. He would never see his daughter again.

David lowered his face to his knees.

When the woman lifted his head in both hands a few moments later, he was surprised by a tear in her eye. She brought his lips to hers as if he were a cup. There was no desire in the kiss. Only a relief.

'I am so glad to see you, David.'

'Likewise.' He studied her face. 'Who are you?'

She placed a gloved finger to his mouth. 'Put this on.'

The rucksack was no larger than an archer's quiver. It had loops for his shoulders. As he struggled into it, he saw that the woman now wore a similar pack.

'Wow, it's heavy.'

'See this, David?'

She was holding a piece of paper in front of him. High, like ID. The pink paper had lost its corners, and the fold lines had almost torn, but David recognised it as the picture he had taken from the fridge door of his house in Oxford.

'Who gave you that?'

'Never mind. Look at the number.' She tapped the corner of the drawing. In ball point pen, someone had written *TS4415*. 'I need you to remember this code.'

'Why?'

She glanced at the helicopter. 'Just do it.'

'Blimey.' *Tom Sawyer with a .44 Magnum shooting a partridge in a pear tree and getting five gold rings as payment.* 'OK, I'll remember.'

She took his hand and led him to the corner of the rock pile. The two policemen were thirty feet away. David glanced at her, ready to panic, but said nothing. Her lips were moving. David looked back. The policemen had split to approach the rock pile from opposite sides. 'Whatever the next part of the plan is,' he said, 'can we please proceed to it?'

'Every police vehicle in the UK is fitted with a trip code in case of hijack. When you send the code, the vehicle locks down and returns to its depot. Check the car.'

David leaned out. He saw the doors of the patrol car close. A moment later, the sound reached the police officers. They stopped and exchanged a glance. The taller policeman touched his throat and radioed to the other.

'The policemen are wondering why that happened,' said the woman. 'The short one has just realised. Now they're wondering if they can get back in time.'

David watched them dash to the car. Their runs were ungainly on the slippery rocks. 'What about the helicopter?'

She seemed to consider his question. 'The pilot took it calmly. He's having a coffee. His co-pilot is agitated. But the flight computer will return them safely to the heliport.'

The helicopter tipped forward and, as David stared, became a receding dot. 'How do you know all that?'

'I can't answer any more questions.' Absently, she moved a lock of his hair. 'There's no more time. I'm sorry. All will be well.'

'Why should I trust you?'

'Take this. I know you want it. I stole it from the evidence locker in McWhirter's suite a few minutes ago.'

She handed him a pink sheet. Jennifer's drawing. But,

as it fluttered in the wind, David noted that its edges were pristine. Fold marks had not yet scored the paper. And, below the crayon house and the three stick figures, no code had been written. David frowned. This woman had two versions of the drawing: one looked as he remembered, while the other was worn and aged.

'Now I understand even less. But thank you. I didn't want to lose this.'

'Let the parachute do the steering.'

'Let the what do the what?'

'See ya.'

She sprinted towards the cliff edge, launched like a long jumper, and was gone. David felt his stomach drop in sympathy. He looked around the side of the granite pile. The policemen seemed angrier than before. They'd returned quickly and were almost upon him. The patrol car had gone. David looked into the cobalt sky and hoped his shoes would keep their grip on the grass. As a talisman, he rolled the pink paper and held it against his heart.

He ran towards the edge.

CHAPTER ELEVEN

Saskia's apartment was a nondescript box in the Schöneberg area of Berlin. It had bare wooden floors, white walls, and black furniture. Its curtains were closed. There was no evidence of a previous owner. On the breakfast bar, she found paper manuals for the boiler, washing machine, and oven. She only stared at them before moving on. She felt like she had died and now haunted this apartment.

At length, her glassy indifference cracked. She lifted her hands. There were calluses where the palms met the fingers. She walked into the bedroom and looked at herself in its full-length mirror. She leaned close, turning her head from side to side. She unzipped the boots and dropped them next to the bed. Then she removed her clothes and underwear.

She remembered the motto of the FIB. *Ex tabula rasa.*

When she had walked out of the building on Behrenstraße, she had passed two overalled workmen taking up the tiles of the inlaid seal. The building was not the FIB headquarters but a nondescript block of office space. Her organisation was covert. Its funding was obscure but linked to BPOL, the Federal Police.

She looked again at her reflection. The individual muscles across her belly were visible. The physique was not bulky – it was suited to running, perhaps swimming – but she could hardly imagine the level of exercise required to maintain it. The torso and thighs were pale, suggesting a one-piece swimming costume. She turned, looking for a birthmark. None; but there was an appendix scar, a vaccination mark and two dots either side of her left nipple, where a piercing had once been. She smiled at the marks until the macabre implication struck her. How different was she from Beckmann, who had commanded her movements in the office the day before?

This is not me. This is the person I control. Something else happened to me. Did they kill me, to read the pattern of my brain?

She opened the wardrobe. There were eight identical FIB outfits along with outdoor gear, gym clothes, plastic-wrapped underwear, several racks of shoes, and bags. She selected a black, short-handled bag and closed the door. Then she took the suit from the bed and dressed. When she had finished, she considered herself a chic, professional Berliner. It felt like a disguise.

She found eye shadow in the bathroom cabinet, along with red nail polish. She looked at the polish and remembered her Russian nickname, the Angel of Death. She brushed her shoulder-length hair until it crackled with static.

She opened the curtains and the windows too. The gloom withdrew with a bow. The black furniture turned grey. She decided to go out and buy food from the Turkish kiosk at the corner of Meininger and Gothaer.

Saskia was on the threshold of the apartment when her phone rang.

'Never mind settling in,' said Beckmann. 'I have your first assignment. It's an Englishman called David Proctor. Don't worry about the jurisdictional issues – I'll handle those. You're to fly to Edinburgh.'

'Don't I need a briefing?'

'Haven't you read the documents I provided? They're in your apartment safe.'

She had a safe?

'I'm… still settling in.'

'Here.'

Like a blooming flower, the knowledge grew in her mind. She gasped and slumped against the doorframe. A distant voice said, 'Consider yourself briefed,' then said no more.

›•‹

Saskia took a taxi to the airport. She shopped for headache tablets. She also bought some tampons. Thanks to Beckmann, the date of her last period was a mystery.

The flight landed in London Gatwick at 10:40 a.m. Waiting for her connection in the lounge, she eavesdropped on a businessman listening to something called *Hamlet* on his media player. Her eyes narrowed in astonishment: there was a fundamental question in the play that found an answer on the echoless steppe of her memories. 'Thus conscience does make cowards of us all; and thus the native hue of resolution is sicklied o'er with the pale cast of thought.' When the businessman rose to leave, she went to grab his hand and said, 'Wait,' but he frowned and backed away.

Who wrote that? she asked of his retreating back, forlorn in her seat. *Can I meet him?*

In Edinburgh Airport's baggage reclaim, she passed an advertisement for something called *Fiddler on the Roof*. Each question reset the bearing of her path through an unknown culture:

What is a musical?

Who was Topol?

What is a Jew?

What was the holocaust?

She fled to a toilet and sat in a cubicle. Her open eyes saw newsreel footage. She felt overwhelmed, as if food were being forced into her mouth faster than she could swallow. There were colourless bodies in drifts. Mounds of hair, shaved. Troves of treasure, surgically stolen. Ash.

The grey blocks that she had seen through the window of her office – the fake office, when she was investigating herself – were a memorial to the holocaust. She had looked at it without seeing.

Stop. I don't want to know any more, she told the chip.

She recalled her conversation with Klutikov. 'You're brand new. You're not answerable for the crimes of your body any more than you can be responsible for the crimes of your parents. Understood?'

No, she thought, wiping her eye. *Not understood.*

›•‹

A man wearing a grey suit waited beneath the sensor that opened the automatic doors of the arrivals area. He held a sign that read 'Brand'. She shrugged. Close enough. Detective Inspector Philip Jago was in his mid-fifties. His cheeks were purpled with blood vessels. He escorted her to a car and they got in the back. It was an unmarked, manual Ford.

'In your own time,' he said to the driver. He spoke in a way that reminded Saskia of Bavarian German: watery sounds running together. 'Your luggage has been sent on. You're staying in Whitburn, as you requested. Any reason? The last sighting of Proctor was further south.'

She would not tell him that the decision to head toward the site of Proctor's original bombing had come to her as inspiration from the sleeping brain of the woman whose body she had usurped.

'Intel,' she said, thinking of Klutikov's explanation.

Jago flicked some ash from the window and looked annoyed. She wondered what he thought of her and was surprised – given the British politeness that ran through her fading memory of Simon – to be told immediately.

'Get this straight, Detective Brandt. When you're on this island, you play nice. You don't use your firearm unless I say so. You tell me everything you're thinking, including hunches, and you'll share your sources. We find Proctor and we deliver him to Special Branch, then we shake hands and say *auf wiedersehen. Alles Klar?*'

'*Alles Klar.*'

They looked at one another.

'I'm serious.' His sigh was blue. 'Last bloke from the FIB shot our suspect and fucked off to Paris. Are you an assassin too?'

Assassin. From the Arabic.

'An eater of hashish. Or a person in the control of Hassan-i-Sabah.' She licked her lips. 'I need a cigarette.'

He seemed amused, and a little surprised. 'I won't stop you.'

'May I have one of yours?'

'Of course.'

'People seldom smoke these days,' she said.

'They do in the police.'

'Why?'

'New to the job?'

'Yes.'

'Light?'

'Please.'

He took out a gold Zippo and struck the thumbwheel. Saskia looked at the flame as she leaned into it. She had seen that trick before her investiture in the FIB. Where? She grabbed Jago by the wrist and studied the flame. But soon the lighter was only familiar. Then, even the familiarity was gone.

Jago stared at her.

'Brandt, you may be sex on a stick, but I've been unhappily married to my desk for twenty years and, between the two of us, I only get it up when the Hibs put one in.'

'When what?'

'When my beloved Hibernian Football Club scores what we term a "goal", my dear,' he said, affecting a pompous tone. He switched back to his native register: 'So turn it off, eh?'

She let go of his hand. 'I didn't mean to—'

'Here's my ID, hen. Next time, ask for it. Any numpty can

hold up a sign in an airport.'

'Sorry.'

Softening, he said, 'You're alright. Here, take a look.' He showed her his warrant card. She took it, nodded, and allowed him to inspect her FIB badge. He held it at arm's length and squinted. 'Ex tabula rasa?'

'Just so.' Saskia thought of the emptiness inside her. She was no police officer. Beckmann had employed her for her gut instinct. 'DI Jago, I would please like to go to the West Lothian Centre.'

'Where?' The annoyance returned to his face. 'The community centre?'

'No. The scene of the terrorist activity.'

'You mean the Park Hotel. Waste of time.'

'Why?'

'Our contact there has government connections and doesn't have to cooperate. The situation is covered by the Official Secrets Act.'

'What's that?'

'There'll be something like it in Germany. Once you've signed a secrecy contract, they can stop you talking about certain things. The act means that we can't know everything about the murder.'

'That makes it rather difficult to investigate, DI Jago.'

'Yes, Detective Brandt, it does.'

'Kommissarin.'

'Our job, *Kommissarin*, is to find him, not to investigate anything. My super and a sheriff looked at the evidence. They're satisfied he's guilty and have authorised all reasonable force in grabbing him. We should start at the shed where he landed.'

'No,' she said, surprised at the ease with which her certainty came. This was the voice of her instinct, homed in that blood-infused organ behind her eyes, the brain that was not hers.

'No?'

'DI Jago, please. Trust me. This is my job.'

'We're going to be thick as thieves, I can tell.' He tapped the driver. 'Park Hotel. Just out of Whitburn, on the way to Harthill.'

›•‹

A low sun hung in reflections, across stonework, on the patina of snow that had fallen during the night. Saskia stepped from the car. She blinked in the sudden cold. She could hear water running nearby. The battlements of trees loomed and she was held, albeit briefly, by the urge to run into that woodland and just be, where it was silent and safe. She turned to the hotel. Its wings flanked the car park. At the centre, Saskia noticed a fountain set with a stone Prometheus, frozen as he passed the gift of fire to man.

'Brandt?' prompted Jago.

Prometheus, who had been chained to a rock by Zeus for his treachery. Prometheus, who had suffered as a hawk pecked away his liver. The liver that grew back; the hawk that returned.

The chains…

'Revenge should have no bounds.'

Hamlet echoed across her mind again.

The Zippo lighter. The gesture.

The hawk that returned.

Why did these thoughts feel significant? Were these the weeping wounds of her brain, silent in the dark of her skull?

Not now. This is a different chase. Whom do you hunt? Proctor or Brandt?

The hawk that returned.

She remembered the dream from her first night as Brandt. The Fates: Clotho, she spins the thread of life; Lachesis, she measures a length; Atropos, she cuts it.

Spin, measure, snip.

Saskia took a case from her handbag. Inside was a pair of glasses. She put them on. She knew – though she could remember no training – that the glasses would capture video of everything she saw. The statue was a key, and she wanted an impression of its shape.

'Brandt, are you OK?'

'Yes. The wind is turning, I feel.'

'Northerly. It'll be a cold night. Come on.'

CHAPTER TWELVE

That morning

David awoke in a field. He was partially wrapped in his parachute. His uncovered face had deadened to a mask. His hands were tense balls of bone and sinew. In the left was Jennifer's crayon drawing. His back ached and he needed to urinate. He wriggled from the canopy and got to his feet.

Ahead, a dark shape in the dawn, was a wooden shed.

First things first. His fingers moved only at explicit, clumsy command. Finally, he opened the overalls' zip. Piss steamed gloriously onto the colourless grass.

Cold. My core temperature is too low.

This had implications, he knew. He had to get warm. And eat. Something like a hot soup. He remembered a favourite from his youth, when he had hill-walked with his wife, Helen. Oxtail soup from a Thermos. Yes, oxtail at the pinnacle; pushing back the cold as it went down, stratum by stratum.

He looked at the shed.

It was wooden, four metres by six, painted white. On top was a solar panel. The door was padlocked but the key had not been removed from its base. He detached the padlock, held it as a weapon, and went inside.

'Hello?'

An old-style fluorescent tube started up. There was a tool-laden workbench. To his right was a partition of old sacking. David approached the bench and saw a stack of folded, silver material. He picked it up. A space blanket.

'Things are…'

A vacuum flask fell from the blanket. Slowly, he picked it up. He unscrewed the lid. With a twist of steam came the memory of peaks climbed and cold defeated: Oxtail soup, his favourite.

'…getting weird.'

'Hello.'

David looked down.

There was a tablet computer on the workbench. As he tipped soup into the flask lid, an impressionistic face appeared on the screen. He slurped the soup. It hurt going down.

'Are you Professor Proctor? If so, you'll remember the code that needs to be written on the pink sheet.'

David poured himself another cup. He had burned his palate and was already tired of his rescue plan. *Tom Sawyer…*

'TS4415. Happy?'

'Thank you. Immediately below this computer is a heated box containing clothes. Please do not touch any of the other clothing in this storage shed.'

'Why not?'

'It does not belong to you.'

David downed the last of the soup and let the space blanket fall. He opened the crate, took a warm T-shirt, pushed it into his face and sighed. He found hiking boots, thermal underwear, jeans, an over-shirt, gloves, a heavy-duty sports jacket, a scarf and a woollen hat. There was also a rucksack containing cash, a credit card in a false name, some official-looking registration documents, and a stun gun – still in its retail packaging.

'What's the plan, computer?'

'Beyond the partition you will find a motorbike.'

'Oh.' David's excitement was undercut by the thought of his Matchless G80, a custom-restored beauty that he kept in lock-up near his home.

'Watch this, please. The bike is an advanced model.' The computer screen changed to show a cartoon motorbike. 'It has a key ignition. The keys are in the bike. Turn the key to the second position and press the start button. The right-hand grip is the accelerator and its lever is the front brake. The left-hand lever is the back brake. Always use both brakes simultaneously.'

David began to dress. He was careful to transfer Jennifer's drawing, which was damp but otherwise intact, to his new clothes. 'I've ridden a bloody bike—'

'Remember, the left-hand lever is not the clutch. The bike has automatic gear transmission. The on-board processor will select the appropriate gear based on speed, predicted traction, orientation and so on. In the event this processor malfunctions, the bike will revert to a mechanical automatic transmission.'

David pulled on the gloves. 'Will there be an exam?'

'Your left foot will rest naturally with the metal tab under the heel and another tab over the toes. The same for your right foot. If you move your feet like so,' the stick figure on the computer screen squeezed its heels, 'then the engine output will increase significantly for a short period.'

The stick figure raced away.

'Cool feature.'

He parted the sack-cloth divider and whistled. The bike had a low profile and wide, spiked tyres. Hydraulic pistons connected the chassis to the steering column. The colour scheme was chrome silver. Fuel cell-electric hybrid. On the tank, in the precision flourish of an artist's signature, was the word *Moiré*.

'That'll do nicely.'

CHAPTER THIRTEEN

The empty hotel lobby had twinned staircases that rose like the edges of a cobra's hood. Saskia crossed dark and light tiles: milky veins in the brown, black cracks in the white. Her small heels made clacks. Deliberately, she lifted her gaze. The ceiling was shot through with lights.

A man hurried towards them.

'No, no, fucking no,' he said.

He had the countenance of a soldier who had learned to march in his youth and had never recovered his relaxation. He was beyond retirement age, but the tightness of the skin around his throat suggested fitness. His eyes travelled up her legs, stopped briefly on her breasts, and flitted to Jago. 'You're bloody persistent if nothing else.'

'Thank you, Colonel McWhirter,' replied Jago. He was motionless. They did not shake hands.

'You have not met me yet,' said Saskia. 'Frau Kommissarin Saskia Brandt, *Föderatives Investigationsbüro*,'

McWhirter stared at her hand as though he wished to

break it, and a branching diagram of self-defence sprouted in her mind's eye, discreet as a menu offered by a butler. It varied on dimensions of incapacity (light, moderate, severe), completion time (7 seconds, 30 seconds, a minute), and weapon type (unarmed, pencil, McWhirter's sweater).

Saskia raised her fist to her mouth. She coughed lightly. The menu slid away.

'The continental FIB hereby requests your full cooperation in the capture of Professor David Proctor, Colonel.' She moved closer to him. She saw the blackheads and the bloodshot sleepiness of his eyes. She looked at his lips and tilted her head. 'I will give you five minutes. Call the person who pays you. Ask them to confirm my identity with the Berlin section chief – Beckmann. You already know my deputy.'

McWhirter frowned. His anger was imperfectly contained. Saskia imagined him as an actor who was dumbstruck by the improvisation of a fellow performer. He spun on his heel, crossed the foyer, and was gone.

Jago turned to her.

'Deputy now, is it?'

'Sorry.'

'Don't apologise. I've never been a sidekick. It'll be a new experience.'

'A sidekick?'

'You know, a sidekick. He asks the hero dumb questions so the audience knows what's going on.'

'Ah, I understand.' A memory – a precious jewel – glinted. 'That happens on *Enterprise*, the 60s TV show. You beam down with the captain. If you are wearing a red shirt you will be subject to a fatal special effect.'

'You'd better call me Scotty, then. He never gets killed.'

'Do you think my speech worked?'

Jago found his smile, then lost it. 'We'll get the gen, or a bullet in the head. Either way, it's progress.'

›•‹

The rear lawn was pressed and smooth, sloped like a fairway, and tree islands put winter half-shadow across Saskia, Jago and McWhirter as they walked.

'What about the woman on the motorbike?' Saskia asked.

'We can see from the security video that she's Caucasian, medium build,' said McWhirter, frowning. 'We would have her in custody if it wasn't for the local police.'

To Saskia, Jago said, 'We like to be useful.'

'Colonel, I presume you had Proctor's possessions stored somewhere,' she said. 'Was anything taken?'

'We're still looking into that.'

Saskia and Jago exchanged a look.

At the peak of the garden, where one could look back across the shoulder of the hotel to the widening valley, a large, camouflaged tent flexed in the wind. A man in civilian clothing stood next to its porch. His hands rested on an assault rifle. He saluted McWhirter as the party entered. Inside, a dozen men and women were packing computer and office equipment into crates. Unlike the guard, they did not acknowledge the visitors.

'It's lucky you came today,' said McWhirter. 'We would have been gone by tomorrow.'

Saskia moved to the centre of the tent, where a huge shaft had been sunk. Its mouth was large enough to admit a car.

Four coloured ropes dangled into the hole from a pyramid scaffold.

'Is this the only way?' she asked. The inspiration from her body, filtering through her chip, was clear: she must go down. But it looked dangerous.

'I'm sure the detective inspector and I wouldn't think any less of you if you satisfied yourself with the crime scene photos rather than a trip down there. Am I wrong, Jago?'

The DI peered into the hole. Then he looked at the rig. He seemed unimpressed. 'Saskia, you should think twice about this.'

She removed her coat, handed it to Jago, and shrugged off her suit jacket. Both men stared at her. 'I came to see the crime scene,' she said.

'There are airborne contaminants,' said McWhirter. 'I really—'

'You let Proctor down.' Saskia removed her earrings and put them in a trouser pocket.

'Listen to me, *Kommissarin*.' He moved close to her. 'I need this hole capped by seven.'

'Then we should proceed now.'

McWhirter held her stare, then turned to open an equipment crate. 'Splendid. Why not? We'll call it "The Magical Mystery Tour" and invite coach parties.'

Jago draped Saskia's jacket solemnly across one arm. As she reached to remove her holster, he gripped her knuckles. She read his expression and nodded. The gun stayed with her.

'Take this,' McWhirter said. He tossed her a helmet. Inside was a tangled bundle. Saskia shook it out to reveal a harness. She was relieved to see that it looked familiar.

Rappelling, then, counted among her implanted skills. Her hands began to manipulate its straps with expertise. She stepped her legs through and ensured the double-sprocket mechanism was attached to the carabiner.

McWhirter put on his own harness. He stepped over the fluorescent cordon and attached himself to a rope. 'Twenty metres. I'm on blue.' He tapped his helmet and the lamp awoke. Then he jumped into the blackness. The rope whistled through his decelerator.

Saskia looked at Jago. Her thumbs itched. 'You want to come too, Scotty?'

'No, thanks. A friend was paralysed using one of those decelerators. Anyway,' he said, hefting her coat and jacket, 'I'm being useful.'

'Right.' Saskia clipped her harness to the rope. She chose the red one, unhinged the decelerator and fitted the line around the two sprockets. She closed it firmly and checked, with a tug, that the rope was gripped. There was a disc attached to the sprocket axle. She pulled it out and turned the dial to twenty metres. Then she snapped it back, checked it was locked, and jumped.

The blackness opened like a mouth. She heard Jago say, 'A friend was paralysed by one of those,' but he was no longer there. It was a memory. She blinked in the rushing, dry air. She was falling too quickly. She would hit the ground fast enough to break into pieces, fragments of a looking glass.

She saw a circle of light. She began to slow. The decelerator squealed and the harness bit into her pelvis. Her weight returned with a thump and her head whipped forward. Gasping, her eyes opened on smoke and dust. She could see her shoes dangling centimetres from the ground. She pinched the decelerator. It sprang open and the rope was released.

She landed on the balls of her feet. A pat confirmed that her gun was still in its holster. She resettled her glasses and tensed as McWhirter stepped towards her. She smelt his stale breath.

'Your helmet light has three levels of brightness. Just tap. Understood?'

Though her glasses had zero-light processors, she did not want McWhirter to know. She tapped the helmet three times. The beam became intense and localised. She had landed in the remains of a corridor. It was a long, grey space choked with debris. She could see furniture, computer equipment, filing cabinets and paper. The air tickled her throat.

'What happened down here?' she asked.

'A fire. Don't be surprised if we suffocate.'

'Was this damage caused yesterday?'

'Most of it by the first bomb, twenty years ago.'

'And you say Proctor was responsible for both?'

'The origin of the explosion was inside the locked powerplant of Proctor's laboratory. It should have destroyed the equipment in Proctor's lab, and only that.'

'But it didn't.'

'No. It started a fire, which soon spread. Ceilings collapsed. Eight people were killed. Proctor was evasive during his initial interrogation and evasive again to the inquiry. In their report, the investigators indicated their suspicions, but there wasn't enough evidence. He slipped through the net.'

'Until now,' said Saskia, probing. 'When he slipped through the net again.'

McWhirter turned his light in her direction. 'Be careful where you put your feet, Detective. I don't want to lose anyone else.'

He stepped through a rough gap that had once held a door. Puddles splashed as she followed. Inside the room, their torch-beams were thickened by the dust. A huge glass tank loomed. Its broken edges winked.

'What was in there?'

'A whole world. A world in a fish tank.'

'I do not understand.'

'Of course you don't.' He gestured to the right. 'That was where the 2003 bomb went off.'

Saskia removed her glasses and polished them on the hem of her blouse. As she rubbed, she felt his stare, and the revolver was close in her thoughts until the glasses were replaced and McWhirter turned away. She looked slowly over the scene to capture it. Later review of the video would reveal the shadowed corners. She stepped forward and something crunched underfoot. She glanced down and saw the eye of a flattened rat. She moved back and bumped into an overturned chair. Her heart seemed to grow large and hot in her chest.

McWhirter's light blinded her again. 'You know, we have a saying in Britain: "The murderer always returns to the scene of the crime." Shimoda was in that room along with the bomb. He still is. Pieces of him, anyway.'

'"Thus conscience does make cowards of us all".'

'Sorry?'

'Another British saying. Shakespeare. Do you feel guilty, Colonel, that this happened on your watch?'

'Should I?'

'It happened twice.'

'Detective, few people win the games they start with me.'

Saskia touched the rat with the tip of her shoe. She remembered crying in the back of a taxi after the break up with Simon, the boyfriend who never was. The burn: a question mark. Question: what power did McWhirter have over the Angel of Death, the serial killer whose bottled genie could erupt from her brain in an instant?

'Are you trying to scare me, Colonel?'

'I'm making you aware of the facts.'

'Facts I have. What I need is the feel. Where is the interface with the computer?'

'See for yourself.'

He pointed towards a doorway in the far wall. She moved towards it. The plaintive cries of the rats became louder. The room was small. There was a power here: it was a room in a room in a room, buried deep in the earth. Saskia was struck by the thought that, after she and McWhirter completed their tour and this place was capped, its silence would return and its power would grow again.

McWhirter breathed in her ear. 'It has an unpleasant *feel*, don't you agree?'

She turned to him. 'It is certainly dusty.'

'Got what you wanted?'

'Please?'

'You wanted to get into Proctor's head. Are you close enough? You can almost smell him, can't you? Smells like… an incinerator. A crematorium, even.'

'I would like to leave now.'

'It has atmosphere, doesn't it? My little Magical Mystery Tour.'

'I would like to leave.' Her voice was firmer. Her hand rested on her gun. 'Now.'

He laughed. 'I'm only pulling your leg. Come on.'

They retraced their steps. When they reached the corridor, McWhirter was quick to attach his rope. He connected the decelerator and climbed upwards in a caterpillar-like motion, alternately grasping the rope with his hands and feet. 'Are you coming?'

'Directly. I want to check something first.'

'Well, don't stay too long. I heard some noises just now.'

'What kind of noises?'

'Just noises.'

And he was gone. His breath echoed down the shaft and sounded close, but Saskia was alone. She touched the edge of her glasses and a Heads-Up Display appeared, overlaying the dark scene with object-parsing halos, and a menu. A cross-hair was locked to her eye movements. She blinked at the cartoonish graphic of a filing cabinet and a preview of her recently recorded footage expanded.

What? she thought. Something nagged at her. *What am I looking for?*

Myself?

No. Concentrate.

She cued through the footage until she found the moment she had descended into the research centre. The dark corners were bright. No objects had thermal properties that the glasses identified as statistically warmer or cooler than the ambient. She stopped on the image of the corridor wall. Her breath stopped too. Her astonished eyes saccaded to the magnifier icon, blinked, and the image rushed out.

It showed the corridor – this corridor, right now – in almost perfect brilliance. There was the wreckage, the charcoaled furniture and loose paper. But on the wall immediately to the left of the doorway, someone had written a message.

The words blazed white on the grey surface. She lowered her glasses and looked sternly at the wall. Nothing. She raised the glasses. The graffiti re-appeared. She swallowed. The writer had used a paint that was reflective in the infra-red portion of the spectrum.

The message read:

Das Kribbeln in meinen Fingerspitzen lässt mich ahnen, es scheint ein Unglück sich anzubahnen.

The glasses were produced in America and their default language was English. Uncommanded, a subtitle ran across the base of her vision.

'The pricking in my fingertips lets me say that bad luck is on the way,' it read.

Her heart tapped at her ribs. The glasses skipped through a Euclidean deep-structure analysis of the sentence and returned a quote that was its nearest neighbour in a multi-dimensional semantic space:

By the pricking of my thumbs, something wicked this way comes.

Shakespeare, thought Saskia. *Macbeth*. The play began with three witches, each an analogue of a Fate: Clotho, she spins the thread of life. Lachesis, she measures a length. Atropos, she cuts it.

Spin, measure, snip. Her dream.

Surely the message had been written for her. He must have known, somehow, that she was tracking him and – she had no idea how – had happened upon a fragment of her past life – a memory that she could not yet fully recall. He even seemed to know she was German. How?

There was one last element to the graffiti: an arrow that pointed to a slab of masonry. Behind it, she discovered a fist-sized rock and, beneath that, a sealed plastic folder. Inside was a white envelope.

'Are you alright, hen?' called Jago from above. 'Sit tight. I'm coming down.'

'Don't worry, Scotty. I'm on my way.'

She tucked the folder into her waistband, reattached her decelerator, and spun upwards.

CHAPTER FOURTEEN

David pulled into a narrow alleyway. He dug for the kickstand and eased his bike to a stable tilt. The glow of the display faded and the engine faltered and stopped. The suspension sighed.

It was nearly 6:00 p.m. That day, he had watched the sun climb. He had ridden through rain, seen a double rainbow, and swerved around road-kill. His shoulders and neck ached from the constant hunch. His kidneys, meanwhile, had been bruised by the vibration. Same story with his wrists.

He sagged against the wall and tried to tune out the drumming in his ears. He slid his helmet upwards and ruffled his hair. His neck had lost some movement, but he resisted the urge to loosen it with a twist.

He walked from the alley into a dusky street. Across the road was a pub called The Poor Players. Coloured lights pulsed in the windows. The music was a fast thumping. According to Ego, it had vacancies, and it was an unlikely destination for a traveller as weary as him, so he crossed the road. He was pushing the door when a voice said, 'Nice bike.'

A young girl stood in the shadows next to the porch. She wore a woollen cap, an Eskimo-style jacket with the hood down, jeans, and bright white trainers. She was bird-like in her movements. Her eyes, when they caught the light, were red-ringed.

'It does the job.' David's hand rested on the door. 'Are you OK?'

'A bit hungry.'

Suddenly, David thought of Jennifer.

He moved away from the door and looked down at her. 'Me too. Fancy a bite?'

›•‹

They ate in McCabe's Fish Palace. David let the girl sit facing the window that looked out on a market square. The 'palace' was empty but for them and McCabe, a Turkish man who whistled over his glass battlement. The air was heavy with grease, the floor slippery with it. In silence, they unfurled their fish and chips.

'Eat it before it gets cold,' David said.

'I'll eat it when I fucking want.'

'Who are you?'

'What?'

Slowly, he said, 'What is your name?'

'Janine, like the singer you've never heard of.' She took a chip. 'What's yours?'

'David, like the king. Heard of him?'

'He was in the Bible. Wasn't he a Jew?'

'I believe he was famous for it.'

'Are you a Jew, too?'

'Yep.'

'OK.' With deliberate indifference, she ate more chips, then lifted the fish with two hands and tore a mouthful from the middle. David watched her. She chewed once, twice and swallowed. 'You have a daughter, right?'

'Sort of. She disappeared.'

She took another bite and she waved him on. 'Me and her would get on like a house on fire, right?'

'Actually, I'm not sure if she's your type.'

Janine smiled. 'Why did she disappear?'

'I could give you facts. She was a real genius. The schools in this country couldn't do anything for her. I decided to send her to a school in New York for gifted children. Jennifer was twelve. That was eight years ago. I think she works for the American government now.'

'New York. Fuck, you have money.'

He shrugged and watched, his mind idling, as a customer walked in and asked for battered cod. An old man in faded jeans. 'Yes, you're right. I have money.'

'So what else could you give me?'

'What?'

'You said you could give me the facts. But that's not the whole story. Am I right?'

David ripped a chip from its sticky pile. He pointed it at her. 'You're good. You could do this for a living.'

She nodded seriously. 'I might. Now what about the rest of the story?'

'I...' he began, and Christ if he wasn't near crying. He felt a tingling in his throat and a juvenile sense of hopelessness.

'Here we go: I am not a good parent. Some people could spend millions on a psychiatrist before they can say something like that.'

'Who says you won't? I'm not cheap.'

David laughed, thrown clear of his self-pity. 'What about your own parents?'

'Ah, the psychiatrist cannot talk about herself. It's a rule.'

'You have rules?'

'Of course. Let's be professional. What happened to her mother? Did she leave you?'

David's smile folded. 'Her mother was killed a few months after she was born. Years ago. There was an accident where we both worked. She died in my arms.'

'Fuck off.'

'It's true.'

She leaned forward. 'Did she wake up just before she died?'

'No.'

'Murder?'

'It's not that simple.' Inside, he was silent. His mind listened to his mouth. 'She looked asleep. I tried to wake her but she wasn't breathing. I remember… screaming. Later, someone led me from the building. I regret that I left her there alone.'

'Regrets,' Janine said, as though that word encompassed everything. Her fish was nearly gone. His was hardly touched.

'You want some more fish?'

'No, thanks.'

David took his own fish and plonked it on the remains of hers. 'Here.'

'What's wrong with you? I don't want your leftovers.'

He smiled and watched her eat it. 'Stop fucking smiling,' she said, spitting fish.

'Guess what?' he said.

She stopped mid-chew. 'Wha'?'

'I'm wanted for murder.'

'And I'm the scourge of Poundland. Small fucking world.'

David said mildly, 'Well, it is.'

Janine resumed her chewing. 'I don't usually do this.'

'Eat with strange men?'

Something swept through David. Was it relief that he had been talking to the worst example of society's failure, only to find that she had beaten him at his own game? She had played on his pity and eaten her meal.

And haven't I done the same to her? Got what I wanted? A dry run at reconciliation?

'So what *do* you do?'

'Told you, I'm the scourge of Poundland.' She reached inside her jacket pocket and pulled out a sealed envelope. She put this onto the table and pushed it across but did not lift her hand. 'Special delivery for Professor David Proctor.'

'Hold on a second.' David leaned back in his chair. This escape plan was far more elaborate than he had guessed. How many people were helping him? How long had this been planned? He looked at Janine. 'All this time, you've been waiting to give me this envelope?'

Janine winked. 'I had to make sure you were my man. And if I get taken out for fish and chips at the same time, where's the harm?'

David sighed. He wondered if children had always spoken

like this. He tried to push his chair from the table. It was stuck to the floor. He eased out and put on his gloves.

'Thanks.'

'No problem, man. Back on your nice bike?'

'I'm going to get some sleep. In the morning I'll ride on.' He took the envelope and stood. 'Can I do anything for you? As thanks?'

'No. Forget you saw me.'

'Well, can I ask you something without you getting angry or saying "fuck"?'

'Anything's possible.'

He placed a gloved hand on her head. 'Will you take care of yourself?'

Janine ran her tongue over her teeth and burped.

'Yeah.'

CHAPTER FIFTEEN

In his room on the first floor of The Poor Players, David opened the rucksack that he had taken from the shed. He spilled the contents on the floor. Among paper copies of the bike's registration documents, and a fake driver's licence, there was the stun gun. He read its instructions while the last song of the band downstairs pulsed through the floorboards. Then he opened the envelope that Janine had given to him. Inside were a passport and what looked like a metallic card. He smiled.

'Hello, Ego.'

'Hello. Who are you?'

'Professor David Proctor, at your service.'

There was a beep as his voice was identified. 'No, I am at yours.'

'Oh, you.' David removed the earpiece that had been taped to the back of the computer and pushed it into his ear. 'Switch to earpiece.'

'Done,' said the voice.

At the bottom of the envelope was a money clip, which he put into the inner pocket of his coat.

'Do you have any instructions for me, Ego?'

'Yes. Get to London Heathrow Terminal Five and open baggage locker J327.'

'Anything else?'

'No.'

David walked into his bathroom and turned the taps. The pipes made a thumping noise and under-pressurised water fell into the tub. 'Who arranged my escape?'

'I have been instructed to withhold that information.'

He nodded. The Ego model used a neuronal network to encode its information. Knowledge was stored haphazardly in a great web. Thus, 'cat' had a connection to 'dog', but also to 'paws', 'lion' and 'boat'. Even the most efficient computer operator would find it difficult to isolate information from all the routes that led to it. David set about probing the barricades.

'Where were you yesterday?'

'I was not active yesterday.'

'Think of a name, randomly.'

'Sam.'

'Why did you think of that?'

'I have no reason. That is what random means.'

'Touché. Tell me about Heathrow.'

'Heathrow Airport is the foremost centre for air travel in the United Kingdom.'

'Is that what you think?'

'No. I am reading verbatim from their publicity material.'

'Do you love?'

'No.'

'Are you alive?'

'No.'

'Do you want to be alive?'

'I neither want nor do not want.'

'Do you have emotions?'

'No.'

'Who programmed you?'

'Dr Nagarajan.'

'Sing me a song.'

'Which song?'

'Daisy.'

'Just a moment.' There was a beep and David heard a crackle. The earpiece was picking up Ego's attempt to access the Net via the wireless telecommunications network.

'Alright, forget it.'

He returned to the bedroom and looked at the passport. He noted the name and thought of one or two biographical facts for his new identity. He stowed the passport in the rucksack. Then he removed his clothes and brushed his teeth. Finally, he sank into the bath and felt the heat permeate his extremities. His genitals began to thaw and assume a respectable size. He considered washing his hair but could not bring himself to encourage the wag who had written the copy for the free sachets: *Rinse and Shine at The Poor Players!*

'Ego, can you monitor local police frequencies?'

'Yes. However, their transmissions are encrypted.'

'You are well informed.'

'Yes, I am.'

David belched. The brownish water washed over his stomach and lapped around his neck. He looked again at his stomach. In all the excitement, he was losing weight. 'Ego, if I make a voice call, can I be traced?'

'I have been given instructions to dissuade you from communicating with anybody until you have reached Heathrow Terminal Five and opened locker J327.'

David slapped the surface of the water. Whom would he call, anyway? He had some friends at the university, family in Wales, and one or two old, good friends near London. Undoubtedly, his small circle would be under surveillance. He had some academic acquaintances in Europe and America. He could contact them anonymously, but what could they do from such a distance?

He wondered how close his pursuers were. What information did they have to go on?

'Ego, summarise all the news stories filed about my escape in the last twenty-four hours.'

'That analysis will take approximately two minutes.'

'Do it.'

He stared at the patches of mould on the ceiling. He wondered what he would next say to Jennifer, and what she would say back. His mind drifted. With his eyes closed, there was nothing to do but listen to the sounds of the pub: the lub-dub of hot water, footsteps, the rumble of conversation, the occasional cough, a car pulling up outside.

There was a knock at the ground-floor entrance used by overnight guests. David opened his eyes. Footsteps travelled across the hallway. He heard two men speaking. Only the low, unintelligible register reached his ears.

One spoke slowly and seriously. A policeman? The other responded quickly and made affirmative sounds. The voice of a sycophant: the landlord.

He remembered the thrill of his confession to Janine that he was on the run. He had felt that excitement when he had ridden from Scotland and he had felt it in the chip shop. But he did not feel it now. This was excitement at another level; a surging energy that was difficult to contain.

David stepped from the bath and towelled himself roughly. He pulled on his clothes, then opened the rucksack and stuffed everything he could find into the main compartment. He did not examine what he packed. He simply checked that the room was empty when he had finished. Then he collected his toiletries from the bathroom.

David crossed to the window. As he had guessed, a police car was parked outside. The six-metre drop was sheer. No escape that way. Across the street, a uniformed officer emerged from a flat, touched his cap at the owner and walked on.

So the local police were carrying out house-to-house enquiries in pairs. The officer in David's pub was still checking.

Silently, he turned off the light. With the darkness came a taste of safety. The moment ended when footsteps stopped on the landing outside and he heard the landlord say, 'There's one in here. Bit of a character. Popped out with a Dodger not more than half an hour ago. Under-aged.'

Another voice: 'Come back, did he?'

The landlord: 'Oh, yes. Came right back.'

David did not move. He needed a plan. The window was not an option. The fall would hurt him badly. He had to think of something else.

His thoughts jammed.

Think, think.

The policeman knocked. David had anticipated it, but he drew a sharp breath. He sank to a crouch. Would it make him more difficult to see? Would it provide a moment's advantage?

'This is the police, sir. Open up.'

David reached into his jacket pocket.

The landlord said, 'I've got the master key.'

The policeman, quieter: 'Go on, then. Unlock it. Just unlock it and step back. Understood?'

David drew the stun gun.

In his ear, Ego said, 'The latest story was filed at the BBC—'

'Ego, shut up.'

'Understood.'

Silence beyond the door.

'Do you hear something?' asked the landlord.

'Only your mouth, Sam. Hurry up.'

David imagined the two of them standing there, wondering what lay before them, what the fugitive would do when cornered. He looked down and saw their shadows move in the gap of light.

A key turned in the lock.

David raised the stun gun. The laser-sight put a red dot on the door. His finger tightened. If he squeezed hard enough, two barbed darts would fire at the speed of air-rifle pellets. Each would trail a conducting filament. On contact with the chest, they would lodge under the skin and unleash 50, 000 volts. The leaflet had been quite specific.

The shadows paused.

Suddenly, a third voice erupted: 'Delta Two from Delta Three, over.'

'Go ahead Three, over,' said the policeman. It took David long seconds to realise that the new voice had come from the policeman's radio.

'Report of a six-four in progress, end of Main Street. Request assistance, over.'

'Three, I'm assisting, over.'

David froze in his marksman's crouch. The landlord asked, 'Aren't we going in?'

The policeman scrambled downstairs. 'A six-four is an assault, Sam. Takes priority. You stay here, eh.'

The policeman's footfalls became quiet, then clear and brisk as he ran out into the street. David kept the weapon trained on the door and his eyes on the shadow of Sam, the landlord. The door was still unlocked. Sam muttered something and stepped away. Finally, he toddled down the stairs.

David held his position until his calves prickled with cramp. Only then did he exhale and stand. He rubbed his legs. He took another breath and pocketed the gun, shaking his head at his outstanding luck.

He walked to the window and parted the curtain. The policeman was leaving the building. David felt a momentary guilt. He had been ready to electrify that man.

David took his helmet, confirmed the presence of his rucksack, and moved to the door. He pressed his ear against it. There was no sound. It opened on an empty corridor. He made his way downstairs, low and sideways. He heard the far-off sound of a jukebox, some laughter, and breaking glass. At the bottom of the stairs, he risked a glance into the bar. The landlord was not there.

David took three huge steps across the entrance and slid

through the door. The street was deserted. He swung the helmet over his head and jogged towards his bike. It was a mistake to act like an escapee, but he had too much spare energy. He slipped into the alley, climbed aboard, and made ready for the long ride, pausing often to listen for running footsteps or a shout of alarm. Finally, he zipped his jacket and kicked up the stand. The alley was too narrow to turn in, so he waddled the bike backwards to the pavement.

'Ego, can you interface with the bike's computer?'

'No. It has not responded to my attempts at communication.'

'Fine. Listen, the bike computer uses a vocal input. I don't want to get the two of you confused. From now on, I'll refer to you by name if I'm talking to you.'

'Understood.'

David cleared his throat. Still no police. He held the brake, turned the key and pressed the ignition. The bike hissed to life. Its windscreen rose and the suspension settled. The display gave him the time, his travel range and a route map. He had enough energy for one hundred kilometres on the straight. The excitement of escape began to lighten him.

'Ego, what do you think will happen when the police learn I've disappeared?'

'The local traffic division will move to a high state of alert. Records indicate that the local constabulary has one helicopter. If it locates you, the probability of reaching Heathrow is almost zero. You need to find a motorway to leave the area before roadblocks are set, then transfer to minor roads to avoid detection.'

'Bike computer, show me the fastest route to the nearest motorway.'

A map appeared. He could be on the A1 in less than twenty minutes. He would pass through settlements called Walshford, Fairburn and Darrington. Names he would never remember. He could make Leicester without stopping.

He rolled to the junction and looked left. The two police officers were standing only metres away. They had their backs to him. Between them, being berated vigorously by one, was Janine. Her eyes briefly touched upon David's. He nodded. Her expression did not change.

He turned in the road and coasted away, retracing his route along Main Street.

'Bike, change colour.'

The motorbike rode through one pool of streetlight with a silver finish. By the next, it was midnight blue.

'Ego, read me *War and Peace* by Leo Tolstoy.'

'"Well, Prince, so Genoa and Lucca are now just family estates of the Bonapartes. But I warn you..."'

›•‹

Mrs McMurray, Saskia's landlady, gave her a key with a plastic St Andrew's Cross on the fob. Saskia took it and closed the bedroom door in her inquisitive face. She had fantasised about collapsing on the bed and sleeping dreamlessly, but her mind had not spent its momentum. It turned over still, rolling facts around, testing them, tasting them. The words on the wall. Shakespeare. The Fates. The death of Bruce Shimoda. The first bomb in 2003. The second bomb. Proctor. Back to the words on the wall.

By the pricking of my thumbs.

Minutes later, she lay stretched on the bed. Her nose was

cold. By the pillow, her glasses were folded and dark. Near her feet was the dusty envelope, unopened. Written on it was: 'Do not open this envelope.'

She walked to the sash window. She might have been looking from the window of an apartment on a quiet, cold night, back in Berlin.

Something wicked this way comes.

The Fates: Clotho, she spins the thread of life. Lachesis, she measures a length. Atropos, she cuts it.

Spin, measure, snip.

The window was jet, smoky with hints to the scene beyond. The impressions merged and snapped into focus. A human face.

Whom do you hunt?

Saskia stepped back, aghast. Her calves met the edge of the bed. She did not see the face as a reflection, but as a visitation. She drew her revolver.

'Only me.'

Saskia screamed as she turned. Mrs McMurray, the elderly proprietor who had asked her not to smoke, there's a dear, dropped her tray of tea and thin British biscuits.

'Why, my dear girl,' Mrs McMurray said. Her mouth worked on autopilot while she fixated on the gun. 'I'm very sorry. I should've knocked, should I not?'

'Frau McMurray—' Saskia began. Why was the woman apologising? 'The tea,' she said, confused.

'Aye. Will you look at that? I should clean it up.'

The landlady remained exactly where she was.

Saskia faked a laugh. She let the revolver tip over her finger. 'Do not worry about the gun. It is not loaded. I was… oiling it. This is my nightly practice.'

Do I look familiar, Frau McMurray? Seen my picture in a news story? Do I give you a sense of—

Saskia stowed the gun in its holster. 'Listen. You clean the spill and I shall make us a fresh pot of tea.'

Mrs McMurray brightened. She was staring at the gun. 'That's a fine idea.'

Saskia crept down the thickly-carpeted stairs, past printed masterpieces and a cross-stitched owl. Her heart slowed with each step. The television became louder. She remembered the ghostly reflection and decided that Jago's last word of the night had been correct. She needed to sleep.

Of course, if the landlady walked into a room without knocking, she'd get what she deserved. What Mrs McMurray really needed was…

A bullet?

She froze on the stairs.

Is that what she needs, Frau Kommissarin? Spin, measure, and… snip!

Saskia cleared her throat and continued walking. That voice was surely just her conscience. But she remembered the words of Klutikov: *'The imposition of the donor pattern must be constant. If not, the original pattern – that is, the personality and identity extant in your brain – will resurge.'*

Was it the mind of her true body straining at its bonds? She could not be sure. But if she even suspected that she could lose her new mind to the old one, then that gun would find itself pointed at her temple. She did not want to become the Angel of Death.

A little off the top? asked the voice. *Snip.*

CHAPTER SIXTEEN

Early the next morning, Saskia sat with Jago in the back of a police car as they drove towards the Special Incident Unit. She wore a borrowed police greatcoat, complete with sergeant stripes. Their driver was listening to a local radio station. She did not recognise any of the songs. She shivered and turned up the collar of the greatcoat. It smelled musty. Into her thoughts stepped Jago, reading from a handheld computer. There had been a sighting the night before, he said. Proctor had checked into a hotel in Northallerton, two hundred and thirty kilometres from Edinburgh and one hundred and sixty kilometres from the equipment shed. Jago had been eager to visit the hotel, but not Saskia. Her instinct told her it would be a waste of time.

Jago shrugged. Local police and some officers from the Edinburgh team were on the case. They were competent enough.

Saskia closed her eyes on Edinburgh and let Jago's beautiful vowels and intermittent trill carry her through the report. The equipment shed, she learned, had provided little evidence. A farmer had discovered the parachute and, inside the shed, the exploded remains of a laptop computer: a Korean model available from hundreds of outlets nationwide. It had been destroyed by a plastic bonded explosive with a generic, untraceable blasting cap.

Saskia yawned.

'What about Northallerton?' she asked.

'Late last night, a constable reported the flight of a man who matched Proctor's description. He had checked into The Poor Players under the name Harper. He was moments from being arrested when the constable was called away on an assault-in-progress, which turned out to be a false alarm. When the constable returned twenty minutes later, after a cup of tea—'

'*Meine Güte*. The English and their narcotic tea.'

'—he found that Proctor had vanished.'

'Go on.'

Jago angled his computer screen against the sunlight. 'House-to-house enquiries uncovered Mrs Taome Gallagher. Tay to her friends. Bit of a wind-bag by the sounds of it. She saw a man matching Proctor's description around the time he checked in. According to the credit card people, that was 6:02 p.m. Said he was riding a chrome motorbike and parked in her alleyway. We have an APW on him.'

'APW?'

'All Points Warning. His description is released nationally.'

Saskia stared at the shops sliding by. 'Surely that compromises the secret nature of the investigation?'

'Perhaps. But the governor phoned me this morning and said he was fed up working with one hand tied behind his back. I'm inclined to agree.'

'Does Proctor's bike match the tracks found next to the shed?'

'Yes, but my guess would be that he was met by a group of his own people. They gave him supplies and rode away, splitting up.'

'No. I think that would be a waste of effort. Why not just have all the supplies in the shed?'

Jago picked at a tooth. 'Maybe.'

'Where else was the card used?'

'Two filling stations between Belford and Northallerton.'

'Do they have cameras?'

'No, we checked. He chose wee one-pump jobs. He's using minor roads. One or two lads saw him, but they can't give a good description. They say his bike was chrome too. Maybe a trail bike.'

'So. A trail bike. Probably the same bike he used to ride away from the equipment shed.'

'Yes.'

'Back to last night. You said there was a falsified accusation of assault?'

'It came over the radio just as the officer was about to interview Proctor.'

'That is convenient. In Germany we say somebody has "cried wolf".'

'Here too.'

'Who was the caller?'

'It turned out to be a kid. Truscott – the reporting officer – said she looked to be on the wrong side of sixteen.'

Saskia felt a memory move, delicate as a baby's kick.

›•‹

The driver stopped midway along a featureless road on an industrial estate. Saskia and Jago left the vehicle and entered a grey campus of office buildings. She could see security cameras tracking them. On instinct, she lowered her face into the raised collar of her greatcoat. The wind sang in the corners. Jago ushered her into the lee of a five-storey building. There were Lothian and Borders Police signs, but the impression was blank, corporate. The occasional flowers looked unhappy.

Saskia relaxed her shoulders as they entered the lobby. There was a security barrier but its horizontal bars were open and its lights green. Jago nodded to the guard and, just like that, they were through.

'The good news is, they found us a room,' said Jago, entering the lift.

'And?'

'You'll want to keep your coat on. They're renovating some of the floor and half the windows are missing. It's a tad "parky".' He used air quotes. 'That means—'

'Parky. Right.'

They shared a smile as the doors closed.

›•‹

'Agent Brandt,' said Paul Besson, removing his mittens, 'what do you know about cryptanalysis?'

Saskia considered this nervous, boyish forty-year-old. She was reminded of Lev Klutikov. The last two minutes had comprised rapid introductions and work allocations for the team of four, all galvanised by the chill in the room.

She was about to tell Besson she had no idea what cryptanalysis meant. Then, the answer came to her.

The study of methods for undoing the encryption that has been applied to a signal, in order to discover its true meaning.

'I'm a beginner.'

'Let me tell you what we know so far.' His tone was flat and he had difficulty meeting her eyes. She could smell the anxiety on his breath. 'Just before he left he entered the hotel, our suspect initiated a communication using his personal computer as the interface, and telecommunications equipment in his taxi as the transmitter. We know that the communication was an encapsulated transmission of video and audio. That it passed through the exchanges at ScotIX and MAE-West. That it lasted less than two minutes. That there were only the two parties involved.'

'And that we very much want to know its content.'

'And that.'

'Milk and sugar, please,' she said.

Saskia watched him pour four cups of coffee. They were standing next to the long conference table that dominated the room. Garland – a red-haired, thirtyish woman who had travelled up to Scotland with Besson – nodded and took one of the coffees, returning to her station at the head of the table, where she donned tinted glasses and re-entered her workspace. Meanwhile, Besson put milk and sugar into another cup – hesitating, his eyes on Saskia's knees – and gave it to Saskia. She smiled and stepped away from the coffee machine.

'Start with the basics,' she said.

'The basics?' Besson sipped his coffee and unzipped his

coat. He loosed a sigh of concentration. 'Encryption is the process of converting publicly readable information into something that can only be understood by the intended recipient. These days, we tend to use something called asymmetric encryption. It's asymmetric because the key used to encrypt the information is not the same as the key used to decrypt it.' Besson hummed. 'It's…'

'Complicated?' she said, sipping.

He grinned and put a hand on the crown of his head, scratching. 'You remember the Enigma machine?'

'No.'

'The Germans used it to encode military transmissions during the Second World War. The cool thing about the Enigma cipher was that it changed itself with each letter of the message. The odds against breaking it were 150 million million million to one. But it was cracked.'

'How?'

'It was systematic. It was predictable. With modern computers we could have broken it in no time. But if there is no system, we have a real problem.' He looked pained. 'I've had a brief look at the data this morning. I'd guess it falls into the unsystematic category. It's a one-time pad. Unbreakable.'

'I do not like the sound of that.'

'Of all the methods of encryption, only one is mathematically impossible to crack, and that's the one-time pad, or OTP. Even given infinite computing resources, the plaintext could never be recovered from the ciphertext. The OTP uses a key that has the same number of elements as the plaintext. Each plaintext element's value – be it a letter or a pixel – is transformed by the corresponding random value in the key. As long as each element in the OTP is truly random, there's no systematic element for a cryptanalyst to sniff out. It's what we call perfect secrecy. You rarely find OTPs in the wild because they're unwieldly, but we do use them to teach students the basics of cryptanalysis.'

'So how does the receiver of the message know how to unravel it?'

'The sender and the receiver must have identical versions of the key.'

'And what form might the key take?'

'It would be a series of random numbers approximately one terabyte in size in this case, based on my guesses about the format and frame rate of the transmission.'

'Paul, tell me honestly,' said Saskia. Her voice was low. 'Can we discover the contents of Proctor's communication?'

Jago's arm reached between them and took one of the coffees. 'You can forget you heard that name. I mean it.'

'Oh dear,' said Besson, looking amused. 'Somebody point out the irony of spilling the beans to a cryptanalyst.'

Saskia frowned at Jago. 'Scotty, I have made it clear that I do not agree with your superiors' policy of restricting information.'

Besson nodded seriously. 'I like your attitude, Agent Brandt.'

'It's *Kommissarin*,' said Jago. He turned to Saskia. 'All the same, we should keep this on a need-to-know basis.'

'Did you manage to find a heater?' asked Besson.

'That depends. Will you manage to forget the name?'

After a pause, Besson said, 'Kommissarin Brandt, you were asking about the *possibility* of cracking an OTP. Well, it has been done. The Signal Security Agency of the US

Army managed to crack the OTP of the German Foreign Office in 1944. It turned out the Germans were using a machine whose numbers weren't completely random. That gave the breakers a foothold. But Proctor's code? We have no foothold.'

'Well, looks like you can go back to Cheltenham,' said Jago, triumphantly. 'Sorry to have wasted your time.'

'Scotty,' said Saskia, 'the transmission is critical.'

Jago took her elbow and walked her away from Besson.

'It's important, maybe. Tell me why it's critical.'

'Proctor got this call before he walked into the West Lothian Centre with a bomb. Did he receive instructions from the person behind the bombing at that point? Or was it the last message to a loved one from a man about to lose his freedom? In either case, we must discover to whom he was talking. The second party might have been involved in his escape. Perhaps they are waiting for him, helping him.'

'That "gut instinct" of yours?'

'I suppose.'

Jago sighed. 'Alright, hen.'

Saskia walked over to Besson, forced him to look her in the eye, and waited for his smile to answer hers. 'You say it is unbreakable. Break it for me.'

CHAPTER SEVENTEEN

Jago led Saskia through the foyer of the building, where a crowd of uniformed police had gathered. 'They're waiting for news about the privatisation,' said Jago, not stopping. Saskia smiled at a young officer. He winked back in the habit of her boyfriend-who-never-was, Simon. She looked at the linoleum floor and recalled her arrival at the FIB building in flip-flops, irritable with heat and curious about a case. Her secretary. The fridge. Beckmann's button hole and its curious yellow flower. Now this cold. This mission.

Only variations on a fictional theme, Kommissarin Brandt. Whom do you hunt? Yourself or Proctor?

They passed through the vestibule, down some stone steps in a grassy slope, and stopped beneath a blue lantern. Smart men and women hurried by. Their heads were turned against the cold.

'Here'll do,' Jago said.

'Do you have a spare cigarette?'

'I do. Could you not buy your own?'

'No. It would shatter the illusion that I do not smoke.'

'You're worse than my boy, Jeremy.'

'How old is he?'

'Fourteen. Spoiled by his mother. Only child. When he comes home stinking of smoke, she blames me.'

He knocked two cigarettes into his hand. He gave one to her and produced his lighter.

The lighter.

The feeling that returned.

Her eyes closed.

Laughter. The flick of a playing card dealt on a table. The smoke transformed from wisps (lit cigarettes) to plumes (burning furniture, wood, an office, mannequins).

Someone saying, 'Revenge should have no bounds.'

'Saskia?'

She opened her eyes. Jago was holding her shoulders. A cigarette dangled from his lower lip. 'Are you all right?'

'I felt dizzy.'

'Migraine?'

'No. It is not that.'

'Do you want something to eat?'

'Eat? No, I'm fine. Light me up.'

Jago seemed to think about that. Then he put his lighter to the cigarette. She glanced at it, but it was just a lighter again. Its mnemonic power was spent.

They watched people walk in and out of the building. She took a drag and held it.

'You muttered something, Saskia. It sounded German: ootah.'

Ute.

'A woman's name,' she found herself saying, knowing.

'Mean anything to you?'

She looked away. 'No, Scotty.'

Jago nodded, his eyes narrow against the smoke. 'But you know she's a woman.'

›•‹

Saskia sat at the head of the conference table. Opposite her, Jago leaned against a portable heater. Besson was tapping a pen on his teeth while Garland continued her research in the realm of her glasses.

'OK,' said Saskia. She pressed her cold feet against the floor, stilling them. 'Let us hypothesise that Proctor did not intend to encrypt this transmission.'

'Why that?' asked Jago.

'Tell me: who sent the transmission?'

'Who? Proctor.'

'Fine, Scotty. Why do you say so?'

'Well—'

Besson pointed at Saskia with his pen. 'You're right. We grabbed the transmission on the basis of a surveillance tape from a camera outside the hotel of Proctor talking in the taxi. We don't know who initiated the call. We know nothing. We just have a terabyte of scrambled data that was received and transmitted by Proctor at that time.'

Jago looked at both of them. 'What are you saying? Someone sent a message to Proctor?'

Saskia nodded. 'My gut feeling, Scotty, is that Proctor would not have waited until he reached the West Lothian Centre to send his communication. I'm certain he knew about the surveillance. Why would he encrypt a transmission and then allow people to see him making it? This only invites us to crack it. Proctor would have chosen to make call from concealment.'

'OK,' said Jago. 'I'll go for that.'

'So, we need to determine the names of any individuals, perhaps of a mathematical persuasion, who may have contacted David Proctor, an Oxford professor. Charlotte?'

'Heard you,' she said. 'I'm on it.'

'Paul,' Saskia prompted, 'you said that the one-time pad would be a large list of numbers.'

'If we were talking about a text message it would be large. But we're talking about a broadband audio-video transmission: a good quality visual image changing up to thirty times a second, plus two sound tracks.'

'So the list of numbers for the pad would be *very* large. What if Proctor used… a list of telephone numbers?'

Besson pouted. 'Sure. That would be a start. But telephone directories are systematic and have a limited range of numbers. When you limit the range, you limit the complexity, and you make it easier for a cracker. Plus, you'd need to widen the net of the telephone directory to a country, perhaps, in order to make the ciphertext the same size as the plaintext.'

'Listen, people,' Jago said, 'we're not talking about Nazi High Command sending out the order to fire torpedoes. He's just one man.'

'Is he?' asked Saskia. 'He was aided in his escape. Charlotte, what do you have on his family?'

'One minute.' The red-haired woman's eyes roamed. 'His parents are dead. He has an uncle living in Israel who turned up after we made an extensive search. I'd bet that they don't even know of each other's existence. His daughter, Jennifer, left for America four years ago, aged sixteen. She attended a school for gifted children in New York and graduated, aged eighteen, with a double degree in mathematics and physics. Her current whereabouts are unknown.'

Jago snorted. 'What do you mean, unknown? I couldn't wipe my backside without a computer somewhere going "beep".'

'Exactly that, Detective Inspector. She has no bank account, no passport, no social security number, and no insurance of any kind. She has no bonds or shares. Her records would lead anyone to the conclusion that she died aged eighteen. But there is no death registration.'

Saskia nodded. It made perfect sense. 'Think of Proctor's life from 2001 to 2003. Are there any similarities with his daughter's situation?'

Charlotte frowned, blinked, and nodded. 'Yes. During that period Proctor's comings-and-goings are blank, just like his daughter's.'

'In that time,' said Saskia. 'Proctor was an employee of a high security research facility known as the West Lothian Centre.'

Jago sighed pointedly. 'Alright. You think we have a daughter who entered her father's profession. And perhaps called her father right before he went into the hotel and down into the lab. Did she come back to England to aid his escape?'

'If this alley is blind,' said Saskia, 'then we can retrace our footsteps. Proctor is moving. I am certain that this transmission is critical to his movements, and we need to act quickly.'

Jago shrugged. 'Fair enough.'

'The identity of the caller is the key. Can we see the surveillance footage of Proctor's arrival at the West Lothian Centre?'

'It's classified,' said Besson sadly.

Saskia lifted the phone handset and dialled a number whose digits she had not thought of until this moment, and waited, a wink for Jago, as a phone rang in Berlin.

›•‹

The headache burst not long after she hung up on Beckmann. She waved away the concerned hand – Jago or Besson, she could not tell through her narrowed eyes – and groped for the glass door. She walked the corridor blind. The metronomic click-clack of her shoes spoke to deep memories, and her nausea grew.

The toilet was arctic. She opened the tap and let her cupped hands fill with water, seething but chill, and she dropped her face into the swirls.

Do I get migraines? she asked her chip. *Is this normal?*

It was silent.

She pressed her temples. If she pushed hard enough, could she override this pain with another?

Whom do you ask? said that unfamiliar voice in her head. *Me or you?*

Saskia looked at her reflection. 'Who said that?'

Whom do you hunt? Proctor or yourself?

Saskia followed the shape of her mouth. 'This. Is. Me. Talking.'

Confused?

'Who are you?'

The hawk.

'The hawk that returned?'

Spin, measure, snip.

She closed her eyes. Her imagination opened on a snowy archipelago. Each memory formed an island bridge: the Zippo lighter in Jago's hand; the statue of Prometheus at the West Lothian Centre; the name Ute.

And smoke.

At first, it would be mistaken for smoke from a cigarette. Then its deep, toxic wave would overwhelm. Plastic. Coughing. Yes: panic.

A building on fire.

'Is this the key to the cipher?' she asked the archipelago. 'Is this *my* key?'

Whom do you ask?

'Who said that? What are you?'

Ute.

'What about her? What about her?' Saskia grasped desperately at the ghost of the memory.

'Kommissarin?'

Saskia gave a start. The archipelago slipped aside like an inner eyelid. She blinked. She was still in the toilet cubicle, in the basement of the police station, and Charlotte Garland held her arm. She was not in…

'Saskia?'

…in Cologne.

CHAPTER EIGHTEEN

Besson opened his clamshell computer. The heat of his fingertips summoned a keyboard on the lower part of the shell, red-glowing, as Jago, Saskia and Garland watched a projection on the wall. One pane showed a taxi against the frontage of the Park View Hotel. The other was crowded with a set of image processing tools.

'I'll say this for you,' murmured Jago. 'You're well connected.'

'I am,' Saskia replied. 'Paul, go.'

They watched the video from beginning to end. The story was simple: a car drove in from left of frame and stopped; Proctor opened the door, hesitated, then closed it. The windows remained opaque with reflected sky. Five minutes later, he opened the door a second time and walked out of the frame. The taxi drove away. For a period during those five minutes, he had made the transmission.

Saskia asked, 'Ideas?'

'The door,' said Jago. 'Why did he open it twice?'

'Yes. He is the only person in the car. What model of car is that? Does it have an advanced computer?'

Besson shook his head. 'That's a Merc with a hands-off driving module. The computer is thick.'

Saskia approached the projection. 'McWhirter said that Proctor used an industrial prototype to detonate the bomb. Perhaps his computer handled the communication too. Picture it: Proctor arrives, he opens the door, then the computer calls him back in. He closes it again and receives the transmission.'

Jago grunted. 'Maybe the computer announced the caller.'

Saskia clicked her fingers. 'One day, you will make a fine Kommissar, Deputy.'

'Gee, thanks.'

'Paul, can we see a plot of the sound at that point?'

Besson nodded. On the projection, Proctor reversed towards the car and opened the door. Besson wound it back still further. The door closed. He kept cuing. Thirty seconds later – for Proctor, five minutes earlier – the door opened again. 'Alright,' Besson said, 'here's a visual of the sound.' The image was replaced by two graphs, each with a tiny peak halfway along. 'I'll play it.'

As it played, Saskia heard something deep inside the sound. It might have been a footfall, a snapping branch or a voice.

'Anyone?' she asked.

'Hold on, I can enhance it.'

They waited for Besson to select a smudge in the spectrogram.

'This is it.'

David Proctor's voice, swept with wind, said, 'I'm

supposed to be stealthed.' There was a pause. 'Could be my daughter.'

Saskia clapped Besson on the back and shared a nod with Garland.

'Not bad,' said Jago.

›•‹

While Jago spoke to his boss about arranging an interview with Jennifer Proctor, Saskia donned her glasses and monitored the virtual workspaces of Besson and Garland, who were engaged in a review of communications between David and Jennifer Proctor. Pictures and text fluttered into the foreground and disintegrated, or joined to represent relationships suggested by Nexus, the semantic parser used by the UK Police Service.

'Interesting,' said Garland. 'David Proctor is flagged for surveillance. Turns out this isn't the first time he's blown something up at the West Lothian Centre.'

'How does that help us?'

'Here,' said Besson. In Saskia's glasses, a data tile rushed towards her. She stopped it with a blink. It was a scan of a paper document, headed 'GCHQ'. 'Proctor has been flagged since 2003. Some analysis has already been carried out on his correspondence.'

'Can we use that to our advantage?'

'It should speed up the process. Hey, Charlotte, is that video of our man?'

'Yeah. A robotics conference in Amsterdam in '21. Looks like Proctor was the keynote. Nothing doing, though.'

Saskia tuned out. Beyond the graphical interface – which

she could slide away on command – was a world where she had committed murder. There would be data for that too. Photographs. Video footage. Court documents. Witnesses.

In Cologne.

And yet she could not investigate any of it. The previous morning, when she had stood with the revolver in grisly salute, Beckmann had marked her limits. Any attempt to investigate herself would not be tolerated.

Forget it, Brandt.

'Wow,' said Garland, 'look at this.'

It was an email. Garland highlighted some text in the centre and tossed it towards Saskia.

b2kool 2 use an encrypted transmission, dad

'What did her father say to that?' asked Saskia.

'The reply is missing.'

'Shame.'

'Kommissarin,' said Besson. 'Read these.'

It was a collection of their final communications. Proctor was seldom writing more than two lines. They were invariably apologetic: 'Sorry I can't write any more right now,' 'CU Gotta go,' 'Write more soon, I prooomise!', and so on, but the follow-ups were never sent. Jennifer's emails shortened. She made jokes about her father's tardiness, jokes that became sardonic and accusatory. At the same time, Proctor's replies became defensive, hurt and confused. The messages described a dying relationship. Saskia could not suppress her sadness.

The emails dried up. There was no code.

'Okay,' Saskia said. 'Time out.' She removed her glasses and look at their faces. 'Charlotte, the email about the cipher. When was that sent?'

'Back in '21,' said Garland.

'The cipher would have to be complicated,' Besson said.

Saskia turned to him. 'You said something earlier about using one-time pads to teach students the basics of cryptanalysis. Maybe she completed it as part of a school project. What was the name of her school? The one in New York?'

'Wayne's College,' said Garland.

'Find their electronic documents archive. Search for projects by Jennifer Proctor.'

Garland smiled. All three replaced their glasses. Garland tore through the data and Besson and Saskia followed in her slipstream. A list of projects appeared. One was titled: 'An algorithm for one-time pad encryption using the *Homo sapiens* haploid genome, by Jennifer B. Proctor.'

Quite unexpectedly, Saskia thought of Simon.

'Bingo,' she said.

'David Proctor's DNA was sequenced in 2017,' said Garland, 'as part of a research project at the Institute for Stem Cell Research, University of Edinburgh. The sequence was copied by an MI5 surveillance bot in 2020. There's a copy bundled with the GCHQ data. Besson?'

'Got it. Looks like about 750 megabytes. Not a strong OTP after all, though it might have taken us years to crack using a brute force method. What does Jennifer's project say about a hash function? I'll start with no hash and a simple XOR of the data against the DNA sequence.' Besson smiled. 'That was easy. We have it.'

CHAPTER NINETEEN

Detective Superintendent Shand took a box of paperwork from a chair and placed it next to his desk. Saskia settled into the empty seat. Politely, she smiled around the narrow, high-ceilinged office. Jago sat on the windowsill.

'Always good to meet our continental counterparts,' said the DSI. He had a grey goatee beard and a lopsided, friendly expression. 'Are we treating you well?'

'Saskia made the breakthrough in the Proctor case,' Jago said.

'Team effort,' she replied. 'We now have a full transcript of the conversation that took place in the car between Proctor and his daughter.'

Jago gave him a sheaf of loose A4 paper, creased lengthways. The DSI glanced through. 'Nothing jumps out. You two have had time to think about it. Talk to me.'

'I have a hunch,' said Saskia. 'I think that, despite the APW, Proctor has left the country, perhaps via an airport.'

'Why?'

'He was warned. His daughter says, in effect, "Watch your back. Something may happen." This warning comes true, does it not?'

The DSI arched an eyebrow. 'I thought that the "something" was a result of Proctor's own actions.'

Saskia said, 'I realise, sir, that we are not in a position to verify or falsify Proctor's charges. But we are also not required to accept them. I mean, we must not accept conclusions unless we make them ourselves from available evidence. Nobody, so far, has been able to produce evidence to show that Proctor is responsible for anything. It is conjecture. A jury might not convict him.'

The DSI was grim. 'You should attend more trials.' Seeing Saskia's expression, he pulled a face, as if to dismiss his own comment.

'If Proctor is an innocent party, then I believe he will wish to gather more information about his predicament. At the very least, more information would bolster his defence against the charges. Under EU law, it is not illegal for an innocent person to attempt an escape.'

Jago gave her a warning look but the DSI nodded. 'Well, I can't argue with your research, Detective.'

'Kommissarin,' Saskia said. She felt her voice strengthen. 'Proctor is a university professor. It is a comfortable existence. We know from his emails that his relationship with his daughter is strained. The last few days will have proved to be very difficult, even life-altering. Proctor will undoubtedly feel the need to leave the country. Here he is hunted. In America he is not. His daughter is in America. In addition, she gave him the warning. If he is indeed innocent, then his search for answers must begin with her.

Flying out would "kill two birds with one stone". We must assume it is within his capability.'

The DSI said, 'I'm with you. Jennifer is his daughter. The person who helped organise his escape is someone who would risk everything for him. Jennifer fits the bill. Was she the woman who broke Proctor out of the Park Hotel? Who knows? Maybe her employers – if they are the US government, like you say – helped to falsify her passport and formulate Proctor's escape plan. If we get her, we get Proctor. But is she still in the country?'

'I think it is unlikely,' Saskia replied. 'If you are correct and she has the backing of the American government, they would advocate a plan with minimum risk. Perhaps she has already risked a great deal by personally overseeing her father's escape. If they were to attempt an escape together, the probability of their apprehension would increase. In that case, I would suggest that she left immediately via the nearest airport, Edinburgh.'

Jago shook his head. 'I don't know. If the Americans really wanted Proctor, why not smuggle him out by military transport?'

'Secrecy,' the DSI said. 'And cost. How much do they want him? What can he be worth?'

Saskia replied, 'Perhaps everything, perhaps nothing. However, with the correct advice and documentation, there is no reason why Proctor should not be able to leave the country through an airport.'

'Edinburgh?' Jago asked. 'You think he showed up in Northallerton to throw us off the scent?'

'Why not?'

'No,' said the DSI. 'We had Edinburgh locked down tight.

To get lost in the crowd he would need somewhere bigger.'

'Like where?' Saskia asked.

'Heathrow, Gatwick, Luton, Stansted,' Jago said. 'Take your pick.'

'Which is the largest?'

'Heathrow,' said the DSI. 'And its surveillance is poorest due to the volume of traffic. We've had a team researching this scenario. If he took a car or a train, he would have left the country by now. If he's still on the bike, and using minor roads, he could catch a flight at midnight – if he rides hard. Personally, I think he'll lie low for a week.'

'Those flights need to be checked, sir,' said Saskia.

'I agree with you, Brandt. Check each person who flies to America between midnight and 6:00 a.m. Check them by hand. If you don't find Proctor, we can assume he's already gone or he's lying low. We have other people working those leads.'

Jago said, 'Check them by hand? Can't we leave that to the Met?'

DSI Shand shook his head. 'Think. If Proctor takes his holiday tonight, I want us to nab him, not our Cockney friends. No sense having the Met solve our cases.'

'But Saskia is a neutral party.'

The DSI grinned, revealing a gold canine. 'It's that kind of clear thinking that stops you advancing through the ranks, Phil. Saskia is a neutral party accompanied by a Lothian and Borders liaison officer.'

'Yes, sir,' Jago said quietly.

'You two can hitch down to Heathrow with a friend of mine, Sam Langdon. He comes up here for the golf. My secretary will give you his number. Have a nice trip.'

He held open the door. Saskia and Jago walked through. In the waiting room, Jago said, 'I was his mentor when he joined the service.' He checked the time. 'Right, we'd better find this Langdon character. Saskia?'

She was watching Besson and Garland at the coffee machine. They looked up and smiled. Even the loneliest person has the memory of company, but she did not even have that.

›•‹

David glanced at the bike's dashboard. It was 4:00 p.m. He had been riding for nearly nine hours. It was time to gather the elements of his disguise. He took his lead from Ego, who had downloaded three SAS survival guides and related them to David in a digested, if sensational, form. Ego wanted him to change his vehicle and his clothing. David disagreed. Clothing, yes; vehicle, no. The bike was uncomfortable but it was fast, all-terrain, and easily camouflaged.

Now he stood next to the parked, cooling Moiré and considered Ego's advice. He leaned towards the microphone in the helmet, which he had secured to the fuel tank. 'Bike, change to green,' he said. 'Do it gradually, over the next hour.'

David walked into town. The pedestrians cut unpredictable zigzags in front of him. After only two days on the bike, he had forgotten how to walk in a crowd.

Inside the first shop, the owner's smile froze on contact. To be sure, David had a thickening beard and grimy clothes. His head was bowed to avoid surveillance cameras. And he paid cash. Physical money was risky, but he had to assume that the credit card had been blown since his escape from The Poor Players. Prudently, the passport carried a different name.

He abandoned his old coat in a public toilet and walked on. He purchased new clothes and, item by item, left their predecessors around the city centre. In a gentleman's outfitters he bought a suit and shoes. In another he bought a beige briefcase, a pair of tinted glasses, a shaving kit, some paper overalls, a wedding ring, and a startlingly expensive belt. In each shop he lamented the loss of his bank card and shrugged wistfully at the need to carry so much cash. The shopkeepers made clicking noises and were sorry to hear that, sir, and said no more. Finally, he bought some aftershave and a universal storage crate for the bike. At the invitation of the last sales assistant, he stuffed his shopping into the box. Both he and the assistant stared at the crumpled suit for moment.

'Travel iron, sir?'

'Can't hurt.'

Shopping completed, David returned to the bike. The universal box was not as universal as its manufacturers had enthused. It took fifteen minutes to attach. He rode away with his new clothes and a bike that was nearly green. He rode away a different person.

Different enough?

He was still a man on a bike.

'Ego,' he said, pulling out into traffic.

'David.'

'Does it strike you as odd that I haven't been captured?'

'You have been lucky to an extent, but it is not surprising that you have evaded capture. Though there is an All Points

Warning out for your arrest, the description is rather vague. According to the recent spy novel *A Very British Deception*, which contains a well-researched escape similar to yours, I do not believe that the police have the manpower to find you unless you make a serious mistake: that is, break the law. They do not know your location, your destination, your purpose; nor do they have a current physical description. If you continue to ride under the speed limit and use minor roads, your chances of reaching locker J327 are good.'

David snorted. 'I'm sure I broke the speed limit once or twice.'

'No, you did not.'

'Maybe up near Sheffield. I was going pretty fast.'

'I have global positioning and accelerometer data that prove you have not broken any speed limits.'

He turned onto the southerly road. In the sunshine, his visor darkened. 'You've saved me,' he said glumly.

'I do not understand.'

'Like a data file. Saved.'

'It is a precaution designed to provide an objective source of information in the event of a trial. It will guard against tampering. Perhaps I may also act as a black box if you have an accident. The probability of my survival is far greater than yours.'

'Ego, how much battery life do you have?'

'Eight weeks.'

'Well, switch off for now.'

'I am still monitoring radio stations and Net sites.'

David revved the engine and accelerated. It was time to break the speed limit. 'Switch off. Now.'

CHAPTER TWENTY

Saskia reached into the pocket behind the driver's seat and found a blister pack of travel sickness pills. Three seemed a good number; four a better one. She crunched them to a bitter dust. Her head still pounded. Jago was beside her, gripping the handle above the door, unconcerned as the back tyres locked briefly. The two police officers in the front of the car shared a smile. In the back, Jago gave Saskia a nudge and flourished his eyebrows.

The airport was ten kilometres from the station. In the early evening traffic, it would take half an hour. The co-driver activated the siren intermittently but they were soon slowed by congestion.

'How are you armed, Saskia?'

'This,' she said, showing her gun.

'I should have got you something more modern from the armoury.' He smiled. 'Like a bow and fricking arrow.'

'A revolver is preferred for... ideological reasons.'

'You surprise me.'

Silence returned as Saskia counted the kilometres.

›•‹

When they reached the airport, Jago said, 'Straight through, they're expecting us.' The car drove into a huge, fenced enclosure where private planes were parked in rows, then stopped hard.

'This is where you get out,' said the driver. He reached back to shake Jago's hand, but the DI had already left the car.

Saskia shook it on Jago's behalf. Her smile was crooked.

Outside, the cold air was rank with fumes. Lights defined the terminal building, the roads, and the fences. As she watched, a jet landed with mesmeric slowness. Its exhaust blurred the air. She felt the vibration in her chest.

'Saskia, get a shift on,' Jago called, jogging backwards.

They climbed into a small four-seater aircraft. Jago settled in the back and Saskia sat next to the pilot. It was too dark to see his face. 'These are for you,' he said. He handed Saskia a headset with microphone. 'Sam Langdon.'

'Saskia Brandt.'

'Did we make it?' rasped Jago.

'Your timing is impeccable,' said the pilot. He gunned the engine. Through her headphones, Saskia heard him say, 'Control, this is Golf Tango Foxtrot Two-One-Two requesting clearance for take-off, over.' There was no audible reply. 'Roger, Control, I'm taxiing to runway two, over.'

'We appreciate this,' Jago said.

'No problem. I was flying back anyway.'

Saskia relaxed. The darkness was reassuring. 'There's a blanket under your legs,' Sam said as they rolled forward. 'Careful not to touch the control column.'

'Foodibles?' Jago asked.

'Behind you.' Langton turned to Saskia. 'Latest weather report shows poor visibility over the south-east. There's a low pressure front moving north. Expect a bump in the night.' He switched on a red reading light and noted the time in a paper logbook. He held the column between his legs.

'How long to Heathrow?' she asked.

He laughed. 'We're not going to Heathrow, sweetheart.'

'Oh?'

'I'd need to sell the plane just to afford the landing. No, we're going to Farnborough.'

Jago tapped her shoulder. 'Sandwich?'

Saskia looked around. Obligingly, Jago peeled back the white bread to display the filling. Sliced sausages.

'English sausages?'

'The finest. Plenty of brown sauce.'

'What is brown sauce?'

'Good question.' Jago took a bite. 'Must be one of the fun things about foreign travel. New foods.'

Langton said drily, 'How long have you two been married?'

'I'm thinking about a divorce.' She tapped his log book. 'Please tell me where Forbrough is.'

'Farnborough,' the pilot corrected. 'Three hundred miles to the south. In new money, five hundred kilometres. They expect us for 9:00 p.m. Sit back.'

She watched the runway lights stream by as they took off. The acceleration made her drowsy. She became aware of a crowd of English nonsense voices inside her head. All *ths* and *ruhs*. She fell asleep in their company.

›•‹

Later, the pilot explained that the Grantham, being a light aircraft with no oxygen cylinders, could not climb above the weather. It flew low where the winds were thick and the rain constant. They touched down at 9:30 p.m. Saskia had not moved since climbing aboard, but when she stepped onto the wet concrete of the holding lot, she felt ready to collapse with tiredness.

'Thanks, Sam,' shouted Jago above the propeller noise.

'I have to park. See you.'

Saskia gave him a salute and searched for a terminal. She could see none in the fierce rain. 'Where now?' she asked. She ducked to avoid the wing as Sam taxied away.

Jago pulled his suit jacket over his head. 'Look, there.'

They watched as a traffic patrol car approached. It sharked through the aircraft and stopped before some heavy cabling. A female officer approached carrying an umbrella. She opened it over Jago. 'Piss off,' he said, climbing in the back.

It was a twenty-minute drive to Heathrow. Saskia had fallen asleep against the window before the car pulled away.

CHAPTER TWENTY-ONE

Sharp braking threw Saskia out of her dream. She wiped her mouth and looked ahead. The car had stopped. The traffic was a crimson mass of braking lights. Her watch read 10:30 p.m.

'We're late,' she said

She looked at Jago. He was sweating and a vein throbbed on his forehead. 'An accident,' he said. 'It happened just in front of us.' He dabbed at the vein with a handkerchief.

'Scotty?' She put a hand to his forehead, expecting it to feel hot. It was cold.

He grimaced. 'Heartburn. You know, acid indigestion. The bloody sandwiches.'

Saskia heard the co-driver talk urgently into her radio. The words were abbreviated and unintelligible. The car pulled onto the hard shoulder. Jago said, 'They're the closest unit. They have to secure the scene.'

The vehicle shook as their co-driver slammed the boot, shrugged a fluorescent jacket over her shoulders and jogged ahead to the driver. Saskia gripped the handle. She felt an urge to help, but, seeing Jago's exhaustion, she stayed in the car.

'We will wait for the next unit.'

'…Alright.'

'Alright.'

›•‹

David was thinking of his daughter. He had taught her to ride in a cul-de-sac near the old house in Oxford. He had pushed her endlessly, a constant commentary to reassure her of his grip. Finally, when he let go and she wobbled all the way to the turning space, he felt proud. He felt like a real father. At the end of the road, he heard her faint voice say, 'I nearly did it that time, Daddy.' He cupped his hands and shouted, 'You did! I'm back here!' and she turned around and fell off with a scream. He ran down and picked her up, bike and all, and took her inside. He sat her on the washing machine and dabbed her grazes with antiseptic. Between her sobs, she smiled. 'Did it.' That became her catchphrase. When she passed her advanced maths at the age of nine; when she published her poems; when she got into the New York school, she always said, 'Did it.'

A blue light flashed on the dashboard. He glanced down. No, it was a reflection. He turned his head. There was a police car approaching at twice his speed. He indicated left and drifted from the lane, slowing.

'Ego, wake up.'

›•‹

'What is it now?' Saskia snapped. She was exhausted. They had been delayed at the accident site for over an hour and Heathrow was, at last, only minutes away. Beside her, Jago awoke and scratched his cheek.

'What's the description of Proctor's bike?' asked Teri, the co-driver.

'Vague,' said Jago. 'It could be a trail bike. Green, but possibly a different colour by now.'

Teri whistled. 'That new?'

'Yes, that new,' Saskia said. 'Why do you ask?'

'Look at the bloke in front of us. Can't be that many Moirés on the M4 at this time of night being ridden by a weekender. This year's registration, too. Fair-sized luggage container on the back.'

'A weekender?' asked Saskia.

'He couldn't ride a bike to save his life. Obvious from the way he's sitting on it.'

'Pull him over,' said Saskia.

'Easy, hen,' Jago said. 'We can't pull over every bike we see.'

'What do you want to do?' called Dan, the driver. 'He's changing lane.'

Saskia touched Jago's elbow. 'Scotty, pull him over. It will cost us five minutes if I'm wrong, but if I'm not—'

'Fuck it. Teri, give him the blue news.'

The siren whooped. The headlights blinked. The rider glanced back, wobbled, and changed lane. He seemed uncertain whether to pull onto the hard shoulder or come off at the next exit. Teri activated the siren once more. The two vehicles crossed onto the hard shoulder and stopped.

Dan opened his door. The interior light was abrupt and

dazzling. Saskia said, 'Be careful. He may be armed.'

Dan paused. 'Armed?'

Saskia sighed. The preferred weapon of the British police was a stern finger.

'Wait here,' she said.

She slipped from the car and moved forward until she was standing between the headlights and the motorcyclist, who still sat astride his machine. She touched her gun.

'I am armed. Switch off your engine.'

The man did not turn. The engine revved. Saskia heard Scotty and the two uniformed officers get out of the car.

Stay back, she thought. *I'm in control.*

She exhaled and took a pace closer. 'Armed police. Turn off your engine and show me the key.'

This time a gloved hand disappeared in front of the rider's torso. Was he reaching for a weapon? The engine cut. She relaxed. She had to think slow. She was in control. She was prepared to draw and fire. Ignoring the Brits behind her, the occasional car roaring by, and the on-off wash of blue light, she drew her gun. The rider's hand appeared again. It held the keys. The keys dropped to the ground.

Saskia gave further commands and, as she spoke each one, the rider obeyed. 'Deploy the kick stand. Get off the bike. Move to the right. Face away from me. Remove your helmet. Slowly. Place it on the ground so that it cannot roll away. Lie down on your face. Put your hands behind your head. Cross your legs.'

Only at this point did she look behind her. The two uniformed officers had their shotguns trained on the suspect.

'Finished, dear?' Jago asked. He walked past her and sat on the rider.

Saskia waited for him to apply the cuffs, then holstered her gun. 'Well?'

'See for yourself.'

She approached. Her breathing stopped as the man's head came into view. For a moment, their eyes locked. She smiled apologetically. He looked away.

Jago stood. 'Satisfied?'

'Okay.' Saskia turned to the uniformed officers. 'It's not him.'

'Smashing,' said Dan. He and Teri gave their shotguns to Jago and hoisted the man to his feet. Saskia followed Jago to the car. She was sleepy and embarrassed. She overheard Dan's raised voice. They were haranguing the rider over a technicality.

'I did not think British police were armed,' she said.

'Welcome to the twenty-first century.'

They leaned against the bonnet and watched the traffic. The air was crisp and smelled of exhaust gases.

'Sorry, Scotty.'

He snorted. 'We had to take the chance. What if it had been Proctor?'

Saskia watched the traffic some more. A police car fired past and its blue lights were a racing heartbeat. Seconds later, she saw another motorcyclist.

No. She would not cry wolf again.

›•‹

David noticed the parked police car and motorbike. A man and a woman were watching the traffic. He checked his speedometer. It read 65 mph. He slowed and drove past, looking straight ahead.

CHAPTER TWENTY-TWO

Hard upon midnight, David entered Heathrow's Terminal Five. He tooled around the multi-storey car park until he found a secluded bay for the Moiré. The engine sighed away and he slid off. He tugged the bike onto its lay stand. He removed his helmet and slapped his face, firmly. He shook his head like a dog throwing off water. He needed to be awake. He needed to be careful.

'Ego, I'm at the airport.'

'Excellent.'

David had long abandoned reading human emotions into Ego's voice, but it was hard to ignore its surprise. 'Change your clothes. Then find locker J327 in Terminal Five.'

'Am I going to fly?'

'I am not in a position to tell you that. If you are captured, it is better you know little in case you jeopardise a future escape attempt.'

David watched his condensing breath. His eyes followed the vapour and continued to stare long after it vanished.

Then, after another slap, he crouched in the shadow of a van and removed his jacket. He took off his waterproof trousers, his riding trousers and his hiking boots. He placed them in a heap. He opened the universal storage crate on the back of the bike and retrieved the briefcase. He placed his essential items inside it. There were some non-essential items too. In the escape, he had transported most of the bathroom from The Poor Players.

He grabbed a fistful of underwear from the container and stuffed it into the briefcase. In another bag, he picked out the items he would need: a pair of tinted glasses, shoes, a shaving kit, a wedding ring and a belt.

The overalls were at the bottom. He put them on carefully, though the material felt tough. There was a telecoms logo on the lapel. He put his boots back on, but not his bike jacket. Instead, he took a light coat and threw it across his shoulders. Along one side of the container was a dry-cleaning bag with a complete suit inside. He rummaged some more and found a bottle of aftershave. He tossed it into the briefcase, closed it, and set about stuffing his old clothes into the bike container with one hand. In the other, he held the suit.

Finally, he closed the container and detached it. He smiled and patted the headlamp.

'Ego, can you hear me?'

The computer was inside his briefcase. 'Perfectly.'

'Is it all right to leave the bike?'

'Where better to hide a tree than a forest? There are more than four thousand spaces in this car park. And, because payment is requested on exit, it will be days before suspicions are raised.'

'Did you read that in a spy novel?'

'Yes.'

David carried the container and the briefcase towards the terminal building. The pain of the past few days seemed to trot one pace behind. He was nearing the next stage. After miles on the bike, things were moving again. He hailed a Personal Rapid Transport pod and, when it arrived, settled into the driverless four-seater alone.

'David, the PRT computer is asking for your destination. I've told it that you are bound for Terminal Five, but have not given any other information.'

For that, he had to watch an infomercial about women whose lives had been transformed by a brand of moisturiser.

›•‹

David stepped onto the third floor of Terminal Five. The rush of flight reminders and conversation reminded him of an orchestra tuning up. His eyes rose to the distant roof, then dropped, exhausted. Passengers stood in deep lines at the check-in desks. Beyond them, the shopfronts were brilliant.

'You must proceed directly to the toilets,' prompted Ego. 'The computers linked to the security cameras are quite capable of recognizing you, but they sample randomly. The probability of your capture is increasing.'

The toilet was a two-minute walk away. He passed through its gleaming entrance and stepped over a robot loaded with cleaning tools. The stalls were either side of a wall of basins. There were no shower cubicles. On the far wall was a store cupboard. David nodded. He had a good chance of assuming his disguise without incident. As Ego might say.

He selected a basin in the middle of the row. He whistled to fill the air and smiled at a teenager two basins down. The teenager quickened his ablutions. David opened the container and retrieved his washing kit. He shaved. Nothing strange about that, he told himself. Just a chap having a shave.

When he had cleared the last of the foam, he leaned into the mirror. Not bad. He was beginning to assume his old, respectable – and, he realised, vain – self.

Next, he doused his hair with hot water, relishing the warmth as it drew the cold from his fingers. He found a sachet of shampoo in the remains of his shaving foam. He washed and rinsed the soap away. He was still just a chap washing his hair. He whistled some more.

With his hair clean but dripping, he gathered his things and retreated into a stall, locking the door. He slipped off his boots, his nylon coat and the overalls. He used the toilet and then set about his transformation. Soon he was wearing the suit. The tie would need straightening in front of a mirror. He splashed some aftershave around his neck. Then he opened the briefcase.

He checked the contents: his wallet, which contained Ego and some cards; the watch; the passport; cash. He had no physical business documents. That was normal. Everything would be stored on his computer. He dropped the wallet into his inside pocket and closed the briefcase.

He opened the door and walked to the store cupboard. It was locked but the mechanism was a simple magnetic strip reader. Ideal. There were only two people nearby. They were looking in the opposite direction. He took Ego from his wallet, whispered, 'Ego, crack this magnetic strip lock, will you?' and swiped it twice through the reader. On the third pass, the door clicked. In the cupboard were paper tissues, a replacement hand drier, an assortment of bottles, and some mops and brushes. He shoved the container inside. A glance around the room reassured him that he had not been seen. The two people had left. He opened the door again and threw a package of toilet rolls over the container. Only the cleaning robot would use the cupboard on a regular basis. It would simply work around the obstruction. He closed the door and heard it lock.

He took his briefcase from the cubicle and left the room, pausing to straighten his tie in the mirror. Then he flattened his hair with his palm and walked on his way. Just a chap walking out of a toilet.

CHAPTER TWENTY-THREE

Saskia closed her eyes on the crowds and settled against a poster, though she still felt every centimetre of the cavernous and crowded terminal. Nearby, somebody dropped a guitar. Its chamber echoed, and in the moment that followed the dampening of the sound, Saskia became aware of a similar vibration within herself. Had the sound reached the steppe-like expanse of her mind? She opened her eyes. The guitarist had vanished. In his place, a boy whispered into his mobile phone.

Saskia watched the glow on his cheek.

Perhaps the sound in her head was electromagnetic interference. There were so many phones, music players, and computers on the concourse that her brain chip inducted their activity.

She remembered her conversation with Klutikov. *'You need to protect that chip. If you switch off the chip, you switch off 'you'.'*

'Saskia.'

'Finally, Deputy. How can it take you so long to find a toilet? There must be many on this stretch of the concourse.'

'Actually, there's one.' His face was close and ashen. 'And Proctor just used it.'

'What?'

Jago showed her a crumpled plastic sachet. Saskia shook her head. She did not understand. Then she saw the text. It read: *Rinse and Shine at The Poor Players!*

'Shampoo? The idiot. But when was he here?'

Jago had a thin smile. 'It's still sticky. Not long ago.'

'Can it be a mistake? He's been clever so far.'

'You think he *wants* us to find him?'

'I don't know.' In order to concentrate, Saskia looked away from Jago. She turned back. 'The next flight to America. Which is it?'

›•‹

There were fewer than a dozen people in the basement locker area. An attendant slept on the counter of his kiosk with his cheek on a newspaper. As David walked by, watching the attendant, a regiment of lockers emerged on his right. He had substituted his boots for brogues, and they clicked like a pen nervously thumbed.

'Ego, I'm at the locker.'

'Good. On the keypad, type: upper-case M, four, nine, hash, lower-case D, lower-case X.'

Locker J327 sprang open. David touched all five sides. It was empty but for an envelope addressed to 'You'. He checked up and down the row. Nobody. But he heard footsteps. It took him a moment to confirm they were receding. He tore the seal. Inside the envelope was a piece of paper and a single ticket to Las Vegas.

'What is written on the paper?' asked Ego. 'Tell me immediately.'

'It says, "Sounds like…" Christ, it's fading.'

'A security precaution. Keep reading.'

'"Sounds like a car-parking attendant belongs to the finest." That's all.'

'Information stored and encrypted.'

The fatigue of the bike journey, propelled by the knowledge that he was headed for America, seemed to overtake David. He sagged against the locker. '"Sounds like a car-parking attendant belongs to the finest." What is that? A crossword clue?' The neat handwriting had faded to nothing.

'Examine the ticket.'

David rubbed his eyes. 'McCarran International, Las Vegas. Via Chicago. So what?'

'The time?'

'12:30 a.m.'

'It is now 12:10. I suggest that you leave immediately. It is unlikely that you will still be at liberty for the next flight.'

›•‹

As they ran, Jago shouted that the simplest approach would be to buy their tickets and arrest Proctor in the air. They found the check-in and jumped the queue. Saskia did not linger on the aggrieved expressions of the waiting passengers. This close to departure, Proctor would be on the flight already. Jago slapped the counter and demanded two tickets. The attendant shook her head.

'That flight leaves in ten minutes, sir.'

'Yes, with us,' Jago said. He produced his warrant card. The attendant studied the passport. In the pause, Saskia placed her FIB wallet alongside Jago's. As her fingers left its surface, Saskia was a chess player committing to a move. If she left the EU without Beckmann's permission, she would be executed. But if she allowed Proctor to escape, she would be executed for that. She prioritised the fugitive pursuit.

The attendant looked over Saskia's shoulder. The glance was deliberately indifferent. Saskia turned. A plain-clothes security guard was standing behind them. Jago turned too. The queue became still.

Jago said, 'Who are you, the bloody prefect?' He looked at the attendant and stabbed a thumb in the direction of the security officer. 'Tell him to piss off.'

›•‹

David Proctor, who was standing not far behind the two police officers, detached himself from the queue. His hands, which had been dry, began to drip sweat. His face, recently shaved, itched. He walked to the next desk and said, 'Excuse me. My flight leaves in a couple of minutes. May I check in for Las Vegas from here?'

'You got lucky, I was about to open up.' She started her computer with a touch. 'Are you feeling alright, sir?'

He turned to face away from the police. 'I haven't flown for a long time.'

'Thought so. Luggage?'

He tried to swallow but his throat was too sticky. 'Just the briefcase.'

To his left, close enough to touch, the middle-aged officer said, 'Jesus, we're only in pursuit of a criminal. Take your time.'

David released his air. His hand crept towards his jacket pocket. Then it dropped. The stun gun was gone. It was in the bike container, which was in the gent's toilet, which was a lifetime away.

'Sir?' asked the attendant. Their eyes met.

'Yes?'

'I asked if you are carrying anything in your briefcase for somebody else.'

'No.'

'Your boarding pass.'

'Thank you.' He reached for it, but she pulled it back. He swung from victory to defeat. Had the police officer seen him? Made a signal? Pulled a gun? But the attendant smiled. David released another breath. The air was stale and hot.

'Here is the gate,' she said, pointing to the boarding pass with her pen, 'and here is the seat.'

'Look, I've just about had a titfull of you,' shouted the police officer. 'Get a move on.'

'I've put you near an emergency exit,' David's attendant continued steadily. 'So you'll have more leg room.'

David reached for his documents. They stuck to his sweaty fingers. The attendant said, 'Deep breaths,' and he nearly laughed. He began to walk away. He inclined his head. With each step he felt the certainty build, the certainty that a voice would shout, 'Stop! This is the police!'

It never came.

He watched his feet. It was the only way to be sure that he would not fall over. After twenty metres, he knew that he had escaped.

For now.

›•‹

'Come on,' said Jago.

They headed towards passport control. Saskia checked her watch. Jago saw her. 'How long have we got?' he asked.

'Five or six minutes.'

'We can make it.' He broke into a jog. Loose objects jangled in his pockets. Saskia followed, but hung back. She did not want to make him run faster. The tails of his suit jacket whipped back and forth.

'Scotty,' she said, trying to sound breathless. 'Let's slow down.'

'Just a bit of running. It'll look great in the report.'

They reached passport control. It was congested. Jago stopped and removed his coat. He took great breaths and leaned forwards. 'Let's,' he said, swallowing, 'let's jump the queue.'

'Are you feeling all right, Scotty?'

'Indigestion. Those bloody sandwiches,' he said. 'We should keep moving.'

'No. Take a moment to recover. I can see the plane. The gate is very close and we have several minutes. We have time.'

Jago nodded. 'I'll just catch my breath.'

Saskia loosened his tie.

'Do that.'

›•‹

David told himself to breathe as his retina was scanned. When the machine thanked him and asked for the next passenger, he watched the passport control officer frown at something on his terminal. The man's eyes flicked from the passport to David, from David to the passport. The silence was building. Or was it?

'You seem nervous, Mr…' The officer cocked his head. It had to be a deliberate affectation. It suggested control. David saw himself reflected in the man's designer glasses. He glanced at the official's name tag. Christopher Garner. Senior Passport Control Officer. David's hand flexed around the briefcase handle.

What was his own name?

His fake surname?

'Mr Greensburg?' the officer prompted.

David tried to recall his back-story from the scraps he had invented over the past few hours. There was a wife living in Leeds, a son at university, a DB7 Vantage (lovingly restored), a farmhouse kitchen…

'Greenspoon,' he blurted. 'Mr Greenspoon.'

The officer seemed disappointed. 'Of course. Mr Greenspoon.'

'I am a little nervous,' David offered. The regret followed immediately, accompanied by the memory of Ego's last words to him: *'Less is more.'*

'Really, sir?'

'Of terrorism. Terrorphobia, you might call it.'

The man handed back his papers. 'Naturally, we all are, sir.'

David moved towards the detector and felt physical relief when he heard the officer attend to the next person in the queue. His fingers trembled as he dumped his wallet into the pot on the conveyor belt. The briefcase followed. He stepped through the archway. A waiting police officer with a sub-machine gun cast an empty eye over him. Would he be recognised? Nothing happened. He collected his wallet.

›•‹

Saskia was watching a man. She turned to Jago and touched his arm.

'What?'

'The man walking through the detector.'

Jago squinted. His breathing was still heavy. 'Could be.'

'The passport officer seemed interested in him.'

'Did he now?'

›•‹

David took two strides before he remembered his briefcase on the conveyor. He laughed a little too loudly. The armed police officer turned towards him. His face was young and blank. David smiled. The man did not smile back. David reached for the briefcase. He looked directly into the eyes of Saskia Brandt.

CHAPTER TWENTY-FOUR

She did not react immediately. His hair was longer than it had been in his police photograph. His eyes were hooded, shadowed. He had lost some youth. He was thinner. But he was her man.

'Proctor!'

She barged into the passenger in front of her, who tripped, dropping his case. Jago cut in from the other direction. He trod on the case, twisted his ankle, and pitched forward. His shoulder caught Saskia behind the knee. They both fell.

Saskia tried to stand but the owner of the case was sitting on the small of her back. She jabbed her elbow at his thigh and he rolled off. She climbed unsteadily to her feet, drew her revolver and scanned for Proctor.

'Police!' shouted an armed officer. 'Drop your weapon now!'

'*Föderatives Investigationsbüro,*' she said, turning to him.

'Drop it now!'

'*Föderatives Investigationsbüro,*' she repeated. 'Federal

Office of Investigation. I am in pursuit of a suspect.'

The officer stepped forward. '*Now.*'

Saskia hissed with frustration. She dropped the gun and looked at the area beyond passport control. Proctor had gone. A voice over the tannoy asked Mr Jago and Ms Brandt to please board flight IAL 778. Jago, who was being held down by a civilian security guard, swore loudly.

'Let me show you some identification,' she called to the armed officer.

'Left hand. Slowly. Toss it over.'

Saskia skimmed her ID across the floor. She saw three more police officers running in lock-step down the terminal towards her. Each wore the same outfit: a black baseball cap, a bulletproof vest, combat trousers, and black trainers. Each had a sub-machine gun pointing at the floor. Meanwhile, the civilian security officers began to clear passengers away.

Her ID landed on her foot. 'That's yours, Kommissarin. Good to meet you. I'm Sergeant Trask.' He waved to the new arrivals. 'Stand down.'

But Saskia was not listening. Jago, her deputy, was struggling to breathe. He held his chest as though his heart was trying to break out. His skin was grey.

'Scotty? ...Philip?'

A shadow fell across Jago's face. It was Trask. 'Paramedic to my position, over.'

Saskia took Jago's hand. The palm was slick. She turned his chin, hoping to make eye contact, but his eyes were trapped under tight lids.

'Brandt, is it?' Trask said. 'We were told you were coming down. Didn't expect this drama, though.'

She nodded. She kept her eyes on Jago. 'Neither did I.'

'Paramedics are on the way.'

As she pressed Jago's wrist for his pulse, she noticed his watch. It was 12:29 am. Proctor's flight would leave in one minute. She turned to Trask and studied him for the first time. He had a hard, dependable face. 'I am in pursuit of a fugitive. I need to ground his plane.'

'Flight number?'

She threw her boarding pass at him and wiped the sweat from Scotty's forehead. His rictus had sagged to a gape.

'You have a problem,' said Trask. Saskia followed his finger. She saw, through the transparent wall of the terminal, the huge A380 reversing.

'Stop the plane.'

'We could call ahead. Chicago is tight on this kind of thing.'

'But I do not know his name and there are over six hundred people on that flight.'

The man looked at her. 'Control from Bravo Two at Tango Five, I have a priority request to talk to the captain of the A380 now taxiing towards runway four. Flight ILA 778, runway four. Repeat, this is a priority request, over.' He tapped the device on his lapel and the controller's voice became audible.

'Bravo Two, stand by, over.'

Saskia looked around for the paramedics. Jago had lost control of his bladder. His breath had dwindled to tiny sobs. Trask crouched and turned Jago's head. He was encumbered by his sub-machine gun. 'Keep his airway open.'

From his radio, an American voice said, 'Good morning, Bravo Two. This is Captain Jameson on ILA 778. We're moderately busy. Make this quick.'

'Captain,' said Trask, 'I have a request from an FIB agent that you return to the terminal. You have a fugitive on board your aircraft.' He waited. 'Captain?'

'Do you have any reason to believe that he threatens the integrity of my aircraft?'

Reluctantly, Saskia shook her head. Trask said, 'No.'

'Bravo Two, let me put this simply. If we lose our slot, we'll be bumped, and given the capacity restrictions at this terminal, that will cost us at least four hours. My co-pilot and I will breach our duty hours limit if that happens, which I will only permit in exceptional circumstances. Pass his details to my sky marshals. We'll contain it. ILA 778 out.'

For the first time that she could remember, Saskia said, 'Fuck.' She looked at the oncoming paramedics. There was no doubting the push of her instinct: she must board the plane. She kissed Jago on the forehead and whispered, 'I promise to come back.' To Trask, she said, 'Delay the captain for just a couple of minutes. I intend to catch his flight. It is a matter of British national security.'

She snatched her gun and ran through the passport control gate. Trask shouted at the staff to let her pass.

›•‹

She vaulted a barrier that read 'Heathrow Personnel Only', skipped down the maintenance stairs to ground level and burst into the night. This was the eastern flank of the terminal. To her left and right were docked aeroplanes. Only dashes of light spoke to their shape and size. The air was thick with fuel vapour and the wail of jet engines.

Nearby was an orange vehicle with a flight of steps rising from its back. She eased herself into the driving seat, looked over the dashboard, and swore. The steering controls were horizontal hand bars. They had triggers and stalk buttons. Besides that, the fascia was dark. She slammed her palms on her thighs.

'Move over,' said Trask.

She slid into the passenger seat as Trask climbed in. 'At the FIB, our cars are computer controlled,' she said.

He gunned the engine, pulled away, and wrenched the handlebars. The vehicle skidded to face the receding aeroplane.

'*Vive la différence.*'

Saskia attached her seat belt and remained alert for vehicles and aircraft as they accelerated. She overhead Trask's conversation with the ILA captain. 'Yes.' He glanced at her. 'In a heartbeat. What? German, I think.' He turned to Saskia. 'He'll stop just before they get to the runway. He thinks you're plucky. That'll be our one chance.'

'Please keep your eyes on the road.'

'But there isn't a road.'

He swerved left and right to demonstrate. Saskia groaned. At length, she said, 'Trask, I appreciate this a great deal.'

'Dinner.'

'Not that much.'

›•‹

Inside the aeroplane, where the seats were close and the ceiling low, David sipped his cup of whisky. Cabin crew answered questions and patrolled with ambassadorial ease.

The passengers were relaxing and settling; opening snack bags, securing their children, slipping off shoes. Not so David. He looked into his drink and wondered if one could read ice like tea leaves.

'Sir?' asked the stewardess. 'Your cup.'

He gave it up and returned to his thoughts, which seemed to be about nothing at all. When his armrest beeped and its screen opened like a flower to show the flight deck, David looked down wearily.

'Good evening, ladies and gentlemen. We are pausing to take on an officer of the continental FIB. There is no cause for alarm, unless you haven't filled in those tax returns.'

The adrenaline coursed through his tissues in a single, sparkling wave. His jaw locked tight.

'So,' continued the captain, 'allow me to welcome you on board this ILA flight 778 to Chicago. In a few moments, we will leave Heathrow in an easterly direction before turning towards the north-west.'

David lost interest. Halfway down the walkway, three air stewards had gathered. David watched one of them open the door. There was a moment of quiet anticipation, then a woman was helped into the aeroplane. The nearby passengers applauded. The cabin crew slapped the back of their new arrival and straightened her clothes, but she pushed them away. She was already searching the faces of the passengers.

David looked down at the video of the captain.

'Okay, ladies and gentleman, we now have our full complement. On behalf of ILA, the crew, and myself, I would like to wish you a pleasant trip. Cabin crew, final pre-flight check, please.'

David did not believe he would have a pleasant trip. He could only think of what might have been. Had his benefactor arranged a new life for him in America? It made no difference. He would be arrested and extradited.

When they were in the air and the detective was walking towards him, scanning faces, he raised his arm and gave her a little wave.

›•‹

The woman had long brown hair and emerald-green eyes. She was tired and serious, and hopelessly beautiful.

'Professor David Proctor, you are arrested by Frau Kommissarin Saskia Maria Brandt of the *Föderatives Investigationsbüro*, badge number 077–439–001, on two counts of murder. These charges will be pursued under British law. You have the right to remain silent. Anything you say may be recorded at the discretion of your arresting officer and reproduced in a court of law as evidence against you. These data are the property of the FIB. Do you understand? Come with me. I must speak with the captain. I am armed.'

CHAPTER TWENTY-FIVE

Hours later, as the aircraft skirted Greenland, Saskia stared at her blurred reflection in the cubicle mirror and considered Proctor's story. The compass of her mind floated over an inscrutable lodestone – the instinct of a murderer, she guessed – and settled on a decision.

She reached into her jacket and withdrew her badge. She thumbed the golden letters of *Föderatives Investigationsbüro*, . Underneath, 'Brandt' had been stamped on the metal. It was not her real name. The extent of her official biography ended with her nationality, her sex and her age: German, female, late twenties. Her skills were fake. Her knowledge of arrest procedure: inserted. Digital.

Her eyes closed. She saw three women on a dark plain. The Fates: Clotho, she spins the thread of life. Lachesis, she measures a length. Atropos, she cuts it.

Spin, measure, snip.

She folded her make-up kit and pulled expressions at the mirror. Her face was becoming familiar.

›•‹

Saskia found Proctor sitting on a steward's jump seat in the rearmost compartment of the top deck, flanked by stowed trolleys and two emergency exits. He was handcuffed. He looked up as she approached. She did not respond to his brief smile. She wanted to keep the worry bright in her mind.

'I have thought about your proposal,' she said, taking the spare jump seat next to him. She did not unbutton her jacket. She did not want to tempt Proctor with her gun, though it had been unloaded at the captain's request.

'Go on.' His eyes moved around the small space. Occasionally they settled on her. Mostly they settled on his handcuffs.

'It is unacceptable.'

Proctor tipped his head. 'Ah.'

'Professor Proctor—'

'David.'

'It is not within my power. You do not even know your ultimate destination.'

'No, that's true.'

'I have arrested you. It is my duty to return you to Britain. There you will face the authorities.'

'But you believe me. I'm not the criminal you think I am.'

'I do not have the luxury of belief or disbelief, Professor. Tell the authorities what you have told me. That you've been acting under duress. If it is the truth, it will be taken into consideration at your trial.'

The lift opened and a steward emerged. He gave both Saskia and Proctor a professional smile before moving into the economy cabin.

'A trial?' Proctor said, turning to her. 'Kommissarin Brandt, do you remember what I told you about your role?'

'Yes. You said that I have a further part to play. But you cannot tell me how you came to this conclusion.'

'I could tell you,' he said, 'but you wouldn't believe me. I'm not sure I believe it myself. You must come with me.'

Saskia listened to the seashell hiss of the engines. 'Professor, it is within my power to have you chained to a bulkhead in the cargo bay. You can keep the poodles company.'

'I'm afraid I can't allow that.'

Saskia smiled. It was difficult to feel threatened by a likeable, middle-aged man who had protested his pacifism at such length. 'Professor—'

'Your full name is Saskia Maria Brandt. Your FIB badge number is 077–439–001. Your service records begin three days ago.'

Her hand flexed in anticipation of a swift draw, but her gun was empty. She swallowed. 'So you've researched your pursuer, Professor Proctor. Full marks. How?'

'It is being dictated to me by my personal computer, which is always on the lookout for other friendly computers. Like the one in your brain.' He looked at his handcuffs again. 'It would be very easy to deactivate it, and will take only a keyword from me. That, I guess, would have very serious consequences for you.'

Saskia did not blink. She had no bullets. If he deactivated the chip, there would be no time to find some, load the gun, and blow her malfunctioning brains out.

'Professor,' she said, struggling to flatten her tone, 'you have spent nearly two hours explaining your principles.

Have they now deserted you?'

'In the end, it comes back to protecting those principles.'

Saskia rose on her anger. 'How pathetic. That is the age-old drivel spouted by every idiot with a cause, from the religious fanatic to the political terrorist.'

She waited for his retort. Instead, his head drooped.

'I don't want to do this. I'm not responsible.'

'Listen to me. I know you're not a bad man. But you must understand.' She took his chin and turned his head towards her. 'My superior. The way he operates…' She did not blink. 'This chip contains me, the real me. Do you understand? I cannot… go back. I choose to remain like this.'

He looked at her curiously. 'So what does Saskia Brandt *mean*?'

'What?'

'Who are you?'

'I don't know.'

›•‹

As the A380 rumbled into Chicago, Saskia avoided Proctor's gaze, irritated by his questioning expression. She still felt its regard, and the bleeding edge of his pity. It was two o'clock in the morning. She collected the rounds confiscated by the captain and allowed a sky marshal – an ex-police officer – to escort them to the immigration control section, where the blind barrels of automatic firearms tracked them in a small room shared by Middle Eastern women and their children. Accents British, eyes downcast like Saskia's. The marshal touched his cap and told her to go ahead and keep the handcuffs. Proctor guffawed and scratched his head.

Her bound right lifted too. *A salute*, she thought, looking at the marshal, and thinking of Beckmann.

She sat in silence, motionless as the statue of Prometheus, and locked out the noise and constant motion of Proctor as he fidgeted, sniffed, and sighed.

Within half an hour, they were taken to a soundproofed room and left alone. Saskia unlocked the handcuffs. She bounced on the balls of her feet and rolled her neck. She shrugged her shoulders. She appraised the young immigration officer as he entered and closed the door. He read an element of her intention, but Saskia descended upon him before he could gather air for a shout. She punched nerve bundles in his chest and shoulders to undermine his strength, put her elbow into the notch below his ear, and caught his fall.

CHAPTER TWENTY-SIX

It was sunrise before Saskia would speak to him. Proctor dozed in the driving seat of the rental car, slightly reclined. His personal computer was in a dashboard cup holder. The Ego unit had instructions to deactivate Saskia's chip if she did anything other than sit and wait. So she watched the dawn blaze on the landscape, flat as a page. Las Vegas was a ten-hour drive on I-70, but their counter-surveillance precautions would slow them. She saw a billboard slide by. It advertised Iowa sushi. She frowned. She felt empty. The flesh of her memory had been picked clean from her bones. Ahead, a truck's indicator blinked. Siudeck the money launderer had been given a uniform with epaulettes. She raised her fist and looked at the bruised knuckles. She wondered if her unarmed combat skills were intended for the use of harder, more robust hands than those she had grave-robbed.

Klutikov? He had large, good hands.

The traffic thickened. The car slowed into the human

speed band, and its braking tipped Proctor forward. He widened his eyes, stretched his eyebrows, noted Ego still on watch.

'Morning,' he said.

'Professor.'

'I told you to call me David. Where are we?'

'Crossing into Nebraska.'

'We've made good time.'

'I've ordered another rental car to rendezvous with us at the truckstop in six miles. Our current car will follow us for a few miles.' She looked at his white stubble. 'As a double bluff.'

'All this expertise comes with your new chip, does it?'

'You're talking to the chip right now. It's not something separate.'

David looked as though he had said something rude. 'What did you do with the guard's uniform?'

'It's in the boot. Safer if I wear my suit instead. It fits.'

'Saskia, I'm sorry.' He touched her shoulder. 'As soon as I find my daughter, you will be free to leave. I promise.'

She batted his hand away. 'Do you want me to feel grateful? You give me up to a future where I will be hunted like you. To fail my first assignment is to die. My employer told me so.'

'I'm doing what I'm doing for the best reasons.'

'As they seem to you.'

'Yes.'

'You don't even know where you're heading.'

'The plane ticket said Las Vegas, so that's where. For now.' David touched his forehead. 'Oh! Of course. The paper from locker J327. It said, "Sounds like a car-parking attendant belongs to the finest." What do you make of that? It could be phrased like a cryptic crossword clue. They often have part of the answer in the question. One of the words may be an anagram of the answer.'

Saskia closed her eyes and pictured the letters. She thought, *What are the anagrams?* An instant later, she knew that 'attendant' had no rearrangements that made sense, while 'finest' could make 'feints' or 'infest'.

'I cannot find any likely anagrams.'

'Wait. What's another word for a car-parking attendant?'

'You are the English speaker, not me.'

'Ah, but you fake it so well. Another word… would be "traffic warden", or "attendant". No, we have that. Come on, Saskia.'

'I'm thinking.'

'It could be an American word. We're in America. Valet.'

'What's a valet?'

'Somebody who parks your car for you. Could it mean the best example of a valet, like a super-valet?'

'What's a super-valet?'

'Like *Superman*, only cleaner.'

'What?'

David sighed. 'Never mind.'

'Let's stay with "valet",' said Saskia. 'As for finest, in some online indexes of English word usage, it refers to a city's emergency services. Usually the police, but sometimes the fire service.' She felt his interest. 'My chip can connect to the telecommunications network.'

'Wow. Consciously, unconsciously? Can you see a webspace right now?'

Saskia closed her eyes. Her thoughts fluttered, trapped.

She knew that the chip was background processing the relationships between 'valet', 'fire service' and Las Vegas, just as the semantic parser of the UK police had tracked Proctor's emails.

She opened her eyes.

'The clue must refer to the Valley of Fire State Park, on the outskirts of Las Vegas. Your daughter is there.'

Proctor laughed. 'Well done that woman.'

'This is the truckstop,' she said coldly. 'We have to change cars. Pull in.'

'Computer, give me control.'

The car said, 'You have control in five seconds, four, three, two, one. You have control.'

›•‹

Saskia waited beneath a sign that warned of the dangers of hydrogen. She watched David enter the glass-fronted store and lost him in the reflected scrubland. Carefully, she lifted the handset and dialled. The British ringing tone made her think of Simon. Somewhere, perhaps in a zinc tray, a phone played 'Scotland the Brave'.

'Hello?' asked a woman.

Saskia tucked her hair behind her ear. 'May I please speak to Detective Jago?'

'I'm afraid that's not possible,' she said. Her accent was British. Not Scottish, but English.

Saskia almost hung up. Then she said, 'To whom am I speaking?'

'I'm his daughter.'

Jago had only one child and he was called Jeremy. Saskia

swapped ears.

'My name is Sabrina,' Saskia said. 'I heard that your father had been taken ill. Could you please tell me how he is?'

'He's under observation.'

'I see,' said Saskia. She pursed her lips.

'Are you still there?'

'When he wakes up, tell him I'm sorry. Can you do that?'

'...Wait.'

Saskia listened as the phone was handled.

'There is something else,' continued the woman. 'Dad said that Saskia might call. He had a message for her. Is that you?'

Saskia considered the isolation of the gas station and the anonymity of the phone. The surrounding land was flat and empty. She looked into the heights of sky, and thought about the cold stare of a satellite, and the colder eyes of Beckmann.

'Yes.'

'He told me that your former boss has sent a man to find you. Dad was visited by him last night.'

'I see.'

'Saskia? All's well.'

She frowned at the horizon and her reply was spoken before she could think. 'That ends well.'

Shakespeare.

'Wait,' said Saskia, but the woman hung up. When Saskia called back, the phone rang without answer. She lowered the handset gently, though she wanted to smash it. The muscles in her face gathered like a fist. Someone whistled and she looked up. David was sitting at a picnic table on the opposite side of the lot. She collected her tear-diluted mascara on a knuckle and walked the windy gap between them and felt like a gargoyle as she perched on the furthest edge of the bench, waiting for the next rental car.

David studied her.

'What are you staring at?' she asked.

'I'm debating if I should tell you something.'

'Let me know whether the motion is passed.'

'On board the aeroplane, when my computer brought the presence of your chip to my attention, I took a gamble and claimed that I could deactivate it. The truth is that I can't. My computer doesn't even recognise the communication protocol. It's encrypted. You're perfectly safe.'

Saskia turned to face him. 'But you knew my name, my badge number.'

'Just a skin of metadata wrapped around the unencrypted hellos and goodbyes your chip sends all the time.'

'Sends where?'

'The Net.'

'Maybe it's my location. Did you think of that?'

'I did, but consider the possibilities. If compressed, it could send the data of your senses across the Net.'

Saskia took his coffee and sipped. 'What is the taste of coffee, expressed as a number?'

'Now you're getting it.'

'David, do you think I'm even here? Am I lying in a coma in a hospital in Berlin, or London, or Rio – relaying my soul chip-to-chip like,' she looked across the forecourt, 'a conversation?'

'Easy to find out. We'll get you a foil hat and see if you drop dead.'

'No, thanks.'

'I note that you aren't calling for help.'

'Perhaps I just did,' she said, indicating the gas station.

'The phone call? Yes, I noticed that. But Ego doesn't think it's something I need to worry about. He heard the whole thing. Sorry about your partner.'

'Never mind that. Tell me about the woman who rescued you from the West Lothian Centre. Did you know her?'

He stared at her thoughtfully. 'Did I know her, Saskia?'

CHAPTER TWENTY-SEVEN

Jennifer Proctor had worked late the night before. She woke at eleven, made coffee, swallowed her norepinephrine reuptake inhibitors, and checked her inbox. Then she took the elevator to the car park of her apartment building. The traffic was heavy, but manageable if she avoided the Strip. She read some paperwork while the car turned north, then east, then joined I-15 heading north-west. Twenty minutes later, she turned onto Route 169 at Crystal.

The road surface worsened as she entered the Valley of Fire. Sunlight struck the red sandstone formations and they did indeed appear to ignite, but Jennifer did not look up from her notes until she had reached Met Four, the weather station in the north of the park. The car dropped her at the base of a huge rocky column and, as she approached the iron steps, it parked nearby.

She stopped.

'Good afternoon,' said a tall man, blocking her way.

Nothing about him moved but for the tails of his coat. 'Dr Jennifer Proctor?'

'Who are you?'

His irises flared blue. 'Detektiv Lev Klutikov. I'm with the European FIB, the Federal Office of Investigation. Here's my badge and a number you can call to confirm its validity.'

'I believe you. What do you want?'

'One of our agents, going by the alias Saskia Brandt, has turned rogue. She was fitted with neural augmentations containing a donor personality. That personality has become unpredictable. We think she's targeted you. I've been assigned to provide you with personal security, should Brandt attempt to make contact.'

'You're kidding.'

'Not at all. There's a high likelihood she will make contact in the next hour or so.'

'Well, there's no need to worry about me.' Jennifer nodded to the rocky column ahead. 'She can't follow me in there without an army. Neither can you, for that matter.'

'A renegade agent from the FIB is treated seriously.' He waved a blue ID badge. 'I have a level one pass and full co-operation from Helix Base.'

'Man.' Jennifer had never seen such a clearance. Klutikov had the keys to the kingdom.

'We should proceed immediately, Dr Proctor. We—'

'What?' asked Jennifer. She followed his stare to the road, but she could not see or hear anything.

'Get your car. You're in danger.'

'Danger?' she said. Her fear was turning to pique.

Jennifer gasped as he put his hand into the pocket of her jeans. He pressed her key fob. In the corner of the lot, her car started. 'When it comes to pick you up, get inside and lock the door. Understand? Wait for me.'

'Is she here?'

'Brandt. Yes. She's watching us.'

'But I could hide inside the installation.'

Klutikov turned to the zigzag of iron steps that ran the full height of the column. 'You wouldn't make it.'

Jennifer's car stopped at her sneakers. She settled inside and threw the locks. She looked from Klutikov to the unreachable castle of Met Four. Would its cameras be trained on the car park? Certainly. But there were no human eyes behind those cameras, and a computer would only summon help if presented with overtly suspicious behaviour.

Jennifer sank behind the driver's wheel and planned. If something happened to Klutikov, she would run from the car. Her running would alert the computer, which would alert guards, who would come to her rescue. Perhaps she could make the iron steps before the agent reached her. They had told her, in the early days, that something like this might happen. She hadn't believed them.

Through the arch of the steering wheel, she saw Klutikov walk away. He flexed his right hand.

›•‹

Saskia stood in front of her car. Her hair was redrawn gust by gust. She watched Klutikov's eyes. Somehow, she knew that he had hacked his sight to detect electromagnetic radiation above and below the thresholds of human vision. He could taste her heat. Sense the tell-tale metals at the heart of her ceramic revolver. She waited for him to scan her body and the car. Satisfied, he nodded and held up his golden FIB badge. His free hand rested on the butt of his holstered gun. She looked for a ring like the one Beckmann had used to control her, but he was wearing gloves.

In rapid German, he said, 'Frau Kommissarin Saskia Brandt, you are arrested by Detektiv Lyova Klutikov of the Federal Office of Investigation, Russian section, badge number 012–919–001, on the internal charge of desertion. This charge will be pursued under the laws of the European Union. You have the right to remain silent. Anything you say may be recorded at the discretion of your arresting officer and reproduced in a court of law as evidence against you. These data are the property of the FIB.'

Saskia said nothing. Waited. Her hair fluttered across her eyes.

'Did you hear me, Saskia?'

'Yes. Why German?'

'I don't want to make it easy for the surveillance computer to eavesdrop. Things might get more complicated.'

He walked towards her, closing his badge with an easy flick. 'Why aren't you armed?'

'Airport security confiscated my gun.'

Klutikov drew her hair through his gloved fingers. Her scalp shivered. 'Hello, Angel.'

'Hello.'

'Our boss made a serious mistake with you.' He lifted the hair to his nose and sighed. 'After all, what qualifications do you have, apart from getting caught?'

'Why didn't Beckmann use his ring to control me, call me back?'

'That trick works at short range. He chose the long-range trick. Me.' He put an arm around her shoulders and suddenly his gun was at the soft meat below her sternum. She gasped and he pushed harder. His pupils were wide and black. 'Now, tell me again where you put your gun, and don't be,' he grazed his teeth against her forehead, 'clever.'

'Under the passenger seat.' She indicated with her chin. 'Let me get it.'

'No, I think I will.'

With his free hand, Klutikov opened the door. He put one knee on the driver's seat and reached across. Saskia, heaving a breath, hooked his back leg with her own and tipped him inside. At the same time, she shut the door on his forearm. His hand splayed and his gun dropped to the desert. Saskia tucked his arm inside and slammed the door. The locks clicked. Before Klutikov could sit, the car accelerated out of the car park and was gone, its dust thinned by the breeze.

David stepped from behind a van. 'Good work, Saskia.'

'Is the car still under your control?'

David listened to Ego. 'Yes. He kicking at a window right now, but the car is travelling too fast for him to bail out.'

'How long do we have?'

'The car will be out of Ego's range in twenty minutes. Maybe Klutikov can overcome the car's computer. I don't know.'

Saskia nodded and crouched to take Klutikov's gun. Despite the satisfaction of besting him, she was uneasy about the questions that his appearance raised. Why had he been improperly briefed? He should have been told to expect two people, not one. If Beckmann had wanted to recapture Proctor, why would he limit Klutikov's effectiveness by restricting his information? Klutikov was eminently capable of retrieving

Proctor. He was, perhaps, more capable than Saskia.

She pulled at her lip. No. Her reasoning was not correct. There was nothing to suggest that Beckmann had abandoned Proctor. Beckmann had simply tried to remove Saskia from the case.

She studied Met Four. The ghostly traffic of sand rushed about her.

Beckmann had changed his mind. If he did not want Proctor to be captured, that meant he wanted Proctor to reach his destination.

And his destination was his daughter.

'Come on, David.'

›•‹

Jennifer's fingers trembled. She felt for the door handle and gripped it hard. She would make a run for Met Four.

No, she thought. *Just drive away. Play it safe.*

She touched a button on the dashboard. The engine started.

'Car, take me home.'

But the rogue agent called Brandt was in front of the car, looking at her through the windscreen. The car switched to reverse, then stopped immediately. There was a man at the trunk. It was not Klutikov. This was a man she had last seen in New York.

'Park here. Unlock the doors.'

His face was older now, an extrapolation of the man who had cried with her on the steps of Wayne's College long years before. He was trying not to laugh. Jennifer stepped into his arms.

›•‹

In the car, sealed from the airs, slow minutes passed. Jennifer's attention shifted from her father to the rogue agent, and back again. The two sat on the rear seat. They were waiting for Jennifer to speak. Jennifer pointed at the woman. 'Why would Klutikov lie about you?'

'He told you what you needed to hear. His larger aim was to return me to Beckmann, our mutual employer, for execution.'

'That doesn't explain his blue Helix clearance.'

The woman nodded. 'It doesn't.'

'And you,' Jennifer said to her father.

'And me.' The lines on his face, which had recorded all his smiles and frowns, were deeper and browner than ever.

'What happened after I spoke to you, Dad?'

He sighed. 'It's a very long story, but I'm afraid that... Jenny, I killed a man. I'm on the run.' He indicated Brandt with his head. 'From her, actually.'

'Dr Proctor,' Saskia interrupted, 'let me explain our position in brief. I was dispatched to apprehend your father. I did so, but he managed to exploit the situation and brought me here against my will. David had received a cryptic clue, from an anonymous benefactor, which directed us to this location. Does this mean anything to you?'

Jennifer looked through the windscreen at an expanse across which the devils spun. She turned back.

'I'm a physicist. But there are many technologies being developed in our research centre. One of them, Dad, looks like a recreation of your old lab from the West Lothian centre. The project manager has a crush on me and I got the royal tour. He told me that they're trying to reverse engineer some of what you and Bruce Shimoda did twenty years ago, before your technology went up in smoke.'

Her father seemed to deflate. 'Bruce and I had planned to the destroy the technology, electronically first, and physically if that didn't work. We had an idea for a bomb, but we never got that far.'

'I met a person inside the computer. I think you should meet him, too.'

'Jenny, Bruce Shimoda is the man I killed.'

'I know.'

CHAPTER TWENTY-EIGHT

Their footsteps echoed on the iron stairs. Jennifer led, followed by her father, then Saskia. The top of the column was edged by an artificial parapet of rock. They stopped at a chain-link fence with an inset door. Next to its handle was a slot. Jennifer swiped her card and they passed through. Met Four comprised two prefabricated buildings. An array of antennas and dishes sat on top of the first. Above the second, there were two flags: the Stars and Stripes and the pennant of the US meteorological office.

A man emerged from the first building. He was unarmed, but Jennifer knew that his colleague stood by in the second building with a sub machine-gun.

'Morning, ma'am,' he said. If he had said, 'Morning, miss,' this would have been a coded instruction to go home.

'Morning.'

'Guests?'

'That's right.'

They entered the first building. Inside, it was

unremarkable. A ranger sat behind a desk, his hands at keyboard. Nearby, a secretary placed some papers in a filing cabinet. Jennifer had walked into the same room once a day for more than a year. The woman and the man had never changed their positions.

'Good morning, Jim.'

'Morning, Jennifer. Who are your friends?'

'Professors Stiefel and Whitney from Caltech. They should be expected.'

Jennifer was quite confident. After all, she had a man on the inside.

Jim checked his computer. 'They are. Have a great day.'

'Thanks.'

Jennifer led them through a chipboard partition to a cloakroom. She placed her coat on a hanger and did a twirl for the microwave camera. Saskia and her father did the same. Jennifer showed them where to put their thumbs against the wood. Their nail beds glowed pink. Partial sections of her DNA were read and checked. Thanks to the work of Ego behind the scenes, they matched those held by Helix Base. The floor sank. When their heads had passed below the floor, a panel closed the top of the shaft. A gap appeared at their feet as the lift slid into a room.

'Where are we heading?' asked her father.

Jennifer studied her father in the growing brightness. When she had argued for improved computing support at a committee meeting the day before, she had ridden her anger hard, as always, and she knew its source. She had not shouted at the chairman but at her father. At her father, who had dumped her in a school in New York and left for England. But now, in his presence, her fury had died to an ember. He had given her the best education. For him, that was the first priority. It was his one true aspiration. He had put that aspiration above their relationship. He was a principled man.

'Through the looking glass, Alice.'

They spoke little for the rest of the way. They descended further into the rock and took their first steps into the research centre proper. Jennifer explained that the low-ceilinged, busy corridors comprised the Stack, which was the vertical structure that threaded the enormous tunnel of Helix Base. The Stack housed administrative offices, workshops, recreational facilities, a canteen, and a water processing system connected to Lake Mead. Five minutes later, they took a horizontal corridor leading away from the Stack. Jennifer gestured to the door at its end. Its sign read, 'Project N25136'. Beneath this, someone had added 'Looking Glass'.

She said, 'Two days ago – moments before you destroyed the Onogoro computer, Dad – a stream of information was uploaded to a server, then downloaded to here: to Project Looking Glass. This, Professors Stiefel and Whitney, is where your fake identities came from.'

›•‹

Minutes later, with the imager securely attached to her face, Jennifer opened her eyes. She was in orbit around a virtual planet. Clouds wheeled across oceans that glistened in the light of the local star. The vapour met her as she passed through. Beneath were mountains, forests, and the trails of great rivers. She fell further. She looked right and saw the sun set behind the planet's belly. Two evening stars descended with her: Saskia and her father.

The Looking Glass system was equipped with haptic cloud technology, in which swarms of microscopic machines could buffet a user's body to produce realistic virtual environment interactions. Jennifer had not activated the cloud. For this reason, the system rendered the three of them not with bodies but as glowing, shapeless stars.

It was as these stars that they fell to the surface of the planet.

They settled near water at the base of a ravine running north-south into the foothills of a mountain. It was widest at their point of landfall. To their right was an expanse of shingle, which reached out for a kilometre before meeting the wall of the ravine. At its face was a hut. It was crude but solid. From this distance, nothing could be seen except for the bonfire set before its porch. It produced a weak, shifting light.

She closed her eyes and imagined the bonfire. She was transported in an instant. Saskia and her father settled nearby. The fire sounded like rain on glass.

'Computer, my voice is my passport. Announce me.'

The bonfire erupted to twice its height. Then it settled back to a murmur.

Jennifer watched as a man stepped from the hut. He held a spear. He was wrapped from head to foot in fir fronds. She looked at the blurry star that represented her father and wished she could see his face. It was only when Bruce Shimoda smiled and said, 'Welcome to my parlour,' that her father whispered, 'Oh my God. How?'

Bruce approached the bonfire and sat. 'I'm no more than

data on the run, really, but aren't we all? Welcome to the land of the unreal. We need to talk, everyone. Now.' Bruce opened his mouth, then closed it. His jolly expression was gone. 'Damn, something is happening. There's something wrong.'

'What?' asked Jennifer.

Abruptly, the simulation ended. Everything was blank, beyond black. From that darkness seemed to come a sound, almost visible, and its meaning was so profound that it took Jennifer a long moment to place it. The Evacuation Alarm had been activated. It was a scenario unthinkable to her, but conceivable to military minds: something had happened in one of the fringe projects down here, something bad, and the compression apparatus within the subterrene's core was about to send the reactor supercritical.

CHAPTER TWENTY-NINE

Saskia felt the mask disengage from her face with a kiss of negative pressure and rise to its ceiling dock. She was no longer on the virtual planet but in the glass immersion chamber. Through its frosted door she could see red lights pulsing in time with an alarm. Against these lights grew a dark silhouette.

The shape resolved to a figure, a man, approaching and raising his arm. The proximity of his gun to the frosted glass made its barrel and front sight clear, nosing from the fog.

The alarm stopped.

She kicked the door open.

It slammed against the man, glass crystallising, and sent him staggering back. He wore a grey suit and a cowboy hat. His face was expressionless. She could see every centimetre of him now, could track his muscle movements, and perceived – perhaps because of her chip, perhaps because of deeper biological processes – the very moment he chose to fire.

He was within reach. She relaxed, let her arm whip out, and struck the gun. A concussive wave clapped her ears and a confetti of sharp fragments sparkled across the back of her neck.

This bullet had missed.

She was already moving forward. She moved to his right, well beyond the angle of the weapon should it discharge again, gripped the gun barrel securely, twisted, and stepped behind him. She pushed and he fell onto his belly, sliding down the black walkway that divided the cubicles. He came to a rest at David's feet.

'Good, isn't she?' said David. 'Saskia, meet John Crane, part-owner of Helix Base and a portfolio of very expensive technologies. Third richest man in the world.'

'Second,' Crane said, gasping. He had raised himself to one elbow. 'Farrow died in Martian training camp last Tuesday. More money than air.'

Jennifer stepped from her cubicle. 'That's the base alarm. The reactor is going supercritical.'

Saskia swung out the cylinder of Crane's gun, counted five bullets, and snapped it shut. Then she pointed the weapon at him. She could not connect his appearance with the reactor countdown. Looking at him, but talking to Jennifer, she said, 'How long do we have?'

The red lights continued to pulse.

'Fifteen minutes.' Jennifer went to her father and took his hand. 'We do this drill every month. There are evacuation tubes on every level. The exits will be blowing open as we speak. We can make it if we hurry.'

Saskia shook her head. She was still looking at Crane. His blank face was locked on hers. In it, she saw an element of certainty that she did not like.

'Jennifer,' said Saskia, 'what is the result of the alarm?'

'The *result*?' She gave Saskia an exasperated look. 'A lot of heat and light. Come on.'

'No,' said David. 'Not the explosion. The alarm.'

Jennifer looked from David to Saskia. 'It will evacuate the base and disengage the locks. People will re-group north of Mead…'

She trailed off as Crane got to his feet. He smiled – it was wrong, a bad copy – and opened his hands, palms upwards. They were empty apart from the ring he wore. Saskia had last seen a ring like that on Beckmann's hand.

In the reflective surface, tiny and red in the emergency lights, she saw the hawk spread its wings.

The hawk that returned.

Saskia half-closed her eyes. There were three old women on a dark plain. The Fates: Clotho, she spins the thread of life. Lachesis, she measures a length. Atropos, she cuts it. One of the women turned. Her skin was baggy and her eyes empty. 'You will return,' she said, 'as you have returned before.'

Spin, measure, snip.

'I'm here for Jennifer, that's all,' said Crane. His toneless voice made him sound as though he were reading a script. Perhaps, in a way, he was. 'I'll put everything right. This is the beginning.'

As Jennifer put her fist to her mouth, Saskia sensed a change in David. His eyes became narrow and severe. In a clipped voice, he said, 'Jennifer, what did you build for him?'

'I—'

'What, Jennifer?' he said, and Saskia felt the disappointment of a father at his daughter's mistake. When Jennifer shrugged, David turned to Saskia and spoke slowly, as though his words were for the benefit of Jennifer too. 'I used to think that every fringe project Crane ever funded was an elaborate exercise in self-medication. That each one was a big bet with a heavy stake. Until now, each one lost. Onogoro certainly did. But Crane backed a winner in Jennifer. Project Déjà Vu has romped home.'

She frowned. 'What do you mean?'

'Do you remember what I said when we first met?'

'Yes, you claimed to have met me before.'

'It took me until now to fully understand. Before, it didn't make sense.'

'What didn't?'

'You, Saskia, helped me escape from the West Lothian Centre four days ago.'

Saskia waited for him to continue. When he did not, but looked at her seriously, she frowned and shrugged.

'What do you mean?'

'Just that. You rode me away from the West Lothian Centre on a bike.'

There was nothing to say. The absurdity of David's statement made any answer useless. Even for Saskia, whose life had been shattered by her own face reflected in the blade of a murderer, there was no sensible way of construing David's words. And yet the thought was not so easily dismissed. David's conviction was plain. And there was no answering incredulity from Jennifer. If anything, the woman had seemed to shrink further into herself.

'There's nothing impossible about time travel,' said Crane.

'Since Einstein, the Devil of time travel has only been in the detail.'

'Saskia,' said David, 'it didn't make sense because you were twenty years older than you are now. In the time we've spent together, I've thought through the alternatives in an attempt to talk myself out of that conclusion. Did you have an older sister? Could it be your mother? Was it some other kind of *doppelgänger*, a person transformed by plastic surgery? Now, here, I realise that my instincts were correct. It was an older you. You are going to travel backwards in time.'

Saskia felt their attention. They were looking at her like a museum exhibit. She had the gun, but she was suddenly vulnerable – the most vulnerable person in the room. 'This is nonsense. If I had aided David in his escape, I would also have aided myself in the past few days. But my future self has been absent.'

'That's not true,' Jennifer said. 'You contacted Bruce, who contacted me.' She raised her hands at the room. 'We made it here.'

Crane began to laugh. It was a grating, unnatural sound more like the shrill repetition of the siren.

Shoot him, she thought. *Shoot him now.*

Physically, she was capable of it, and she remembered well that he had tried to kill her. She had every right to discharge the gun point blank.

He was looking at her, laughing.

Why couldn't she fire?

Thus conscience does make cowards of us all.

Crane touched the ring once with his thumb. Immediately, Saskia felt the same separation inside herself she had felt when Beckmann had taken control of her body. She tried to move, but she could not.

'Jennifer,' said Crane. 'Step away from your father.'

Helplessly, tears brimming, Saskia watched as her gun wavered, then turned towards David and his daughter.

'No,' said Jennifer, moving closer to him.

'Do it,' said David. He held Jennifer by the shoulders and gently steered her to one side. Then he stood with a straight back on the threshold of the cubicle and raised his chin. He looked seriously at Saskia and put his hands in his pockets.

The thoughts screamed inside her head, pulsing: *No. No. This is his arm, not my arm.*

'Shoot Professor Proctor between the eyes,' said Crane. 'But only,' he continued, 'if he tries to escape, or if his daughter does not fully cooperate with me.'

Saskia looked from David to Jennifer, who had her face in her hands.

'I'll cooperate,' Jennifer said.

'Listen to me,' he continued. 'All of you. The reactor alarm is a decoy. Helix Base will not be destroyed. But it will, shortly, be empty of personnel. Jennifer, I understand that the materials needed for your machine were delivered today.'

'It's ready.'

'Saskia, do we understand one another? Jennifer, David?'

Jennifer dropped her eyes to the floor. David said nothing. Saskia tried to nod but could not.

That's it, she thought. *I've lost.*

As Crane held out his hand for Jennifer, Saskia heard a humming sound. It was coming from behind her. Crane paused.

Saskia could not turn. She was forced to watch the curious, then unsettled reactions of Jennifer and David as the sound increased in volume, together with a cool draught that moved wisps of Saskia's hair forward. It seemed to be coming from the cubicle she had vacated.

Something moved across her neck. It might have been a breath. Then her view darkened as a grey vapour enclosed her from behind. It had to be the haptic cloud, the technology that created solid shapes within the imaging chamber.

The cloud condensed in the space between her and Crane. It became a shifting ghost of a man, not unlike the shape in the frosted glass moments before.

Crane's face remained blank, but his eyes widened as the dark shape made a fist around his ring hand.

The voice of Bruce Shimoda came through hidden speakers: 'Data storage rule number one, Mr Crane. Always have a backup. Here I am.'

Saskia blinked. She could move her eyelids.

'Shoot, Saskia,' said Bruce. 'I can't block the signal for long.'

Sensation was spreading from her eyes in a sparkling cascade down her face and chest, her back. She flexed her fingers. For this moment, they were hers, but even as they flexed, she felt a return of the weakness.

She wanted to tell David to take the gun, but all her mouth could do was swallow.

Saskia turned the gun on Crane. This was the moment. If she waited any longer, her weakness would engulf her. She squeezed the trigger. The gun fired through the haptic cloud, puffing a clear channel, a red star appeared on the wall behind Crane.

He spun. Saskia dropped the weapon. It landed on the floor with a thunking sound. She followed it to her knees, holding her wrist. Her arm felt bruised and weak. Meanwhile, the haptic cloud twisted, making Saskia think of sparrows in a morning sky, before falling to the floor like soot, dead.

Crane was sitting against the wall, a smear of blood behind him, breathing heavily. Saskia could see that she had clipped the top of his shoulder. It was a shallow wound; never a threat to his life. She reached out for the gun again, but her hands were shaking too badly to pick it up.

Crane looked at her without anger or even interest. He said thickly, 'You're forgetting data storage rule number one.'

Saskia focused on the gun. Her fingers had almost reached it when another hand moved into her field of vision and took it. The hand was gloved. Saskia sighed and raised her head. There was Klutikov, holding the gun.

'Caught again, Brandt.'

In this moment, as Klutikov was relishing the intensity of her hatred, David moved forward. His boxing stance surprised Saskia, and Klutikov only had time to frown before David's punch caught him hard on the cheekbone. Klutikov stepped back, blinked, and swung the gun. David raised his guard: fists against temples, chin on chest. If he had not raised it in time, the force of the blow might have broken his skull. In the event, he was knocked off his feet and fell alongside her.

Crane was already standing.

'Stay with them,' he said to Klutikov. 'If Jennifer refuses to cooperate, I'll contact you. Then kill her father.'

'What about her?' Klutikov asked, indicating Saskia with the gun.

'Wait,' said Crane. He touched the ring and closed his eyes. His lips moved slightly. 'There. Saskia, I've turned off your chip. That new personality you so love is no more. Over the next minute or so, you'll become the thing you most despise: the Angel of Death. Enjoy.'

Saskia watched as Crane, holding his shoulder, ushered Jennifer from the room. Jennifer flashed her a pitying glance.

Saskia felt something shift in her mind.

She saw Jago. Poor, dear Scotty. It was night. He was walking towards a small boat, which was tied to a pontoon. On the boat was a hooded man. Saskia called out and Scotty turned. He smiled and said something she couldn't make out (*Don't worry about me, hen…*) and reached into his pocket. He withdrew something (*a Zippo lighter*) from his pocket and struck it on his thigh: the lid opened on the down stroke and the wick lit on the upstroke. She waved. His lips moved but she couldn't hear (*the gift of fire*) his words. He spoke again from (*Remember what you're carrying…*) a faraway place (… *Ute*).

She blinked.

She was back in the room. Klutikov was crouched next to David's unconscious form, rubbing the fines from the haptic cloud between his finger and thumb.

'Klutikov,' she said. 'The lights are going off inside me.'

'Do you want me to feel sorry for you?'

'How sorry did you feel when you killed that Polish fisherman?'

Klutikov stared at her. He pursed his lips, thinking. He

opened the revolver and let the remaining bullets fall into his palm. Then he put one back, closed the cylinder, and put the gun near the door.

'That's for you,' he said. 'If you can get to it in time.'

He walked out.

›•‹

Saskia thought of the moment, an instant before, when she had had Crane in her sights. She had not been able to shoot. Would she now become the kind of person who would be able to shoot? To shoot and never stop?

She crawled to the gun and picked it up, relishing the weight. In the doorframe, she stretched out, bracing herself against the jamb as though bracing herself against the coming loss, the tide of nothingness.

Would it feel like a stroke, or falling asleep? She felt no shift in her mind, but when David next spoke, his words were becoming difficult to understand. Her English was fading. No doubt it was an implanted skill that existed only on the chip, not the brain.

She put the gun to her temple.

I will not become the Angel of Death.

'Saskia,' breathed David. She looked back at him. He lay on his side and his arm was stretched towards her. There was a trickle of blood on his forehead.

She looked at the gun. A six-shooter. Each chamber a side of a die. She checked that the bullet was beneath the hammer. But before she could squeeze the trigger, David gripped the barrel. They fought for control. David pushed the gun towards the floor and it glanced across his thigh, spinning the cylinder. Saskia gave him a weak shove. It was enough to make him gasp and fall back.

Beckmann was there, in her head: 'The purpose of Russian roulette is edification. A lesson that poses the question: is there a bullet or is there not?'

She put the gun against her head and pulled the trigger.

Snick.

The chamber was empty.

She pulled the trigger again.

Snick.

She had hit the second empty chamber.

She squeezed again.

Snick.

The third empty chamber. Anger expanded inside her. She looked at the gun.

For the last time, she pulled the trigger.

The spring creaked. The hammer yawned and the ratchet revolved. Spin. The chamber turned. *Measure.* At the same time, David's hands closed on her shoulders and she heard his meaningless words, felt his breath on her face. The world slowed. David's voice deepened and Saskia imagined the gap between the hammer and the round. In that gap, which might have been a thousand miles across, a flame sprang up, guttered, and died.

A nightmare poured from that darkness: she was in a coffin. She wanted to scream but her dead mouth would not move. Her chest itched from the coroner's incision. She smelled formaldehyde, corrupt meat and wood. Smoke, too. With that, she felt a draught through the dark curtain that separated the present from the past. The light from another world found her, even as she lay inside her box, and she remembered everything.

Here was the nightmare inside the nightmare.

Everything was revenge.

Snip.

CHAPTER THIRTY

Cologne: three months earlier

The tusk-like arches of the main railway station emerged on her left. Opposite was a department store. She stepped between them, a wounded figure. Her eyes, hidden under sunglasses, fixed on the sign for Oppenheim Straße. She found a bench. It was midsummer and the sun was high.

Ute removed a camera from her shoulder bag and retied her long hair into a neat ponytail. She pretended to photograph the passers-by, but she was taking pictures of an office block. Its ground floor housed a perfumery. Above that, the windows were soaped. Ute moved away. She found an alley that led around the back of the building. More photographs. There was a fire escape. Beyond was Father Rhine, steady as the sea.

She returned to the main street. On the same bench, she ate ice cream.

She paused on the way home to buy a padlock and a tube of superglue. The shop assistant asked her out for dinner, his gaze flickering upward to her green eyes. She stared at him until he apologised. She hurried from the shop and vomited into a drain.

The day grew old. She avoided eyes and hugged herself against the air while others relaxed in cafés and commented on the warmth. Ute heard them and seethed. It was not summer; it was autumn. If not that, then winter.

›•‹

She was a student. She was writing a thesis on the use of traditional myths in German literature.

Six nights ago, she had returned to the Kabana Klub. Her friend, Brigitte, had accompanied her, and together they had scanned the crowd. They had not found him. Brigitte had said, 'Why would he come back? He might expect it.'

'He would not.'

'What are you going to do if you see him?'

'First, I need to see him.'

Brigitte had accompanied her the next night too, and the one after that. Then she had stopped. Ute did not blame her. The music was too loud for conversation and, as Brigitte persisted with her questions, Ute persisted with her silence.

On the third night, alone, Ute saw him: a short, moustached man. He stood in the same corner wearing the same clothes. He chatted to two women just as he had chatted to her. He lit their cigarettes with a Zippo lighter whose flame he conjured with a dash across his thigh. But her fate and theirs took different paths; they smiled indulgently at his broken German and walked away, giggling. Ute watched them leave. She wondered whether she should confront the man. She decided not to.

He left two hours later, on foot. He walked for almost a kilometre. He meandered and doubled back on himself. Ute matched him. She had lived in the city her whole life and he had not. She stopped on corners and in shadows. There were few places for him to lose her.

They took the underground at Ottoplatz and emerged at Reichenspergerplatz. They came to the office block. This must be the place. She found a phone booth and dialled Holtz's office at the police station. There was no answer.

The night was cool. She walked back to her apartment via the river. The route was dangerous and she did not care. Fear was nothing next to her anger. She had a stun gun in her bag and a five-inch flick-knife under the sleeve of her right arm. She dared every shadow to attack.

Back at her apartment, she considered calling Brigitte. But Brigitte should not be involved. So Ute did not call the woman who had visited her in hospital on the first night when she was still curled, catatonic, bleeding from her vagina and holding keepsake scrapes of her attackers' flesh beneath her fingernails.

She did not call Detective Holtz again. She removed her clothes and dropped to her exercise mat. She did press-ups to muscle failure, crunches until her abdomen burned, squats with a barbell, and then repeated the routine until she felt nauseated and dizzy.

There was a poster of von Bingen, Germany's top triathlete, on the living room wall. She looked at it for a long minute.

Then she tugged the poster away. She reached for a pen, and, on the blank reverse, drew a plan.

›•‹

On the afternoon before the attack, she had been reading a book. Now she took it to the sofa. She sat there, jacket on, door wide, and opened the book at its marker. The page showed three old women sitting around a spinning wheel. The caption read:

Clotho, she spins the thread of life. Lachesis, she measures a length. Atropos, she cuts it.

She knew she was stronger than Brigitte. Her friend would have been damaged for life. Not Ute. She had no fragile belief in right or wrong, or natural order, or her own invulnerability. She had no creator to blame.

She had nothing.

CHAPTER THIRTY-ONE

She examined her photographs of the office block over breakfast in a nearby bakery. She returned to her apartment and thought, read and smoked for the first time since she began training for the CTW triathlon. She even tried to write some of her thesis. The words wouldn't come. That night, she slept fitfully. At 3:00 a.m., she drank a glass of water, put on her coat, and left the apartment.

She returned at 7:00 a.m. and left again at 8:00 a.m. Part of her knew she should call Holtz, tell him that she had found the office block and let him arrest the suspects. A nurse had collected sperm. It could be matched with any or all of the five men.

The train arrived and she got on. Her thoughts were lost in the crowd, in the pictures sweeping by, in the sensation of her fingertips on the stun gun and its extended capacitor.

There was a chubby boy on the train. He was about ten years old. He was on his way to school. He saw Ute and smiled. She looked away, not trusting herself.

She alighted one stop from her destination and walked the remainder.

›•‹

Ute emptied the glue into the lock. She put the tube in her pocket and left the alley. On the street, she turned right and entered the perfumery. It was precisely 9:00 a.m. The shop had no customers. Ute walked to the back of the shop and stood near a staff-only door. She pretended to inspect a moisturizing soap. When an attendant walked by, Ute clutched the woman's arm. 'Excuse me, please, but could I have a glass of water?'

The woman's bright smile faded. 'Yes, sure.'

She disappeared through the staff door and returned with the water. 'I'll have the cup back when you're finished.'

Ute took two deep breaths, drank the water, and dropped the cup. She swayed. 'I'm sorry…'

'Are you feeling all right?'

'Perhaps some more water…' Ute said. She fell into the woman's arms, leaving her no choice but to steer her into the back room. Ute's downcast eyes saw linoleum and cleaning buckets. She smelled fresh coffee. The woman dropped her on a chair in a small kitchen. Ute heard the running of a tap, and it was then that she withdrew her stun gun.

The woman turned. She held a cup of fresh water in each hand. When she saw the gun and Ute's cold eyes, she let the cups drop. They bounced on the tiles. 'You own the shop?' Ute asked.

'Yes,' the woman said. She was tearful, but her anger kept

her alert. 'What do you want? The takings? We have only been open a few minutes.'

Ute put a finger to her lips. 'What I have to do today has nothing to do with you or your shop. I need to get into those offices.' She pointed at the ceiling. 'How do I do that?'

Ute noticed the highlights in the woman's brown hair, her tan, and the red bandana that was tucked fashionably into the collar of her blouse. Her badge read Sabine Schlesinger. 'The fire escape.'

'No,' Ute said. She pictured her journey that morning, before sunrise, when she had stolen up those iron steps in bare feet, attached the padlock, and felt it click home.

'There *is* another way. Out of here, turn left. There's an interior fire door that opens onto a corridor. Go up the stairs. You realise I must call the police.'

'Of course,' Ute said. She did not lower the stun gun. 'Please do not follow me. This is for your own safety. Evacuate the shop.'

'What's going to happen?'

'Evacuate the shop.'

Ute walked backwards from the room. In the tiny corridor, there was nobody. She pushed through the fire door, closing it behind her. The corridor was empty. At one end was the door with the lock that she had superglued before entering the shop. She tested its handle. Immovable.

Her one problem was the connecting door. It had a push-down bar on both sides. She had to act quickly.

She removed her shoes and walked up the stairs.

There was an interior door on the first landing. The handle turned. It was a cheap door with a cardboard filling that could not be barricaded.

For the second time, she stepped inside.

The empty office space was huge. The air was stuffy with sunlight. There were sheets of paper, old mugs, filing cabinets, chairs and sheets of plastic.

In the centre were scores of mannequins. Faces blank. Gender-neutral bodies naked and dusty. They hadn't moved since that night.

Immediately to her left was a walled office. It had an open doorway but no windows. Nearby was the fire-escape that she had padlocked earlier that morning. She came closer. She felt dust on her bare feet. She heard snores.

Inside, it was dull and hot. She counted six sleeping men. They were lying, two half-dressed, four naked, overlapping by foot and hand. Ute had once been afraid of these men. Now she was disgusted. There was a syringe-littered table in one corner. In another, a television and a games console. There was a duvet in the centre. The stench of sweat and semen was nauseating. She did not care who they were. She did not care why they lived this way.

Ute took the can of lighter fluid from her bag. She squirted it onto the duvet. It was a good feeling. She was pissing on these men. Next, she took a match and flicked it into the centre. The duvet erupted. Benthic smoke poured outward in a carpet, making for the door. She did not hurry to withdraw her stun gun. Humans cannot smell while they are asleep. She had checked.

She saw the moustached man who had led her from the club. He was middle-aged and balding, but Ute had always preferred older men. He had drugged her Martini. Later, he had injected her with something as she crouched to re-tie her shoe – scopolamine and morphine, a doctor had told her later. Life had become hazy and slow. Her resistance had fallen away. For passers-by she was a drunk. The man waved them on with a laugh.

She fired the gun. Two darts flew out and embedded in his thigh muscle. They connected to the stun gun with strong, insulated cables. The darts had barbs. They could not be extracted without ripping. There was a second trigger to activate the charge. Quickly, she fired darts into all of the men.

She pulled the trigger.

The bodies twitched and rolled.

She remembered that, at the conclusion of the ordeal, the moustached man had injected her again. He had put an avuncular arm across her shoulders and led her to the Rhine. One last injection: the rest of the syringe. A gentle push and she fell.

Callused arms had found her in that cold, empty hell, and heaved her onto a barge. Shouted words in a language she did not understand. Wiped hair and muck from her mouth. Shone light in her eyes. Injected her; saved her.

She pulled the trigger again. This time the groans were louder, angrier. Eyes sought her. They were monstrous but pathetic. She realised that they would never be as strong as her. She had returned. Her revenge knew no bounds.

She pulled the trigger a third time. Bodies convulsed. The smoke grew soupy. One of the men tugged at a barb in his chest. Ute watched the flesh draw to a peak. It would not rip. Finally, the man collapsed in the smoke.

The duvets burned blue-green. She watched the flame.

Someone grabbed her ankle and Ute screamed. She pulled the trigger again and the hand tensed. It fell and lay flaccid on her foot.

With each pull of the trigger, she imagined herself raping them, firing into them, inching them towards the edge of an abyss with each dirty push.

'This,' she shouted, 'is what it feels like when you're fucked.'

Behind the burning duvets, a woman rose. She wore only her underwear and a T-shirt. She shimmered through Ute's tears.

Ute cursed her stupidity. She reached forward to help the victim from the room. She would have a straightforward escape through the door to the staircase and, from there, through the perfume shop to freedom.

The woman grabbed Ute's throat and pushed hard. Ute dropped the stun gun and they broke through the door. In sudden daylight, the woman's eyes seemed more animal than human. A cat's eyes. The eyes were familiar; she had been present at Ute's rape. She had looked on.

Ute tripped but the woman followed her down. They slid over the floor. Rolled once. Ute felt the world darken. Above them, the ceiling was on fire. Plastic embers began to fall. Still the world darkened.

They knocked into the mannequins. The dolls were heavy and one struck the woman's forehead. Her grip relaxed momentarily. Ute took a breath before it was re-established. She had come here to kill her attackers. She would not be satisfied with all but one of them.

Inside her shoulder bag, she found the canister of lighter

fluid. She jammed the can into her attacker's mouth and twisted savagely. The thin metal tore and Ute pulled it free, then immediately sliced at her assailant's throat with the metal's edge. The skin opened. The woman's grip relaxed and her cat eyes glazed. She bucked and slithered away. Ute grabbed her ankle. The woman yelled. She jammed the cold ball of her foot into Ute's throat.

The pain stopped time. When finally she moved, she could see only the expressionless mannequins and their hard, plastic fingers. They seemed to mob her. They were dead and they wanted her dead too. From the gaps between one mannequin and the next, there issued only smoke, not air. She screamed.

The nightmare inside the nightmare.

She pushed against something. It was the lid of a coffin. Cracks appeared. The darkness was no longer absolute. She saw her simple funeral clothes in the bloody light. She understood that she was in the furnace of a crematorium. No, she thought. *This memory is false. I survived the fire.* She drew breath to scream again. She would escape her coffin now, oh yes, into a fire that might let her linger, let her relish the last few moments of life with a height of sensation she had never known. The crackling flames. Smoke. Distant organ music. The murmur of David Proctor thanking the priest for a lovely service. Saskia would have wanted it that way.

No. It didn't end like this. It can't end like this.

Saskia.

The hawk that returned.

CHAPTER THIRTY-TWO

Snick.

Ute opened her eyes. The gun had misfired, and she let it slip, dead, to the ground. Memories crowded her. She remembered her first kiss. It had been on tiptoe behind the local supermarket. She saw the face of her best friend at school, Katrin, and some fellow schoolchildren, and the faces of her foster parents. Spending hours learning to hula hoop. A school trip to France. *Dinner for One* on New Year's Eve. Her foster mother's name was Fride. They had lived in Cologne. Her Uncle Manni had once saved her from drowning. He had died within a year from skin cancer.

A whole life returned to her. Ute Schmidt's ghostly passenger – the digital Saskia Brandt – was a dream.

She felt David's breath on her face. He was lying against her, semi-conscious, muttering. Her knowledge of him was once removed. She knew that his words were English but she could not understand him.

'Your ability to comprehend English, as well other

recently-acquired skills, will return in a few minutes,' said a voice. It spoke flawless German and was coming from David's chest. 'David just claimed that you are a, quote, "bloody idiot", unquote.'

'Who are you?' asked Ute.

'I am Ego, David's personal computer. But I was once in your possession. I have a message for you.'

'Tell me.'

'Ute, you must understand that it is a message from Saskia.'

The name stirred something in Ute. It carried a sisterly feeling, one of protection. And one of loss. It was comparable to the death of a twin. 'The message reads, "Look in the envelope".'

'Which envelope?'

'The one you found in the West Lothian Centre.'

'I... I remember.'

Ute knelt and shrugged off her shoulder bag. As she opened it, she noticed the dark polish on her nails in the pulsing red light. Her long hair cascaded over her face. She found the transparent wallet that contained the white envelope. It was fastened with a metal popper. She opened it and withdrew the envelope. It must have once been white, but was now yellow and spotted with mould. On the front it read: 'Do not open this envelope.'

She ripped the seal and shook out a laminated ID card in the name of Saskia Brandt, FIB. The photo was her, Ute. On the reverse was written one word: 'Munin.'

'Munin,' repeated Ute. 'David, does that word mean anything to you?'

The professor's reply was gibberish.

'I shall act as translator,' said Ego.

She heard Ego repeating her words in English and, as David, Ego gave the German equivalent.

'Saskia,' David said, 'I'm afraid that you have to follow Crane. You have no choice.'

Crane. The name conjured the image of a business-like man.

Beckmann.

'You are destined to follow him,' said David. '*Destined* to follow him. When Crane shot at you just now, he fired point-blank, but he missed. When you tried to shoot yourself, the gun didn't fire. It couldn't fire.'

Ute felt the gap in her mind: a jagged hole shaped like Saskia Brandt, whose own body had been dumped at sea, or in building foundations, or fed to pigs. Crane was getting away. He had killed a woman to capture her ghost. That ghost, Saskia, wanted revenge.

Revenge was something that Ute understood. And sacrifice.

'Ego,' she said. 'There is a chip in my skull. I think Crane deactivated it with a signal. Can you reactivate it?'

'Attempting…' said Ego. 'No, I cannot. It requires a password.'

Ute looked once more at the handwritten word on the reverse of her ID card. 'Try "Munin".'

'The chip has accepted the password. Your mind construct has been reactivated.'

Nothing happened.

David said, 'Listen, we need to get after him. We don't know whether he will make it or not. That's not certain.'

The woman felt the presence of Ute as a weight on a

seesaw, heavy but close to the fulcrum, and her mind, still largely unknown to her, lighter but further away.

Balance was returning.

'*Hör zu*—'

'I understand him,' said Saskia. She crouched to retrieve the gun. It was empty, but Klutikov wouldn't know that. 'Let's go.'

You will return, the witch had said, *as you have returned before.*

CHAPTER THIRTY-THREE

Since his nanotreatment for cancer, John Crane's senses had been unable to create a unified percept. He had long since developed a technique of moving from one modality to another, noting what information it held, and this is what he did as he followed Jennifer into Project Déjà Vu. His eyes moved from the red blotches on her neck (he noted fear, excitement) to the vast space of the cavern, where lights in the vitrified roof blazed down (brighter, aiding evacuation).

On the metal decking, glowing lines led to doors in what might have been a huge set of organ pipes. The pipes were personnel evacuation tubes. Crane imagined himself accelerated into the air above the Valley of Fire, carried by an escape shell all the way to Lake Mead, where he would parachute down to a waiting robot flotilla. There were enough shells to accommodate the occupants of the Déjà Vu staff, and they had used them. The cavern was as empty as he had hoped.

Touch: cool air, artificially dry. No information there.

Sound: the hum of electricity. Lacking voices, footsteps.

Smell: a faint ozone. The blood seeping through his shoulder.

Oh, that, he thought, attending to the pain briefly. *A superficial wound.*

'I want you to start the machine,' he said.

Jennifer turned to him. Her anger radiated.

'Who says it will start at all?'

Crane knew that the launch systems, though temperamental, were automated.

'One word to Klutikov,' he said. 'That's all it needs.'

He was indifferent to her emotion, yet recognised it as hatred, and knew the value of engaging with people in human terms, of kindling their hate in a good cause.

She bit her lower lip and turned to a storage chest next to one of the sheds. There were hard hats inside. Jennifer picked one up.

'First, I'll need to physically inspect the centrifuges.'

She is underestimating my interest in her project.

The larger centrifuge, in the lowest tier of the cavern, was called Giver. Taker was the smaller one alongside. When both rotated, the proximity of their masses produced gravitational fluctuations. These were amplified and shaped by a machine called a 'carbon focuser'. Jennifer's genius had been to create such positive interference in gravity waves as to rip the Higgs Field.

Crane knew this and more. Indeed, he had monitored each of the projects in Helix Base, as well as the base itself. His knowledge had allowed him to override the failsafes on the reactor alarm.

'There's no need for an inspection. Put down the hard hat and pick up a T-suit. Quickly.'

Jennifer didn't move.

'I have access to all your tests,' he said, 'all your plans and contingencies. There are four transfer suits inside the storage locker. Why? Because there is a plan to put a test pilot in one of those suits and send him back five minutes, to appear somewhere above Edwards, where he will parachute to safety.'

'I don't know—'

'I'm moving that plan forward. I'll be the first man to travel in time. So hand me one of those suits.'

Crane watched the rise and fall of Jennifer's intention to object. She was so clear to him now. She removed her hat, dropped it in the bin, and walked up the steps of the storage container. She disappeared inside.

Alone in the quiet cavern, Crane found himself thinking of the past.

›•‹

The door of the storage locker opened and Jennifer emerged. She was carrying a folded bundle of clothes with a pair of boots on top.

She said, 'You know, the first scientists to set off a nuclear bomb didn't know whether it would create a chain reaction and destroy the whole planet.'

Crane paused to work out her register, failed, then followed her to the base of the stairs leading to the amphitheatre.

'It didn't,' he said. 'We're all still here.'

She stopped and turned to him. 'But it might have. What

you're trying to do runs the same risk. Every effect has its cause.'

'Do you think that, if I change time, I'll destroy the world?'

'There's a chance you'll destroy much more than that.'

'If you really thought so, you wouldn't be helping me.'

To this, Jennifer said nothing.

Crane did not tell her that he hoped his trip into the past would indeed destroy the future – this one, anyway. He would cure himself long before his cancer became critical. There would be no West Lothian Centre. He would never meet David, or any of the others. He was hastening towards his own death and the rebirth of something that he, even in his acutely psychopathic world, held above anything else: the wish to be real again.

›•‹

Holding her empty revolver, Saskia Brandt crept down the last of the stairs to the empty Level Zero corridor. With each step, she felt a growing dread that the safeguards installed inside her by Beckmann – those designed to prevent her investigation of herself – would trip, and she would fall lifeless down the staircase. Nothing of the kind happened. The dread dwindled, starved as her attention turned to the blue door ahead. In military stencil, a sign read: 'Project N83261'. Underneath this, in magic marker, someone had written:

We like to call it "Déjà Vu".

And underneath that, in a different hand:

But you knew that already. ☺

The door was ajar. Presumably, its lock had disengaged

following the alarm. Saskia stepped through, her eyes widening at the vast space. The lights in the ceiling were like stars.

Ahead, she could see Crane and Jennifer walking up the steps to a high platform. From this angle it was difficult to tell what it was the platform held, but she could just see the uppermost row of banked seating.

Crane was one problem. Another was Klutikov. She had not passed him in the tunnel, and he was not with Jennifer or Crane. He might be watching from concealment.

Saskia raised the revolver and stepped sideways until she was in the shadow between a house-sized storage container and the wall of the cavern. To her left and right were open vertical shafts, like chimneys, their doors lying all around. On one of the doors was a warning about explosive bolts.

At the same time as she processed these details, part of her wondered at the extraordinary discovery within herself: beneath the surface of her identity was another person entirely, a passenger within her head. Ute Schmidt.

No, she thought. *I am the passenger.*

She continued through the shadowed gap, parallel to the interior wall of the main tunnel, until she reached a power plant surrounded by a chain-link fence.

She passed this quickly, keeping her head down, until she came to an inspection platform. From there, she could look onto the middle terrace of the chamber. It was filled with sand. There were at least three trenches zigzagging through.

Further ahead, and lower down, were two circular structures made of intersecting metal struts. The nearer one was the larger. Each had a rotating arm. Neither were moving.

Centrifuges.

Saskia looked at the larger centrifuge. It had a capsule on the end of its arm. The capsule, which was big enough to accommodate a person, had been parked at the base of a ladder that led to a platform between the two centrifuges.

The ground on which the centrifuges had been built was otherwise empty. Nowhere obvious that Klutikov could hide. Saskia found herself considering the capsule. If she had to hide in plain sight, she would do so there.

But it depended on what Klutikov was planning.

Saskia heard voices. She crouched and moved back into the shadow.

Crane and Jennifer were walking along the catwalk to the central platform. Crane was wearing some kind of flight suit.

'…recruited her through Beckmann,' he was saying. 'His agents are useful sometimes. When I heard that your father had left his house, heading to Scotland, I didn't want him to upset my plans. So I reached for the nearest tool. That happened to be Saskia.'

Saskia rippled her fingers against the revolver. The handle was slick with sweat.

Crane. He was a layer of control above Beckmann, the wheel beyond the wheel. Beckmann could have been answering to the German government, some EU body, anything. It should not have mattered to her that Crane was the puppet master. Why should it? But it hurt. It hurt to see him here. He was winning.

She tried to look at his gloved right hand. Did he still wear the control ring underneath? Perhaps not. He had every right to think that Saskia would be wandering around as

Ute. She should be clueless and scared. And he thought that Klutikov was still guarding David.

Saskia frowned. Something wasn't right about that. Why had Klutikov left his post? In order to control Jennifer through the threat to her father, Crane needed Klutikov. It put Crane in a precarious position.

'Klutikov,' said Jennifer, and the coincidence of hearing his name spoken aloud made Saskia start. 'What about him?'

'Another tool. You reach for a sword when a knife breaks, right? I reached for Klutikov.'

Saskia's eyes dropped to a glimmer on the far side of the smaller centrifuge. Whatever it was, it vanished as she looked. Had it been an eye, reflecting light as a man moved from the cover of the metal supports?

'I'm another tool, then,' said Jennifer. She gestured wearily around her. 'Just like this. The whole project owes its life to your dream.'

Crane looked at her. Because his face was averted, Saskia could not see his expression, but Jennifer scowled with frustration and turned to look away. As her blinking, tearful eyes found Saskia, they stopped.

Jennifer's mouth opened.

Saskia smiled.

Crane gripped the arches at the top of the ladder and prepared to enter the capsule.

'Wait,' said Jennifer, breaking from Saskia. 'Do you remember what my father said? He claimed that Saskia helped him escape from the West Lothian Centre four days ago. And, when you tried to shoot her, you failed. Somehow, the bullet missed. Saskia is going to travel in time. In a way, she already has. She's been working against you since the start.'

Crane said, 'It doesn't matter what she's been doing, or what your father said, or will say. Nothing here matters any more. Once I go back and change the past, this future will simply disappear.'

'That's one theory.'

'Are you still worried that I'll create a paradox?'

'Quite honestly, I don't believe the past can be changed. Not in the way you think. I think you'll get into that machine and vanish, and that will be the end of you.'

'Then what does it matter? Start the sequence.'

'Klutikov matters,' said Jennifer. 'I've seen enough of him to know what he's like. Who says he won't kill Dad when you leave? What guarantee do I have?'

Crane smiled. 'My ring controls an agent if I need it to. But, in Klutikov's case, it is also – how do I put this? – a dead man's finger. If it stops signalling, then Klutikov dies. And I can't think of a better way of stopping the signal than sending me back in time. Can you? So start the sequence.'

Saskia looked for the indistinct shape she had seen on the far side of the smaller centrifuge. Klutikov still had a role to play in this, or at least he thought he did. Klutikov: listening from the shadows, just like Saskia, but spinning his own thread. He had left both Saskia and David. Why?

It had to be the machine. He had used Crane as a stepping stone to reach it. Klutikov wanted to be the second man to travel in time. Perhaps even the first. She could not guess how much damage a man like Klutikov would do if given such a chance.

Jennifer said, 'The sequence has begun.'

'It cannot be countermanded?'

'Correct.'

A shadow detached itself from the centrifuge strut. Klutikov was moving. Saskia made to stand, but hesitated. She couldn't approach Crane without him taking control of her body.

The smaller of the two centrifuges began to turn. It was quiet; an electric hum. Saskia watched Klutikov step behind it, reach up, and ride around to the platform where Jennifer and Crane were standing.

Lights rolled yellow in the ceiling. A klaxon sounded and a computer announced, 'The injection sequence is starting. Guidance will lock in one minute. Elastic collision will be one-dimensional relativistic.'

Klutikov climbed the ladder and jumped onto the platform. The skirts of his long black coat billowed.

'No,' said Crane. He had time to raise his arm. Klutikov was taller than Crane by a head and kilos heavier, and Crane was weakened by his injured shoulder. Klutikov simply grasped his wrist. Desperately, Crane reached across to his hand, perhaps to remove the glove, but Klutikov cuffed his hand away.

'What have you done with Dad?' asked Jennifer, stepping back.

'I said I'd help you, Crane,' said Klutikov. 'I keep my word. But I'm going next.'

'Why aren't you with Proctor?'

Klutikov gave Crane a disappointed look. He pulled off the man's glove. Slowly, Klutikov reached inside his jacket and removed a hunting knife from a shoulder holster. Jennifer screamed. Crane made a fist and struggled to get away.

'Dead man's finger, you called it,' said Klutikov, tonelessly, mimicking the robotic voice of Crane. Then put the blade between Crane's fingers and jerked savagely. Crane did not cry out. He hissed like a cat. The first cut produced a glossy run of blood but did not sever the finger. The second did.

Crane fell to one knee. He clenched his mutilated hand and held it against his chest. Klutikov's attention was on the dismembered finger now. He studied it, thoughtfully, as though checking it was real. Then he put the finger into the breast pocket of his jacket. He smoothed his lapel, patting it once.

The gesture reminded Saskia of Beckman. He had made the same gesture when speaking about the secretary in her fridge: he had tapped the stem of the flower in his buttonhole, adjusting it.

Without another word, Klutikov kicked Crane backwards. Crane teetered for a moment, wheeling his arms, and then caught himself against the hand rails of the ladder. He descended in a scramble. Blood slicked his grip. When he reached the capsule attached to the centrifuge, he fell inside it, and the door closed. The centrifuge began to rotate.

Saskia used the growing noise to sprint lightly across the cavern to the central platform. Klutikov had his back to her. She had no idea what he could do with the ring, but, if she was fast, there would be no time for him to use it.

When she was five metres away, and edging closer, Jennifer pointed at Klutikov. 'If you've done anything to my father, I'll sabotage the centrifuge once you're inside it.'

Saskia could not see Klutikov's expression, but she could hear his grin as he spoke. 'You'll find that difficult, since you'll be in there with me.'

Saskia raised her revolver and struck Klutikov on the back of the neck. She struck him so hard that she stunned the muscles in her forearm. The gun dropped to the floor. Klutikov cried out. He raked at Jennifer's lab coat as he fell forward and she was pushed into the guard rail.

Saskia stepped to his side and took him in a headlock. He seized her arm, dropped his weight, and threw her over his head. She tumbled to the end of the gantry and slid under the guard rail on her back. Her hands tried to grip the rail but there was no purchase. She moved her legs apart, whirled them, and used the rotational energy to turn her torso.

She grasped the edge of the platform by her fingertips. The centrifuges were roaring below her. The air pressed against her in gusts, setting her swinging.

As Klutikov crawled towards her, Saskia looked for Jennifer. She was disappearing into a trench in the sand barrier.

'David followed me down,' Saskia shouted. Glancing left and right, she watched the centrifuges. They were only ten or twenty centimetres apart at their closest point, but the platform extended past this by several metres. 'He's right behind—'

Klutikov stamped down at her fingers, but Saskia was already dropping the three metres to the ground. The end of the smaller centrifuge passed over her head so closely that it touched her hair. She landed with both feet together and pitched sideways. Through the grating of the platform, she could see Klutikov feeding rounds into her revolver.

She kept beneath the platform and ran towards the sand barrier. There was a panel like a screen in a bull ring, but transparent, and behind it were steps leading to one of the trenches.

She heard Klutikov land behind her. She began to zigzag. At the screen, she risked a backwards glance. What she saw made her gasp. Klutikov was standing in a marksman's position, ready to fire. His coat was flapping in the turbulence. The space between them shimmered like the air above a desert road. He had not moved closer after dropping from the platform. There was no need.

Saskia saw the revolver kick. She blinked, anticipating the impact of a bullet, but none came. She put a hand to her chest.

No wound.

She turned. Behind her, the bullet was a grey dot in a white star of plastic.

Klutikov frowned. He adjusted his stance and sighted down the barrel. He fired again. And again. Each time, the bullets missed.

Saskia spun aside and hurried behind the transparent barrier. She was halfway up the steps into the sand trench when the platform above her began to retract. She looked back at Klutikov. He was pressing a speed-loader into the cylinder of the revolver.

The platform had retracted fully now. The pulsing yellow lights shone on the air between them, and in that space Saskia saw rainbows.

As she watched, she saw that Klutikov was watching too. His face was even more distorted now. Saskia's focus snapped to the bullets in the transparent screen and finally she understood: the light between her and Klutikov had been bent. Shooting her was like spearing a fish through water. Without an awareness of refraction, and a correction for it, the spear would miss.

Jennifer's voice flooded the cavern. 'Saskia,' she said. 'Get away from the centrifuges. The forces will pull you apart.'

Saskia skipped up the remaining stairs and entered the angled trench in the sand barrier. Its semi-transparent walls rose above her. A series of high shoring rods spanned the gap. There was a revetment against the side closest to the centrifuges, a raised edge on which an observer could stand and look at the equipment.

Saskia was now at the same height as the platform. She looked back to see a shimmering, web-like shape throw bright filaments between the centrifuges, glowing brighter with each pass. Klutikov could not be seen.

Saskia sprinted into the trench. She reached the first corner and ran down the next section. There were equipment stores leading off the trench but their doors were closed and their viewing panels dark. She didn't want to be trapped in one.

'Brandt!' shouted Klutikov.

He was above her. As he dropped through the struts into the trench, Saskia lowered her chin and added speed to her run. She dashed down the next two sections, but she could hear Klutikov gaining on each straight. Finally, an instant before she judged he would grab her, she planted her right foot on a revetment and reached for one of the horizontal support struts.

The strut held her weight. She had given her jump some height, and, holding on with both hands, she was able to kick with her legs and swing herself over the top of the bar. Klutikov reacted quickly but not quickly enough. He gripped her jacket but he was still moving forward. His fingers slipped away. Saskia pivoted and put her knee into the same place on the back of his neck where she had struck him with the gun.

Klutikov grunted and fell.

Saskia fell, too, awkwardly, but she was on her feet and able to whip her head clear before his gun, which he swung in a blind arc behind him, could connect.

Then he was up, and it was the two of them. She let him unleash two punches, weaving around both, before she spun on the ball of her foot and kicked him hard in the ribs.

Saskia took his wrist, felt the micro-movements of his arm as he reached to grapple, and stepped back. His jacket opened long enough for her to reach inside and lift out Crane's amputated finger.

This cost her any defence, and before she could blink, Klutikov had taken her neck and pushed her against the wall of the tunnel. His strength fell upon her as though he were these tonnes of sand. There was certainty now: she would not see the other side of this moment. Her last perception would be these eyes.

They were the same eyes as those of the woman in Cologne who had tried to strangle her.

The same eyes as those of the mannequins, whose plastic bodies had fallen down around her, like so much sand. The crushing. Being unable to take a breath. The smoke.

But she remembered too the exorcism of this memory in the Project Looking Glass immersion chamber. There was dominion in knowledge; the memory had been unlocked, spent.

David had been there.

Hold on, Saskia.

The darkness was returning.

Klutikov's eyes lost their plastic blankness. They became professional and satisfied. Losing interest in her death.

'Hold on, Saskia.'

She had enough strength to turn her eyes upward. David was standing at the edge of the trench wall. His arms were raised for balance.

'Hold on,' he repeated.

Klutikov seemed to hear him for the first time. He turned to look, and his grip lessened. Saskia drank the air as though through a straw and gasped, 'Catch.'

She felt the grisly length of Crane's finger in her hand. David had been frowning at her. He saw her movement as she tossed the finger to him. He cupped both his hands with the concentrated patience of a cricketer and, as the finger fell into them, he clapped them shut.

Klutikov had followed the trajectory of the finger with a desperate stare. He released Saskia's throat and began to climb the side of the trench using a cross-strut as a hold. Saskia sank to the ground. She wanted to cough, and when she swallowed, the movement seemed to jam, as though Klutikov's hands were still locked around her throat. There was a red tinge to her vision.

David was looking at the finger in confusion. It was only when Klutikov's hand grasped his shoe that he moved out of sight.

'David,' she shouted hoarsely, 'throw it into the machine.'

Klutikov stopped. He looked once at Saskia – and it was not anger she saw there any longer, but a wounded expression, that of a man betrayed – and gave up on his climb out of the trench. He jumped down and sprinted towards the centrifuge.

Saskia got to her feet and stumbled after him. She could swallow now; the puffiness in her cheeks was subsiding. Ahead, she could see a watery glow reflected on the trench wall, and when she turned the corner, Klutikov was standing at the entrance to the trench, silhouetted to perfect dark against the whiteness that floated ahead of him like a thousand blooming flowers.

David stood on the platform a few metres beyond him. Like Klutikov, he had stopped.

'Do it!' shouted Saskia. 'Throw it in.'

Klutikov reached out, shouting, 'No!'

But David threw the finger, and its ring, into the whiteness. Klutikov lunged forward. It would be impossible to catch the finger, thought Saskia, but she could understand his desperation. The whipping edges of his coat were the last she saw of him. The light reached such an intensity that she had to turn away, and her thoughts were not only for Klutikov, who had killed that Polish fisherman and his sons to keep the secret of his identity, to bottle up the past, but for the past itself, which would never be bottled again. Here was the genie, enveloping Klutikov, brighter than a star.

She put an arm across her eyes. There was a sound like a thumping guillotine. The electrical smell left the air and she lowered her arm.

The light had vanished. There was nothing now but the roaring centrifuges. She walked to the edge of the platform and stood alongside David. There was blood beneath their feet. It had to be Klutikov's.

Saskia did nothing as David reached gently to her throat.

'Does it hurt to speak?'

'A bit.'

'Does this hurt?'

He pushed either side of her windpipe.

'Yes. But not much.'

The centrifuges were slowing. The larger of the two, which had contained Crane, appeared to be empty. As it slowed, the capsule rotated upright, and Saskia saw that there was an open trap door in its base. Presumably, that was how Crane had been released into the white spider, or whatever Jennifer called it.

Saskia stared. She was too tired to look away.

'Come on, old girl.' David took her by the elbow. 'We need to talk to my daughter.'

CHAPTER THIRTY-FOUR

The high control room was an amphitheatre with rows of workstations facing a huge, semi-transparent screen. The screen showed line graphs, timers, and three-dimensional plots. Like the rest of the chamber, it was empty.

Jennifer was standing at a lectern computer near the screen. When she caught sight of her father, she sagged with relief and hugged him. Then she put a hand to Saskia's face.

'I saw what happened on the monitors.' Jennifer looked from one to the other. 'I thought he was going to kill us all.'

Saskia nodded. There was an opened Hershey's Bar on the desk. She broke off a piece. It hurt to chew. She sighed, looking at the meaningless numbers on the screen.

'So what happened to them?' asked David.

'Crane travelled through time, as predicted.'

David urged her on with a nod. 'And Crazy Ivan?'

Jennifer pointed to the meaningless numbers. 'His angle of entry wasn't orthogonal to the gravitational axis. There are two consequences.' She leaned on the corners of the lectern. 'First, his atoms will have been scattered far and wide.'

Quietly, Saskia said, 'There was blood.'

Jennifer blinked. She looked at her father.

'Second,' she said, 'because the end point of the wormhole is partly a function of the mass injected into it, Crane could not have gone back to the tempo-spatial point he intended.'

'Where and when did he end up?' asked David.

'I'd need to work out Klutikov's mass precisely. Crane will have come out somewhere in the last forty years.'

'Did Crane say when he wanted to go back?' asked Saskia.

'The late 1990s. He wanted to warn his younger self of the cancer before the experimental nanotreatment became necessary.'

Saskia shrugged. Her head was clearing. She took another bite of chocolate. 'Obviously, it didn't work. Nothing has changed about the present.'

'There's more to it that that,' said Jennifer. 'It's quite possible that Crane's plan won't work because you're going to stop him.'

'I've seen you.' David's tone was eager. 'You were older than you are now. There's no doubt of your fate. You still have a part to play.'

Saskia looked through the transparent screen. 'By getting into that machine.'

'It's still experimental,' said Jennifer. She took a breath, as though considering whether or not to say anything more. Then she said, 'The odds of it failing catastrophically, particularly with something of relatively high mass, like a human body, are greater than 50%. To be honest, I'm surprised that Klutikov's interference didn't destroy it.'

'Jenny,' said David, 'let's not—'

Saskia interrupted him with a shake of her head. She was remembering her phone conversation with the woman in the ambulance with Scotty. She was sure now: that woman must have been herself.

All's well that ends well.

She said, 'The machine can't fail any more than Crane's bullet could have killed me earlier in the immersion chamber. Everything is set. I have no choice.'

'You have a choice,' said Jennifer. She looked very tired. 'But within certain parameters.'

'Ute Schmidt didn't have a choice when she was attacked,' said Saskia. She realised that her voice was raised, but she didn't care. 'I, whoever I am, had no choice when I was implanted into this body. What choice do I have now? Beckmann is still out there. From where I stand, escape does not sound like a bad option.' Saskia folded her arms. 'Perhaps you should fully brief me on the procedure.'

Jennifer looked as though she might embrace Saskia, but her expression of pride changed to something more professional as she turned towards the huge screen.

'There may not be time for that. There are automated systems designed to alert the base to unauthorised use of the machine, and Crane's jump is sure to have triggered them. Security will soon be here. The short version is this: We will accelerate you to a speed of forty metres per second. That's one hundred and forty-four kilometres per hour. The Einstein-Rosen bridge will manifest and you'll be thrown through.'

'What does that feel like?'

Jennifer smiled. 'Only Crane knows.' To herself, she

added, 'I just hope the carbon focuser holds true. We've brought in the extra berkelium, but Harkes said the thing was held together with spit and bailing wire.'

As Jennifer set to work, Saskia moved to the back of the control room and paced slowly along the row, arms folded, ignoring the pain in her throat, trying to list things that tied her to 2023. There were few. She looked at Jennifer, who was busy at her terminal, and David, who was writing on a sheet of pink paper. Jago was in a hospital somewhere. She crossed her fingers for him.

›•‹

The T-suit was tight. It pushed her arms back and her chest out. The trousers felt like orthopaedic stockings. There were reinforced pads at the knees and elbows.

David tapped her collar. 'Stowed in here there's a "hard" hood. On the forearm is your computer display, but the information there will also project onto the interior of the hood when it's closed. There won't be any Galileo satellites, so the suit will get your location from the American GPS. OK?'

Saskia pulled her hair back, made a topknot with elastic bands, and secured it with pins. When she was done, David showed her what looked like a Swiss Army knife.

'Tell me again,' he said. 'You need to put something into the West Lothian Centre for your future self to find?'

'Yes, I need to…' Saskia paused, unable to hold together the sense of her thoughts, what they represented, but voiced them regardless: 'I need to place an envelope in a store room. The envelope contains the password to my brain chip. That's how Ego reactivated it just now.'

David was frowning. 'This is beyond my understanding. It makes my brain ache.'

'I worked with a detective called Jago. He had a heart attack during the chase, and I called his mobile a few hours ago to find out how he was doing. A woman answered. She claimed to be his daughter.' Saskia let her mind slip its anchor. 'He doesn't have a daughter. I think that woman was me.'

'All's well that ends well.'

'You spoke to *yourself* on the phone?' asked David. His eyes were unfocused with wonder.

'I remember the conversation we had, word for word. When I reach the point in my life at which I must supply the other side of the conversation, how will I choose what words to say?'

'You won't have to choose.'

'That's my point. Who chose them? They are just words I must say. Like a script that's already been written.'

Quietly, David said, 'Crane would argue that you have a choice.'

Saskia smiled at him and her vision blurred. She realised she was crying. 'It's funny. When Beckmann recruited me, he made me investigate the murder I committed. I've come to America after you, David, only to find I'm investigating myself a second time.'

The hawk that returned.

'Well, your next trip will be an even bigger deal. Let's get you prepped.' He showed her the pen knife. 'This is a 'Pemberton'. It looks like a Swiss Army Knife but it lies. Pop off the end, like so, and you'll see a square connector. Slide this into any computer of the period, wait a few seconds for the code to propagate, and the system will be under your control. According to Jennifer, Bruce cooked it up for you.' He passed her something that looked like a metal business card. 'Meet Ego, my inflexible friend. He can connect wirelessly to the Pemberton, and control it.'

'OK.'

'That won't help with concealment, though. Check out the red button on your sleeve. It'll lower the refractive index of the suit to zero.'

'What does that mean?'

'Press the button and the suit will become almost invisible – like a clear plastic bag filled with water. Treat it like instant camouflage.'

'I see.'

Jennifer called, 'We'll send you back shortly before Crane.'

'Give her a few days head start,' David shouted back.

'I don't have time to calculate another safe injection point. A past Earth is a moving target. It's either fractionally before or after.'

'I'll find him,' said Saskia, in a tone that tried to reassure herself. 'I'm a detective, after all.'

'And when you find him?'

'I'll stop him curing himself.'

'Saskia saves the universe!' said Jennifer. She looked excited. 'Paradox avoided.'

David smiled at his daughter so busy with her machine, then turned to Saskia. The smile faded.

'The past is full of naff technology, you know. You wouldn't believe what they let the doctors do.'

Saskia raised an eyebrow. 'But the music's better. I am correct?'

David sighed. He was tired, like she was, and his expression revealed the boy he had once been. He shrugged. 'Just take care of yourself.'

Saskia put a gloved hand to his cheek. 'David, you could shoot me right now and the bullet will miss. There is an effect whose cause I must supply, remember?'

'Hurry,' said Jennifer, rushing to join them. 'The security guys are coming.'

Saskia looked from father to daughter. Jennifer had David's mouth, but it was harder for her to smile. Saskia considered asking them, as a favour to her, to stay together, but it was a decision they had to make for themselves. '*Auf Wiedersehen, meine Freunden*,' was all she could say.

But as she turned, David said, 'Wait, almost forgot.' He passed her a pink sheet. It was a child's crayon drawing of a house. Inside were a stick mother and father, and, between them, a girl. 'This has been stuck on my fridge door for years. I guess it's a key to… memories. That's all any of us is.' David looked at his daughter. 'I was going to return it to Jennifer, but you'll need it, Saskia.'

'For what?'

'The number on the back, TS4415, is a hijack trip-code used by the Lothian and Borders Police Service. It's difficult to explain, but you give me the picture during my rescue from the West Lothian Centre.'

'I hope I don't forget.' Saskia unzipped the map pocket on her thigh and pushed the paper inside.

Jennifer turned at the distant sound of a man shouting. 'Hurry,' she said.

Saskia gave them a mock salute and backed away. As she jogged down the stairs, she heard more raised voices from the entrance. She ran into a sand trench and skipped onto the platform, being careful to avoid Klutikov's blood. She jumped into the capsule. It rocked as she clambered inside.

She heard Jennifer's voice in her ear. 'Saskia, communication check.'

'Go.' The capsule door closed as it lurched forward. Saskia sank further into the acceleration couch. The capsule made one revolution, then two. The surrounding air wailed. Through triangular windows, the world tilted. Cavern lights seemed to strobe. She tapped her wrist computer to close the hard hood. Its arch-like sections blended to form a seamless, transparent bowl, muting the noise.

'Whatever you do,' said Jennifer, 'don't turn your head to either side or you'll be sick. You're at two gees. Still reading me?'

'Reading you, yes.' Her jaw ached and her cheeks felt baggy. Her hairpins pressed against the back of her head.

'We've almost finished figuring out Crane's injection time, Saskia. Stand by.'

'OK.'

'Three gees,' David said. 'Remember, you'll appear high in the air. When you land, put your feet together and roll.'

'Reading you.'

She struggled to take a full breath. The strobing lights were a flicker now.

'Four gees.'

Her vision began to lose colour. The ceiling of the capsule blurred.

'Saskia,' said Jennifer. 'I'm sending you back one half hour before Crane. That will give you the best chance of intercepting him.'

'Rea'ing you.'

David's voice: 'My God, Jenny. Look at her injection time. That's only…'

CHAPTER THIRTY-FIVE

A hatch opened in the bottom of the capsule and Saskia slipped into the blazing tendrils of the wormhole. Instantly, she was falling through a bright sky. It was damp, cold, and loud. As she tumbled, the sky and ground seemed to swerve. She felt nauseated and afraid, but she opened her arms and legs to form an 'X'. Webbing stretched between her elbows and her chest, and her tumbling stopped.

There was a Heads-Up Display on the inner rim of the helmet. It read:

Attempting to contact GPS… stand by.

Saskia looked down. Through streaks of cloud, she could see uneven tiles of green dotted with grey buildings.

New text:

Contacted. Acquiring locks… stand by.

She could see individual houses now, and traffic on the roads. The horizon flattened.

Locks acquired.

The display marked her drop-zone with a green circle. A

ghostly figure representing her body overlapped with a solid figure. Saskia hesitated, too anxious to understand, before she realised that the computer wanted her to align the two virtual figures. She tilted; wobbled, overcompensated; the ground grew.

Shit.

The two figures aligned.

The parachute opened and she was jerked skyward. The sudden quiet was startling. Cords fell near her hands and she used them to steer. As she pulled right, she banked steeply and swung towards the ground. She had barely enough height to curse the design of the parachute before her boots hit grass. Remembering David's instructions, she held her feet together and rolled to one side.

She detached her parachute, gathered it into a pile, and switched off her hood.

She had landed in a field in the valley on the south side of a sloping hill. Saskia frowned. The scent of fir trees was familiar. It reminded her of the moment she had arrived at the West Lothian Centre. Hadn't she felt compelled to run into the woodland?

She looked at the road that ran through the valley. There was no traffic. She followed the line of the road back to the—

You will return, the witch had said, *as you have returned before.*

There was a checkpoint at the end of the road. Alongside it were a cabin and a car. The checkpoint was the kind you might see at a stately home. Not particularly high security. However, the two men who were emerging from it were conspicuous in their professionalism. They did not hurry to their Land Rover. Their suit jackets were buttoned to keep their shoulder-holsters concealed.

Saskia now recognised that road. It led into the grounds of the West Lothian Centre.

'Why?' she said aloud, watching the Land Rover drive over the grass towards her. 'Why here?'

Somewhere beneath her feet, the young David Proctor and his colleagues were working. She looked at her forearm computer. The date was 1.34pm on 14 May, 2003. She was familiar with that date. She had read it in the notes Beckmann had given her about David's case.

It was the date the West Lothian Centre exploded. But when, exactly?

Klutikov had told her that all she had to do, when she needed an answer, was ask her chip.

At what time on May 14, according to David Proctor's case notes, was the West Lothian Centre bombed?

A heartbeat later came the answer: 2:04 p.m.

Saskia waited as the Land Rover pulled up alongside her.

'Afternoon, miss,' said Colonel McWhirter, stepping down from the vehicle. He had black hair, sun-bleached eyes and a heavy moustache. 'If you'll come with us.'

She hesitated. Why hadn't he recognised her in 2023, if that had been the second time they had met? Then she remembered. She had worn glasses, and he would have expected someone older. Nevertheless, she adopted a cut-glass British accent and said, 'This is my first solo jump. Sorry if I landed somewhere I shouldn't.'

'We'll soon have this sorted out if you'll come with me.' McWhirter opened the rear door of the Land Rover. Saskia took her parachute and climbed in. There was a young man on the bench opposite. He said nothing. McWhirter moved behind the steering wheel and drove them towards the hotel.

Rocking, she looked through the window at the blue sky.

Help was twenty years away.

She thought of Ute, who was just a girl, somewhere out there across the sea.

›•‹

Saskia closed her eyes and assembled the facts. She knew that an explosion would destroy the West Lothian Centre at 2:04pm, in less than half an hour. She also knew that Jennifer had sent her back half an hour before Crane. It was indubitable, then, that Crane would arrive at the moment of the explosion.

She could think of only one way to connect these events. One had caused the other. Had the explosion ripped the fabric of space and time somehow, capturing Crane like a ship pulled towards a whirlpool? No. That was too complex an explanation. It was simpler to reason that Crane had caused the explosion himself.

Jennifer had said that calculating the insertion point was difficult because the past Earth was a moving target. And Crane's trajectory had been warped by the mass of Klutikov.

Crane was going to materialise underground: a projectile fired from the future striking the bullseye of a power generator or gas tank.

Saskia struggled to understand how Klutikov's actions could have been so precisely timed to have sent Crane here, and now, but she could not. In the end, there was nothing else Klutikov could do. He was the cause for an effect that had already happened. The bullseye had been struck long ago. He, the arrow, had no choice but to be launched.

The car passed the fountain with its stone Prometheus. She imagined him chained to a rock, tormented by the hawk sent from Zeus, but the thought was the key to a room that was long unlocked.

Jennifer had said something else.

'You have a choice. But within certain parameters.'

How much freedom did Saskia have now? She had to write a message on a wall down in the research centre, and she had to orchestrate David's escape from custody many years from now. But what else could she do?

She looked around the car. The security guard opposite would not look at her.

I have a certain future.

I am immortal until then.

The car pulled up at the steps in front of the hotel. There was nobody around. McWhirter got out and opened the door for Saskia.

'I'm really sorry about this,' she said.

McWhirter shook his head, dismissing her propriety, and told the guards to return to the checkpoint. As they drove away, Saskia walked up the steps and entered the hotel. Again she saw the twinned staircases that rose like the edges of a cobra's hood, and the brown and black tiles. McWhirter passed her and went to the empty desk, where he started typing on a keyboard.

'My name is Harrison McWhirter. I'm in charge of the hotel.'

Saskia saw a square hole in the keyboard. It would fit the

connector on her Swiss Army Knife.

'Sophie,' she told him in return. 'Sophie White.'

'Perhaps you could tell me how you came to be parachuting into our grounds.'

'I'm with a parachute school. I managed to get lost.' She laughed. 'It was windier than I thought.'

'That's an unusual jumpsuit you're wearing.'

Saskia shrugged.

'I thought they were all like this.'

'I'll get you a taxi,' he said, turning to the telephone.

Saskia said, 'Thank you,' and moved silently around the desk. She put a hand on his shoulder and pulled him backwards. On instinct, McWhirter countered the force by leaning forward, and Saskia switched her grip to his neck, using his movement to help drive his forehead onto the edge of the counter. He sighed and fell slowly, pulling the telephone to the floor. Saskia checked his head. There was a light contusion above his eye. Then she pushed him under the desk, put the telephone back on top, and connected her Swiss Army Knife to the slot on the keyboard.

Something buzzed in the thigh pocket of her suit. It was the Ego computer. She pulled it out.

'Hello, Saskia.'

'I'm trying to disable the computers here.'

'Yes, I already have root access to the system. My first act will be to erase the surveillance—'

'Can you get me into the centre undetected?'

'Perhaps. I can deactivate the alarms, but the lift is secured by a tamper-proof unit that scans DNA sequences.'

Saskia thought about McWhirter lying between her feet. She pulled the Swiss Army Knife from the keyboard.

Klutikov might have been able to cut off a man's finger, but not Saskia. She put the knife in her pocket. 'What do you advise?'

'It's possible I can spoof the scanner into accepting a single input as two, but you'll need to ride down with an authorised user. I don't think this is feasible. Saskia, you need only come back at a later date and paint your message on the wall. I advise you to leave immediately.'

'No.'

'You are in danger here. Note the date and the time.'

'I'm going down now. You can maintain a wireless connection with the computer system here, correct?'

'Yes.'

'Switch to internal communications via the suit.'

'Very well.'

Saskia put Ego back into her thigh pocket and struck her camouflage button. Her hood flipped over her head and she became transparent. The suit's invisibility worked by diverting light through passive nano-optics, but her eyes needed those rays. Without them she was blind.

'Computer, take the video from the surveillance cameras as I pass through their zones and project them onto the hood display.'

'Very well.'

Abruptly, she was looking at a grainy image of the hotel lobby. She could make out her body as a distortion behind the desk.

'Computer, can you process the image to make me stand out?'

'Yes.'

The distortion tinted red.

'Excellent.'

'Remember that I'm a prototype. Sometimes I don't work as expected.'

'Join the club.'

'You need to pass through the lobby and enter the second room on your left.'

'Understood.'

Concentrating on the image of herself, Saskia moved across the lobby in a crouch. She was on the threshold of the lounge when she heard a sound from the hotel's entrance. She backed into a space between a sofa and a tall plant.

In the pause, Ego said, 'Saskia, would you like me to remove the safeguards on your chip?'

'Safeguards?'

'I have discovered processes that audit your thoughts for key biographical information about Ute Schlesinger. Though your knowledge of her is indistinct, these processes almost reached activation threshold twice in the past few minutes. They are now rising again and—'

'Do it. Remove them.'

She realised that Beckmann had never expected her to gain knowledge of Ute through the deactivation and reactivation of the chip. The safeguards must have been designed to detect explicit learning about her body's former life. Saskia waited as Ego made the changes within her. She felt no movements in her mind.

'By the way,' she said, 'thanks.'

'You're welcome

The camera showed Saskia a man entering the lobby. He had a cane. He looked familiar. She waited until he passed in front of her, then fell into step a few paces behind. The carpet helped to quieten her footsteps.

At last corner before the cloakroom, the man turned. Ego showed her the view through another camera. Its quality was much higher. Saskia could see the half-closed, restless eyes of the man she was following. His long cane had a plastic toy dangling from its wrist strap: a wizard with a grey hat.

Saskia was not surprised at his youthful appearance. Inside the computer, realised as a twenty-one-year-old, he would be no different.

'Hello,' said Bruce Shimoda. 'I believe we're walking the same way.'

> • <

When Saskia emerged from the lift into the West Lothian Centre proper, she took a lab coat from the reception area and removed her gloves. She was surprised by the vibrancy of the main corridor, which stretched ahead in ten-metre sections marked by transparent bulkheads, all open. It was crowded in both directions. White-coated scientists stood in groups of two or three, chatting over mugs of coffee. Some, looking more managerial in expensive suits, were forging through, smiling and nodding as they recognised colleagues. The contrast with the tomb-like silence of the hotel was marked.

Bruce was ahead, walking past a large abstract sculpture, grinning each time a person slapped his shoulder and called his name. She moved to take his arm. 'Me again. I actually had a meeting with Helen Proctor. Can you tell me where her office is?'

'She's a friend of mine. It's A14, about twenty metres ahead. Don't worry about the throng. This is what happens when you tell a bunch of academics their funding has been extended. Just push through.'

'Thanks.'

'Saskia,' said Ego, 'you are out of time. I suggest you take cover.'

Before Saskia could move any further, she saw a familiar figure ahead. It was Jennifer Proctor: smiling, arms folded, more relaxed and confident than Saskia remembered. Saskia smiled to herself, then remembered that this was 2003, Jennifer was a baby, and this could only be—

'You're still holding my arm. Is everything alright?'

'I'm fine.' Saskia was mesmerised by the similarity. 'Just a feeling of…'

The woman laughed. Her hair was darker, she was older, and she had a grace that had escaped her daughter. Helen Proctor. The connections formed. Saskia thought back to the moment she had said farewell to David and Jennifer. The mother was the best of Jennifer, but there was something of David in her joy.

The lights flickered and extinguished. Emergency lighting washed the corridor red. Saskia heard the infrastructure groan and saw dust fall from cracks. The abstract sculpture next to Bruce toppled over, knocking him against her.

Then silence, echoing, only breathing and anticipation.

Bruce got to his feet.

'Let's go,' he shouted. 'Everyone out.'

A concussive wave passed through the air and the emergency lights went out. The floor dropped an inch. The air pressure increased. Saskia screamed.

CHAPTER THIRTY-SIX

'Saskia,' Jennifer said, leaning into the microphone. 'I'm sending you back one half hour before Crane. That will give you the best chance of intercepting him.'

David did not hear Saskia's reply. He was looking at the target prediction that the computer had just calculated. There was something significant about the time. It was so extraordinarily significant that it took him a few moments to handle the thought. 'My God, Jenny. Look at her injection time. That's only half an hour before the explosion.'

Jennifer stared at him with confusion, which transformed to wonder as she considered the date. 'We can't change anything now, Dad. She's gone.'

David looked at the large screen. There was a close up of the capsule. Its trapdoor was open. The light of the wormhole had faded.

He slumped in his chair. 'I think the twenty-year mystery of the bombing is solved. Would his arrival be sufficient, you think?'

Jennifer folded her arms. 'Let's do the math.'

'Maths, love,' David corrected.

'An object leaves this centrifuge at one hundred and forty-four kilometres per hour. It enters the wormhole at the same speed. For a mass of, say, seventy-five kilograms, that's a kinetic energy of almost one hundred kilojoules, which is more than enough to trigger an explosive chain reaction if the target is selected carefully. Crane must have materialised near a power plant.'

'How very accommodating of him.' The circular nature of this business was bewildering. After everything: the trial, the accusations, the damage – even the death of his wife – Crane had been the true cause.

No, she thought. That was not an accurate statement. The cause could be traced back to the person who had forced Crane to veer so fatally off course. That was Klutikov. Or David, throwing the finger with the ring into the wormhole. Or Saskia, tossing him the ring to begin with.

'Turns out the Novikov self-consistency conjecture is more than a conjecture,' Jennifer said. 'The probability that Crane would create a paradox was always zero.'

A group of security guards entered the control room. Their sidearms were pointed at the floor. Behind them came a suited, jovial man. He approached Jennifer. By turns, he was staring in awe at her and at the large screen.

'Syncomp is green,' he said. 'Y-vib is off-the-scale low. Could be worse.'

'Harkes,' Jennifer said, flatly. 'I should have guessed you'd never abandon ship.'

'What have you done?' He looked excited. 'Castle is going to throw ape shit.'

›•‹

Within the hour, David and Jennifer had been seated at a conference table in a secure room high in the Stack. Rembrandt's *The Philosopher in Meditation* hung behind them. David lacked the energy for lies. Half-thinking, he took his daughter's hand, and waited for the third occupant of the room to speak.

'Let me summarise,' Castle said. She was a sharp, professional woman in her early sixties, and had introduced herself to David as the person in charge of Helix Base. 'Jennifer, you used government resources without permission, created an Einstein-Rosen bridge without presidential authority, and aided the illegal entry of two other persons into a secure government property. Professor Proctor, you entered both this country and this property illegally. All those issues need to be dealt with first. In good time, I would also like to discover the whereabouts of John Crane and,' she consulted her notes, 'Saskia Brandt.'

'Ms Castle,' said David, 'I could answer most of your questions if you just let me talk. May I?'

Castle sipped her tea and raised her eyebrows. 'You have fifteen minutes.'

Jennifer looked on as David used a terminal to access a web service. 'This is the most recent backup of my Ego unit, which I gave to Saskia. I'll show you some pictures, and audio and video where possible.' He turned to the women. 'My computer was recording my journey. It is equipped with iWitness software. The British police use it. I take it that is satisfactory?'

'It is,' said Castle. 'Go on.'

'Very well. Here is a picture of my house on Tyndale Road. This, Ms Castle, is where our story begins.'

›•‹

Fifteen minutes later, Jennifer looked at her father. He was smiling. 'Crane's path through time was warped by Klutikov's mass. Crane thought he was going back to save himself using the updated nanotreatment, but his insertion was altered to the precise point of the explosion. In other words, he became the cause.'

'When I ask you my next question, bear in mind that each injection costs us the Gross Domestic Product of a small Latin American country. Why did you send Brandt back?'

'Without the older Saskia around now,' said Jennifer, 'none of this would have been possible.'

'Define "this".'

Jennifer looked down. She said nothing. There didn't seem to be any point.

'Your case,' said Castle, turning to her father, 'would be aided by physical evidence. After all, even with a plausible story, we must fall back on the available facts. You were complicit in the death of this man, Klutikov.'

David lifted a hand and let it fall. 'Well, whatever. All I can do is provide you with the information I have.'

A new voice came from the conference speakers: 'Excuse me. I am a proxy program left by Ego, David's personal computer. I am now authorised to tell you that one year ago today, Saskia Brandt sent three hand-written copies of her testimony to legal firms in New York, London and Geneva. They will be released for your perusal at midnight.'

Castle smiled. 'Perhaps we could also meet Ms Brandt.'

The program said nothing. There was a long silence, at the end of which Castle said, 'Well, I have other things to attend to.' She stood and collapsed her computer.

'What happens now?' asked Jennifer.

'For the time being, Dr Proctor, you will stay in guest quarters here. They are quite comfortable, as you know. I have to speak to the board about this. At the very least, we need to discuss future funding proposals, if Mr Crane's absence proves to be permanent.'

'I've no doubt about it,' David said.

'I will also need to speak to our legal team. However, I will advise the board that no charges be pressed. Public knowledge of the disappearance of Klutikov would be prejudicial to our work here. Professor, you will be expelled from the USA tomorrow. You will answer any charges in Britain. I will ask the board to provide legal representation for you. Dr Proctor, you will have your security clearance suspended. Again, I'm sure this will be temporary.'

Jennifer asked, 'How temporary?'

'Two months. Take a holiday. I hear the weather in Britain is awful.'

'And my funding?'

'Jennifer, you've invented a time machine. You'll get your money. And I want you to stay here long term, front of shop, with the machine. I'm cancelling its transportation to Boulder until the dust settles.' Castle shook their hands. 'The guards will take you to your quarters. You can speak to nobody apart from each other. I'll see you tomorrow. Oh, David?'

'Yes, Ms Castle?'

'The evidence you showed me is quite important to your case. I'd advise you to make a back-up.'

›•‹

MI5: Intelligence and Security Committee Special Report
Presented to Parliament by the Prime Minister by Command of His Majesty, January 2023

Appendix Four:

It will be understood that the Intelligence and Security Agencies may request the redaction of sensitive material in the Report that would damage their work, for example by revealing their targets, methods, sources or operational capabilities. The following statement has thus been redacted from the public version of the Report. The ISC finds that, while corroborating evidence exists for some claims within the statement, the putative author SASKIA BRANDT is likely to be fictitious. Neither does the committee consider a 'time warp' to be a credible explanation for the death of JOHN CRANE, KBE.

The statement below was filed with Brélaz and Mächler, Geneva, on 29 September, 2022, and obtained by this department 30 September, 2023. It reads:

To whom it may concern:

You know me as Saskia Brandt. You, or someone you are associated with, have my friends David and Jennifer Proctor in custody. With this statement, I hereby accept responsibility for the murder of John Crane. I told David Proctor to throw an item into a dangerous machine, in the full knowledge that an individual named Klutikov would do his utmost to retrieve said item, and, in this way, bring about the death of John Crane as an accident of time travel.

There are other facts I must withhold for several reasons. However, where I can be clear, I will be so. I will describe recent events from my own perspective. My purpose is not personal exoneration – indeed, this document incriminates me – but the exoneration of my friends by providing background to their claims.

Before I continue, let me say this. There is a fundamental, human need for causation. It has been an unhelpful drive within myself throughout my life. For you to understand the events I will now describe, you should put this notion aside. The events have no true beginning, just as there is no true beginning for the 'will to act'. Everything is circular. Nothing ends, or begins.

On 22 September of this year, I tracked Professor Bruce Shimoda to a Bristol hotel room, where he intended to make good on a promise of suicide made to himself as a younger man. He had become, by his own lights, a weak and dependent individual. I made entry into the hotel room and, after a short struggle, talked to him. I offered a complete version of the abbreviated story I am now telling you. And I told him he could live again.

By dawn, we were en route to Scotland. In West Lothian, I helped him infiltrate the ruined research centre and connect his mind to the virtual reality known as Onogoro. Autonomous systems monitoring the Centre sent an alert to the Home Office. That evening, a team was assembled under the command of Colonel Harrison McWhirter and dispatched to West Lothian. This action added credence to the false information about David Proctor's association with the Neohuman Cooperative, and led to Crane urging Jennifer Proctor to contact her father.

I knew that McWhirter had made attempts over the years to confront Proctor, who he blamed for the bombing of 2003. The complexity of the situation involving Shimoda would provide him with the reason he needed to bring Proctor back to the scene of the crime. Proctor's summons duly arrived via the Home Office and made clear that Shimoda had broken into the West Lothian Centre.

Proctor and Shimoda had grown estranged over the years. I knew that Proctor would accept the summons, but in order for him to kill Shimoda – that is, complete his suicide – I needed to motivate him sufficiently. So I travelled to Oxford. Without revealing my true identity, I introduced myself as a militant NeoHuman opposed to experimentation on artificial organisms. I gave him the second Ego computer, and instructions on how to most effectively disable Onogoro once and for all. This would complete the plan to destroy Onogoro that both Proctor and Shimoda had committed to many years before; a plan that was interrupted by the explosion in 2003.

The reader will detect a conceptual difficulty here. Why, you might ask, would I feel the need to act as though I am part of the chain of causation, when I know that Proctor must go to the West Lothian Centre, and that I must travel in time? As an older Jennifer Proctor once told me: if the arrow strikes the target, the archer must have loosed the shot. One cannot have the former without the latter. All my arrows were loosed before I became aware of their flight.

This is no small madness. My statement is not the place to explore my psychology, but I am stalked by these indifferent monsters. You, reader, cannot see them clearly. For me, the light of time travel illuminates them. For you, they remain shadows.

Following Proctor's escape, other events took place as they have been described to you by him. In Proctor's possession was another Ego unit. It contained instructions to reach locker J327 at Terminal Five, Heathrow Airport. It also contained a programmable logic controller rootkit that would compromise the Helix Base security system, as well as those computers dedicated to Project Déjà Vu.

John Crane was the first person to travel in time. An error redirected his body to the power plant of the West Lothian Centre in 2003. This will help explain why no bomb fragments were found. You will find elevated levels of calcium and phosphorous if you care to look. There have always been rumours that a person infiltrated the West Lothian Centre prior to the explosion, despite the efforts of McWhirter to discredit them. These are true. That was me. All traces of my presence were erased by my Ego unit.

The circle closes. Nothing ends, or begins. This is the last you will hear from me, and the last time I will use the name

SASKIA BRANDT

CHAPTER THIRTY-SEVEN

Saskia lifted her head and licked her dust-covered lips. Her eyes stung with grit and her ears rang. The emergency lights were working again. She looked around for Bruce and saw that he had gone. With luck, he had already escaped.

The structure of the corridor seemed solid again. Though, moments before, the walls and ceiling had ground together like teeth, they were now still. The illusion of immobility had returned. Shakily, Saskia stood.

As much as she was scared, she was satisfied. The coincidence was extraordinary but the explanation clear. Crane was dead. The time machine had redirected him.

Ahead of her, there was a section where the emergency lights were broken. She had seen Helen Proctor fall into that blackness. Saskia clambered towards her over cabling, masonry and other debris. Her plan struck her as a brilliant. She would save this woman's life and repair the lives of David and Jennifer. She would give them the opportunity to avoid the pain that was in store.

That is, as long as such an act was within the parameters of freedom that had Jennifer spoken about. Saskia didn't yet know. She would try.

She reached a woman's body on the floor. A masonry-encrusted joist had fallen across her face and chest. She was surely dead.

Saskia knelt heavily, defeated. A tear cut through the dust on her cheek.

She was still kneeling when she felt a hand on her shoulder.

'Are you okay?'

Saskia followed the hand to the familiar-unfamiliar face of Helen Proctor. 'Listen to me,' said the woman, 'you're going to be fine.'

The ceiling stirred. Both woman looked up. Saskia saw another joist shift. As it did so, clumps of concrete fell to the floor, where they smashed and billowed.

What are the parameters of my freedom?

'Listen,' she said. 'Your daughter, Jennifer—'

Helen frowned. 'Jennifer?'

'Yes, Jennifer. Your daughter will grow into a beautiful young woman. I am from the future – Jennifer loves you.'

When Helen smiled, Saskia smiled too, with relief. She had got through.

Slowly, as though to a child, Helen said, 'You're going to be all right. You've had a knock on the head.'

Saskia's smile switched off. 'No, *listen* to me.'

Another piece of concrete fell. It struck Saskia on the shoulder and the pain was immense. She fell to one knee. From there, she glanced at the ceiling and saw a black gash, splitting open.

She reached for Helen and bundled her to the floor.

She pressed against her squirming form. The woman was covered. If anything was going to fall on her, it would have to come through Saskia.

She turned to look up into the abyss. The joist was in balance. Daggers of twisted steel reinforcement pointed down.

The gash was widening.

Kill me, then. Prove me wrong.

She screamed as the ceiling buckled and fell. The joist slammed to a stop centimetres from her back, bridged by the masonry that killed the woman she had first mistaken for Helen.

Carefully, she slid from the gap between Helen and the joist. 'Come on.' But as the murk thinned, and Helen's silence stretched out, Saskia grew to know that the woman was hurt, had always been hurt, and would die. She checked Helen's chest and stomach. There were no obvious injuries. She touched her forehead and felt something sticky. Looking closer, she saw that a chunk of reinforced concrete had struck Helen's skull above the eye, rolling against her after it had dropped. The blood pool was thick and growing.

Saskia put a hand to her cheek. 'I am so sorry.'

Helen's eyes opened.

'The… the…'

The witches, the fates.

There was no freedom here. Helen was destined to die and Saskia was destined to survive, just as the young woman called Ute Schmidt was destined to be raped and implanted with a chip – with Saskia.

She heard a man calling, 'Helen!'

It was David. His face was young and desperate as he

crawled over the debris. Saskia retreated into shadow. David looked at her once, perhaps seeing a shape in the darkness, then turned to kneel by his wife. He took her hand and held it to his lips.

Saskia pressed on into the darkness.

Going by touch and the red glow of emergency lighting, she found the door she wanted in a corridor that was blackened but otherwise undamaged by the explosions. She stepped inside. The lighting was white and harsh. The room was full of equipment shelves. One of them had a box of spray canisters. She put her hand among the canisters, closed her eyes, and pulled one at random. She checked the label. She had picked a security paint visible only in infra-red light. She remembered her confusion when she had read that cryptic message on the wall, seconds after McWhirter left her alone in the darkened corridor. And she remembered the envelope.

There was a door at the back of the room, and it led to a walk-in cupboard of office supplies. She felt drunk with fatalism. Even the hand of the architect had not been his own. She acquiesced to the long strings that pulled her.

She took a pen, an envelope, a plastic folder, and printed the word 'Munin' on the reverse of her FIB identity card, which was an otherwise useless souvenir in the year 2003. The word would be read in twenty years' time. She tried to write something else – as an artistic flourish, a token rebellion – but could think of nothing to add. She sealed the envelope, addressed it, and returned to the corridor.

Saskia put the envelope inside the plastic folder. She put the folder underneath a piece of masonry. On the wall, she sprayed, in German: *By the pricking of my thumbs, something wicked this way comes.* She included an arrow pointing to the rock.

She dropped the paint and moved away as fast as she could. Her breath stuttered with sobs. She reached an emergency stairwell and, from there, emerged at the rear of the hotel in weak daylight. The lawn was covered with army ambulance crews. Shocked people walked slowly and silently nowhere. Some cried. She saw McWhirter on a stretcher. He wore an oxygen mask. Inspired, Saskia feigned a breathing problem. An ambulance took her to a nearby hospital. Within the hour, she had escaped.

›•‹

Night came to the woodland. Saskia collected firewood beneath a large moon. She remembered the life of Ute as though it were a huge, cherished novel from her youth. One of Ute's many foster parents, Hans, had been a *Wandersmann*. He had taught her how to make fire using a wooden bow drill. Instead, Saskia selected the fire-starter in the small survival kit in her T-suit. Nothing else in the suit worked. The Ego unit was smashed. She collected moss, dry kindling, and some logs. The fire-starter was a ferrocerium rod, down which she scraped the striking blade. The fire caught her moss and she lifted it to her lips, blowing.

The stars were closer in 2003 than they would be in 2023. The sphere of humanity – the reach of its radio and television signals – was smaller. She looked now at the trees around her. Conifer, oak, sycamore, beech and horse chestnut. She remembered them all from the life of Ute.

She noticed the pink sheet protruding from the map

pocket on her thigh. The crayon drawing reminded her of David and Jennifer. On the reverse, David had written a list headed 'Financial Times for the Lady What Bets'. It contained a list of British prime ministers and American presidents since 1990, some British Grand National winners, and all of the football world cup winners, each prefixed with 'bloody'.

At the bottom were these words:

So good luck and bon voyage!

Love David

P.S. If you could stick one of those 'space blankets' like they have in marathons into the shed for when it gets chilly, I'd be much obliged. And a flask of soup!

P.P.S. Nothing vegetarian, mind – I'll be weak enough as it is!

CHAPTER THIRTY-EIGHT

Westminster, London: November 6th, 2023

From his bench next to the Thames, David saw a pigeon flutter to a stop near his feet. The special committee was due to reconvene at 2:00 p.m. He had fifteen minutes to finish his lunch. He watched the pigeon fly away. The MPs had been unimpressed by his ethical choices. It would take more than Ego's pictures and crackly audio to exonerate David from the crime of detonating that second bomb in the West Lothian Centre. David's best intentions were of little import.

It was as he reached for an apple that her shadow fell across him and she said, 'Hello.'

David laughed. She was there, finally. 'You look—'

She kissed him and sat on the bench. 'I know.' She wore a black greatcoat with the collar turned up. Her hair was short. She smiled as he stared, and he noticed the lines at the corners of her eyes and dimples in her cheeks. She was older but her face was leaner and more striking.

'It's been a while,' he said.

'I thought it was best.'

'I'm on parliament's time. Walk me back?'

He broke up the remainder of his sandwich and scattered the pieces. He and Saskia then made their way towards Westminster Bridge.

'You lost your accent,' he said.

'It's still there. Today, I'm playing British.'

'And what could be more British than a stroll along the river?'

'Quite. What's this about parliament?'

'Yes, that,' David said. Unconsciously, his hand rubbed his chest, where cancerous growths had been found a month before: a vestige of the atmosphere in the West Lothian Centre. His nanotreatment was scheduled for January. 'I'm still trying to explain myself.'

'To whom?'

'A closed parliamentary inquiry. Closed to the public, that is. Ostensibly, they want to find out what happened at the West Lothian Centre. The Chairman is Lord Gilbert. A Lib-Dem guy. He's OK.'

Saskia looked at the Palace of Westminster. 'What are you telling them?'

'I'm singing like a bird.'

She nodded. 'That's good. Don't worry about me. I have a new life.'

'So what do I call you?'

'I'm afraid you don't.' She linked her arm in his. 'I suspect that we are under surveillance. Now, what would be the best outcome?'

David sucked air through his teeth. 'They'd advise the state prosecutors not to proceed with a criminal trial. Unofficially, that is. Even better, they might clear my name. Then I could get my job back at the university. I've got another ten years before I retire. Or I could retire now. Why not?'

They walked in silence for a while.

'Tell me about Jennifer.'

'She's back in America. I'll see her again at Christmas – and her new boyfriend, worst luck. Do you have any plans for Christmas?'

'Some. I'll be visiting a friend in Berlin. Then another in Moscow.'

They continued towards parliament. The Westminster Bridge was quiet. Cold air had come down from the North Sea. They turned against it. After ten minutes, they came to an old building near the Ministry of Defence. 'I'll see you very soon, David.'

'Where?'

In reply, she placed a finger to her lips. Then she touched his with the gloved tip.

'You know,' David said, 'I could do with some help in there. Another witness.'

'I'm sorry, David. Take care.'

He waved. 'I understand. You take care too. And thanks.'

He showed his ID to the duty officer and passed through into the main courtyard. The committee chamber was a small room with an oval table and chairs upholstered with green leather. Conversation ceased as he entered.

'Ah-hah,' said Lord Gilbert. He looked at David over the top of his glasses in the way that David would look at a late student. 'The man of the moment.' Gilbert chuckled. The men on the panel chuckled back. The two women pursed their lips.

Tony Barclay, the MSP for West Lothian, took a nod from Gilbert. 'Perhaps we could go back to the woman whom you met that day, Professor Proctor. The woman who supplied the explosives.'

The stenographer watched his computer screen.

David sighed, and began again.

›•‹

David's hosts were confident that he would not try to leave the country, so he was not held in custody. His hotel was a small one north of the river. It was dingy but, he guessed, not cheap. As he entered the room and locked the door, he decided to bloody well cheer up. He was making progress with the committee, after all. He threw off his coat and walked into the bathroom. 'Lights,' he said.

He took the measure of himself. He was a rumpled, tired version of the man who had arrived at the remains of the West Lothian Centre two months before. But he felt no different. He washed and returned to the living room.

There was an envelope on the floor near the jacket. It must have fallen out. Then he remembered Saskia linking her arm in his. The envelope was addressed to 'You'. He opened it and withdrew a single sheet of paper.

Down in Marseilles there's a nice bar run by a man called Dupont. It is famous for its cat, which turned up one day and never left. The cat thinks she's a loner but, really, she likes company. Now, can you remember all that?

David smiled and watched the text fade until the paper was blank.

ACKNOWLEDGEMENTS

Dear reader,

Thanks for finishing my book. I appreciate it. Really. I lose count of the books I've abandoned halfway through. I've tried to make Déjà Vu the kind of book that you can't put down. To do this, I took Elmore Leonard's advice and removed all the bits that readers tend to skip, printed them out, and sent them to Dan Brown as suggestions.

Oh, you like Dan Brown? Aaaawkward.

And back to me. I have lots of people to thank. First, my publisher, George Sandison, who took a chance on the book and worked so hard behind the scenes to produce the physical (or virtual) object you now hold (or think you do); the many and various elves of Unsung Stories; Olivia Wood, my editor, who is to adverbs as Bruce Lee is to the minions of Mr Han-Man in *Enter The Dragon*; Aliya Whiteley, fellow author and, in bizarre time-loop fashion, original editor of Déjà Vu's first edition; Sandro Ryback for his awesome cover; proofers Daniel Graaskov, Karen Jensen, Alex Mears, Lee Penney and Arie van der Lugt; the Psychology Department Book Club at the University of Exeter (props Rachael Carrick and Kate Fenwick); Consultant Neuropathologist and Senior Lecturer in Neuroanatomy Dr Paul Johns, who helped out with some of the medical conditions and procedures described in these pages – and who, more than twenty years ago, stuck a pin in my thigh during Mr Laud's maths class because he wondered what would happen; David Gardiner who checked my physics, rubbished it, and redid it from scratch; Andrea Lowne of the UKA Press, Scott Pack of The Friday Project, and agents John Jarrold and Katherine Flynn for their support; and my partner Britta, for making all this possible.

But most of all, thank you for your eyeballs, and may your capacitor remain fluxed.

Ian Hocking, Canterbury, UK, 2014

ihocking@gmail.com
@ian_hocking
ianhocking.com